Praise for Yoko Ogawa's

the memory police

"Quietly devastating. . . . Ogawa finds new ways to express old anxieties about authoritarianism, environmental depredation and humanity's willingness to be complicit in its own demise."
—*The Washington Post*

"Timely, provocative reading. . . . A harrowing parable about the importance of memory and the profound danger of cultural amnesia."
—*Esquire*

"One of my favorite novels of the decade. . . . It's a perfect correction to the overwrought politico-apocalyptic fiction so fashionable in These Times. . . . It clarifies all the things our wired society muddles, especially, and most profoundly, the saving grace of the human touch."
—Hillary Kelly, *Vulture*

"A searing, vividly imagined novel by a wildly talented writer. . . . Dark and ambitious."
—*Publishers Weekly* (starred review)

"The novel is particularly resonant now, at a time of rising authoritarianism across the globe. Throughout the book, citizens live under police surveillance. Novels are burned. People are detained and interrogated without explanation."
—*The New York Times*

"Ogawa lays open a hushed defiance against a totalitarian regime by training her prodigious talent on magnifying the efforts of those who persistently but quietly rebel."
—*The Japan Times*

"Profoundly powerful. . . . It has the timelessness of a fable, yet feels like an urgent warning about the need for resistance in a world that seems all too quick to forget the lessons of the past."
—The A.V. Club

"Strange, beautiful and affecting." —*The Sunday Times* (London)

"*The Memory Police* truly feels like a portrait of today. To await the future is to disappear the present—which only accelerates the speed with which now turns to then, and then turns to nothing. . . . A lovely, if bleak, meditation on faith and creativity—or faith *in* creativity—in a world that disavows both." —*Wired*

"Haunting and imaginative." —Refinery29

"Ogawa crafts a powerful story about the processing of loss and the importance of memories." —Annabel Gutterman, *Time*

"Eerily surreal, Ogawa's novel takes Orwellian tropes of a surveillance state and makes them markedly her own." —Thrillist

"A taut, claustrophobic thriller." —*Salon*

Yoko Ogawa

the memory police

Yoko Ogawa has won every major Japanese literary award. Her fiction has appeared in *The New Yorker, A Public Space,* and *Zoetrope: All-Story.* Her works include *The Diving Pool,* a collection of three novellas; *The Housekeeper and the Professor; Hotel Iris;* and *Revenge.* She lives in Hyogo.

the memory police

the memory police

YOKO OGAWA

Translated from the Japanese by Stephen Snyder

VINTAGE BOOKS
A DIVISION OF PENGUIN RANDOM HOUSE LLC
NEW YORK

FIRST VINTAGE BOOKS EDITION, JULY 2020

English translation copyright © 2019 by Pantheon Books,
a division of Penguin Random House LLC

The Library of Congress has cataloged the Pantheon edition as follows:
Names: Ogawa, Yōko, author. Snyder, Stephen, translator.
Title: The memory police / Yoko Ogawa ; translated from
    the Japanese by Stephen Snyder.
Other titles: Hisoyaka na kesshō. English
Description: First American edition | New York : Pantheon Books, 2019.
Identifiers: LCCN 2018057224
Subjects: LCSH: Loss (Psychology)—Fiction. | Memory—Fiction.
    Novelists—Fiction.
Classification: LCC PL858.G37 H5713 2019 | DDC 895.63/5—dc23
LC record available at https://lccn.loc.gov/2018057224

Vintage Books Trade Paperback ISBN: 978-1-101-91181-5
eBook ISBN: 978-1-101-87061-7

Book design by Maria Carella

www.vintagebooks.com

Printed in the United States of America
12th Printing

the memory police

I sometimes wonder what was disappeared first—among all the things that have vanished from the island.

"Long ago, before you were born, there were many more things here," my mother used to tell me when I was still a child. "Transparent things, fragrant things . . . fluttery ones, bright ones . . . wonderful things you can't possibly imagine.

"It's a shame that the people who live here haven't been able to hold such marvelous things in their hearts and minds, but that's just the way it is on this island. Things go on disappearing, one by one. It won't be long now," she added. "You'll see for yourself. Something will disappear from your life."

"Is it scary?" I asked her, suddenly anxious.

"No, don't worry. It doesn't hurt, and you won't even be particularly sad. One morning you'll simply wake up and it will be over, before you've even realized. Lying still, eyes closed, ears pricked, trying to sense the flow of the morning air, you'll feel that something has changed from the night before, and you'll know that you've lost something, that something has been disappeared from the island."

My mother would talk like this only when we were in her studio in the basement. It was a large, dusty, rough-floored room, built so close to the river on the north side that you could clearly hear the sound of the current. I would sit on the little stool that was reserved for my use, as my mother, a sculptor, sharpened a chisel or polished a stone with her file and talked on in her quiet voice.

"The island is stirred up after a disappearance. People gather in little groups out in the street to talk about their memories of the thing that's been lost. There are regrets and a certain sadness, and we try to comfort one another. If it's a physical object that has been disappeared, we gather the remnants up to burn, or bury, or toss into the river. But no one makes much of a fuss, and it's over in a few days. Soon enough, things are back to normal, as though nothing has happened, and no one can even recall what it was that disappeared."

Then she would interrupt her work to lead me back behind the staircase to an old cabinet with rows of small drawers.

"Go ahead, open any one you like."

I would think about my choice for a moment, studying the rusted oval handles.

I always hesitated, because I knew what sorts of strange and fascinating things were inside. Here in this secret place, my mother kept hidden many of the things that had been disappeared from the island in the past.

When at last I made my choice and opened a drawer, she would smile and place the contents on my outstretched palm.

"This is a kind of fabric called 'ribbon' that was disappeared when I was just seven years old. You used it to tie up your hair or decorate a skirt.

"And this was called a 'bell.' Give it a shake—it makes a lovely sound.

"Oh, you've chosen a good drawer today. That's called an 'emerald,' and it's the most precious thing I have here. It's a keepsake from my grandmother. They're beautiful and terribly valuable, and at one point they were the most highly prized jewels on the island. But their beauty has been forgotten now.

"This one is thin and small, but it's important. When you had something you wanted to tell someone, you would write it down on a piece of paper and paste this 'stamp' on it. Then they would deliver it for you, anywhere at all. But that was a long time ago..."

Ribbon, bell, emerald, stamp. The words that came from my mother's mouth thrilled me, like the names of little girls from distant countries or new species of plants. As I listened to her talk, it made me happy to imagine a time when all these things had a place here on the island.

Yet that was also rather difficult to do. The objects in my palm seemed to cower there, absolutely still, like little animals in hibernation, sending me no signal at all. They often left me with an uncertain feeling, as though I were trying to make images of the clouds in the sky out of modeling clay. When I stood before the secret drawers, I felt I had to concentrate on each word my mother said.

My favorite story was the one about "perfume," a clear liquid in a small glass bottle. The first time my mother placed it in my hand, I thought it was some sort of sugar water, and I started to bring it to my mouth.

"No, it's not to drink," my mother cried, laughing. "You put just a drop on your neck, like this." Then she carefully dabbed the bottle behind her ear.

"But why would you do that?" I asked, thoroughly puzzled.

"Perfume is invisible to the eye, but this little bottle nevertheless contains something quite powerful," she said.

I held it up and studied it.

"When you put it on, it has a wonderful smell. It's a way of charming someone. When I was young, we would use it before we went out with a boy. Choosing the right scent was as important as choosing the right dress—you wanted the boy to like both.

This is the perfume I wore when your father and I were courting. We used to meet at a rose garden on the hill south of town, and I had a terrible time finding a fragrance that wouldn't be overpowered by the flowers. When the wind rustled my hair, I would give him a look as if to ask whether he'd noticed my perfume."

My mother was at her most lively when she talked about this small bottle.

"In those days, everyone could smell perfume. Everyone knew how wonderful it was. But no more. It's not sold anywhere, and no one wants it. It was disappeared the autumn of the year that your father and I were married. We gathered on the banks of the river with our perfume. Then we opened the bottles and poured out their contents, watching the perfume dissolve in the water like some worthless liquid. Some girls held the bottles up to their noses one last time—but the ability to smell the perfume had already faded, along with all memory of what it had meant. The river reeked for two or three days afterward, and some fish died. But no one seemed to notice. You see, the very idea of 'perfume' had been disappeared from their heads."

She looked sad as she finished speaking. Then she gathered me up on her lap and let me smell the perfume on her neck.

"Well?" she said.

But I had no idea what to answer. I could tell that there was some sort of scent there—like the smell of toasting bread or the chlorine from a swimming pool, yet different—but no matter how I tried, no other thought came to mind.

My mother waited, but when I said nothing she sighed quietly.

"It doesn't matter," she said. "To you, this is no more than a few drops of water. But it can't be helped. It's all but impossible to recall the things we've lost on the island once they're gone." And with that, she returned the bottle to its drawer.

When the clock on the pillar in her studio struck nine, I went up to my room to sleep. My mother returned to work with her hammer and chisel, as the crescent moon shone in the large window.

As she kissed me good night, I finally asked the question that had been bothering me for some time.

"Mama, why do you remember all the things that have been disappeared? Why can you still smell the 'perfume' that everyone else has forgotten?"

She looked out through the window for a moment, gazing at the moon, and then brushed some stone dust from her apron.

"I suppose because I'm always thinking about them," she said, her voice a bit hoarse.

"But I don't understand," I said. "Why are you the only one who hasn't lost anything? Do you remember everything? Forever?"

She looked down, as though this were something sad, so I kissed her again to make her feel better.

My mother died, and then my father died, and since then I have lived all alone in this house. Two years ago, the nurse who took care of me when I was small died as well, of a heart attack. I believe I have cousins living in a village near the source of the river on the far side of the mountains to the north, but I have never met them. The mountainsides are covered with thorny trees and the summits are always cloaked in mist, so no one ever attempts to cross them. And since there is no map of the island—maps themselves having long since been disappeared—no one knows its precise shape, or exactly what lies on the other side of the mountains.

My father was an ornithologist. He worked at an observatory at the top of the hill to the south. He spent several months a year there, collecting data, photographing the creatures, and trying to hatch eggs. I loved to visit him and went as often as I could—using the excuse that I had to deliver his lunch. The young researchers were kind to me and spoiled me with cookies and hot chocolate.

I would sit on my father's lap and study his creatures through his binoculars. The shape of a beak, the color of the feathers around the eyes, the way the wings moved—nothing escaped his notice as he worked to identify them. The binoculars were too heavy for a little girl, and when my arms grew tired, my father would slip his hand under them to support the weight. When we were cheek to cheek like that, watching them take flight, I always wanted to ask him whether he knew what was in the drawers of the old cabinet in my mother's studio. But just as I was about to speak, I remembered her profile as she gazed at the sliver of a moon through the transom window, and I never found the words. I contented myself instead with passing along my mother's instructions to him to eat his lunch before it spoiled.

When it was time for me to go, he would walk with me as far as the bus stop. At a spot along the road where the creatures came to feed, I would pause to crumble one of the cookies I'd received from his assistants.

"When are you coming home?" I'd ask him.

"Saturday evening, I think," he would tell me, looking uncomfortable. "Be sure to give my love to your mother." He waved good-bye so vigorously that he nearly lost the red pencil—or the compass or highlighter or ruler or tweezers—stuffed in his breast pocket.

.   .   .

I think it's fortunate that the birds were not disappeared until after my father died. Most people on the island found some other line of work quickly when a disappearance affected their job, but I don't think that would have been the case for him. Identifying those wild creatures was his one true gift.

When the hats were disappeared, the milliner who lived across the street began making umbrellas. My nurse's husband, who had been a mechanic on the ferryboat, became a security guard at a warehouse. A girl who was a few years ahead of me in school had been employed at a beauty salon, but she quickly found work as a midwife. None of them said a word about it.

Even when the new job was less well paid, they seemed to have no regrets about losing the old one. Of course, had they complained, they might have attracted the attention of the Memory Police.

People—and I'm no exception—seem capable of forgetting almost anything, much as if our island were unable to float in anything but an expanse of totally empty sea.

The disappearance of the birds, as with so many other things, happened suddenly one morning. When I opened my eyes, I could sense something strange, almost rough, about the quality of the air. The sign of a disappearance. Still wrapped in my blanket, I looked carefully around the room. The cosmetics on my dressing table, the paper clips and notes scattered on my desk, the lace of the curtains, the record shelf—it could be anything. It took patience and concentration to figure out what was gone. I got up, put on a sweater, and went out into the garden. The neighbors were all outside, too, peering around anxiously. The dog in the next yard was growling softly.

Then I spotted a small brown creature flying high up in the sky. It was plump, with what appeared to be a tuft of white feathers at its breast. I had just begun to wonder whether it was one of the creatures I had seen with my father when I realized that everything I knew about them had disappeared from inside me: my memories of them, my feelings about them, the very meaning of the word "bird"—everything.

"The birds," muttered the ex-milliner across the way. "And good riddance. I doubt anyone will miss them." He adjusted the scarf around his neck and sneezed quietly. Then he caught sight of me. Perhaps recalling that my father had been an ornithologist, he gave me an awkward little smile and went off to work. When the others outside realized what had disappeared, they too seemed relieved. They returned to their morning duties, leaving me alone to stare at the sky.

The little brown creature flew in a wide circle and then vanished to the north. I couldn't recall the name of the species, and I found myself wishing I had paid better attention when I'd been with my father at the observatory. I tried to hold on to the way it looked in flight or the sound of its chirping or the colors of its feathers, but I knew it was useless. This bird, which should have been intertwined with memories of my father, was already unable to elicit any feeling in me at all. It was nothing more than a simple creature, moving through space as a function of the vertical motion of its wings.

That afternoon I went to the market to do my shopping. Here and there I saw groups of people holding cages, with parakeets, Java sparrows, and canaries fluttering nervously inside, as if they knew what was about to happen. The people holding the cages were quiet, almost dazed, perhaps still trying to adjust to this new disappearance.

Each owner seemed to be saying good-bye to his bird in his own way. Some were calling their names, others rubbing them against their cheeks, still others giving them a treat, mouth to beak. But once these little ceremonies were finished, they opened the cages and held them up to the sky. The little creatures, confused at first, fluttered for a moment around their owners, but they soon were gone, as if drawn away into the distance.

When they were gone, a calm fell as though the air itself were breathing with infinite care. The owners turned for home, empty cages in hand.

And that was how the birds disappeared.

. . .

Something rather unexpected happened the next day. I was eating breakfast and watching television when the doorbell rang.

From the violent way it rang, I could tell that something unpleasant was about to happen.

"Take us to your father's office," said one of the officers from the Memory Police whom I found standing in the doorway. There were five of them, dressed in dark green uniforms, with heavy belts and black boots. They wore leather gloves and their guns were half hidden in holsters on their hips. The men were nearly identical, with only three badges on their collars to tell them apart—though I had no time to study them closely.

"Take us to your father's office," echoed a second man, his tone the same as the man who had spoken first. This one wore badges in the shapes of a diamond, a bean, and a trapezoid.

"My father died five years ago," I said as slowly and evenly as I could, trying to remain calm.

"We know," said another man, wearing insignia shaped like a wedge, a hexagon, and the letter "T." As though his words had been some sort of signal, the five officers marched into the house without even removing their shoes. Suddenly, the corridor was filled with the clatter of boots and guns.

"I've just cleaned the carpets," I said. "Please take off your shoes." I knew I should have said something more forceful, but this simple request was all that came to mind. It hardly mattered, since they paid no attention to me and were already climbing the stairs.

They seemed to know exactly where they were going, and a moment later they were in my father's office on the east side of the house, setting to work with remarkable efficiency. First, one of them opened all the windows, which had been sealed shut since my father's death. Meanwhile, another one used a long, thin tool like a scalpel to force the locks on the cabinets and the desk drawers. The rest ran their fingers over every inch of the walls, apparently in search of secret compartments.

Then they all began to riffle through my father's papers, pawing at his notes, drafts, books, and photographs. When they came upon something they considered dangerous—in other words, anything that contained the word "bird"—they threw the item unceremoniously on the floor. Leaning against the door-frame, I fiddled nervously with the lock as I watched them work.

The Memory Police, just as I'd heard, went about their assigned tasks in the most efficient manner. They worked in silence, their eyes fixed, making no unnecessary movements. The only sound was the rustling of papers, like the fluttering of wings.

In no time at all, a mountain of paper had formed on the floor. Nearly everything in the room had to do with my father's work in some way. Documents covered with my father's familiar handwriting and the photographs he had taken at the observatory flew out of the officers' hands one after the other. There was no doubt that they were creating chaos, but they went about it in such a precise manner that they gave an impression of careful order. I felt I should try to stop them, but my heart was pounding and I didn't know what to do.

"Please be careful," I murmured, but they ignored me. "These are the only things I have from my father." Not one of them so much as turned to look at me, and my voice was lost in the pile of memories on the floor.

Then one of the officers reached for the handle on the bottom drawer of the desk.

"There's nothing in there that has to do with birds," I cried out. It was the drawer where my father kept family letters and photographs. The officer—this one wore a badge made up of concentric circles, as well as one shaped like a rectangle and another like a teardrop—continued his search. The only offend-ing item in the drawer was a photograph of our family with a brightly colored rare bird—I no longer recall the name—that my father had managed to hatch from an egg he had incubated. The man carefully gathered up the remaining photographs and letters and put them back in the drawer. That was the only kindness shown that day.

When they had finished sorting through everything, they took the items piled on the floor and shoved them into large black plastic bags they pulled from pockets inside their jackets. It was clear from the brutal way they stuffed the bags that they were going to dispose of everything they took. They had not been looking for anything in particular; they had simply wanted to eliminate all trace of anything relating to birds. The first duty of the Memory Police was to enforce the disappearances.

I realized at some point that this search was unlike the day they took my mother away. Today, they seemed to have found everything they wanted, and I was fairly sure they would not be back. My father was dead, and the memory of the birds was gradually fading from the house.

The search had taken an hour and had yielded ten large bags. The office had grown quite warm from the bright sun that streamed in. The polished badges shone on the officers' collars, but none of the men appeared to be sweating or suffering from the heat in any way. They shouldered two bags each and carried them to the truck they had left parked outside.

The room had changed completely. The traces of my father's presence, which I had done my best to preserve, had vanished, replaced by an emptiness that would not be filled. I stood in the middle of that emptiness, feeling myself on the verge of being drawn into its terrible depth.

3

I make my living now from my writing. So far, I've published three novels. The first was about a piano tuner who wanders through music shops and concert halls searching for her lover, a pianist, who has vanished. She relies solely on the sound of his music that lingers in her ears. The second was about a ballerina who lost her right leg in an accident and lives in a greenhouse with her boyfriend, who is a botanist. And the third was about a young woman nursing her younger brother, who suffers from a disease that is destroying his chromosomes.

Each one told the story of something that had been disappeared. Everyone likes that sort of thing. But here on the island, writing novels is one of the least impressive, most underappreciated occupations one can pursue. No one could claim that the island is overflowing with books. The library, a shabby single-floor wooden building next to the rose garden, has only a handful of patrons, no matter when one visits, and the books seem to cower on the shelves, fearful of crumbling to dust at the slightest touch. They will all, in the end, be tossed out without being cared for or rebound—which is why the collection never grows. But no one ever complains.

The bookstores are much the same. Nearly deserted, and the managers appear almost surly behind their stacks of unsold books with yellowing covers.

Few people here have any need for novels.

I generally begin writing at about two o'clock in the afternoon and keep at it until nearly midnight, yet I rarely finish more than five pages. I enjoy writing slowly, filling each square on the paper, one character at a time. There's no need to hurry. I take my time.

I work in my father's old room. But it's much neater and more orderly now, since my novels require no notes or other materials. My desk holds only a stack of paper, a pencil, a small knife to sharpen it, and an eraser. Though I've tried, I've found no way to fill in the voids left by the Memory Police.

When evening comes, I go out to walk for an hour or so. I follow the coastal road to the dock, and on the way home I take a path over the hill that passes the observatory.

The ferry has been tied to the dock for a very long time and is now completely covered with rust. No passengers board it and it can no longer take them anywhere. It, too, is among the things that have been disappeared from the island.

The name of the boat is painted on the bow, but the salt air has scoured it away, leaving it illegible. The windows are coated with dust, and the hull and anchor chain and propeller are covered with mussels and seaweed—as though it is an enormous sea creature that is slowly turning to stone.

My nurse's husband had once served as mechanic on the boat. After the ferry had disappeared, he worked as a watchman for a warehouse by the docks. But at some point he retired and he lives now on the abandoned boat. On my walk, I invariably stopped in to chat with him.

"How have you been?" he asked one evening, offering me a chair. "Are you making progress with your novel?" There are lots of places to sit, so depending on the weather or our mood we might find ourselves occupying a bench up on deck or relaxing on a comfortable couch in the first-class lounge.

"Slowly," I told him.

"Well, the most important thing is that you take care of   17
yourself." He nodded to himself and added, "There aren't many
people who can sit all day at a desk and make up such complicated things right out of their head. If your parents were here to
see you, they would be so proud."

"A novel isn't as marvelous as all that. To me, taking apart
a boat engine, fixing it, and putting it all back together again is
much more mysterious and wonderful."

"No, no. The ferry has been disappeared and there's nothing
more to be said about it." We fell silent then for a moment.

"Ah," he said at last. "I've managed to get some excellent
peaches. Why don't we have one?" He went into the tiny galley
next to the boiler room, where he laid out slices of peach on a
plate lined with ice and topped them with a sprig of mint. Then
he made a pot of strong green tea. He was truly gifted when it
comes to machines, food, and plants.

I've always given him one of the first copies of each of my
books.

"So this is your new *novel*," he would say each time, pronouncing the word with great care and taking the book in both
hands, as though he were receiving a sacrament. "Thank you,
thank you," he would repeat, as his voice grew almost tearful and
I felt increasingly embarrassed.

But he has never read a single page of any of my books.

Once, when I told him I'd love to know what he thinks of
them, he demurred.

"I couldn't possibly say," he said. "If you read a novel to the
end, then it's over. I would never want to do something as waste-
ful as that. I'd much rather keep it here with me, safe and sound,
forever."

Then he placed the book in the little altar to the sea gods in
the ship's wheelhouse and joined his wrinkled hands in prayer.

As we enjoyed our snack, we talked about all sorts of things—but most often we spoke of our memories. Of my mother and father, my old nurse, the observatory, sculptures, and the distant past when one could still take a boat to other places. But our memories were diminishing day by day, for when something disappeared from the island, all memory of it vanished, too. We divided the last bit of peach and repeated the same stories to each other, allowing the fruit to dissolve, ever so slowly, on our tongues.

When the sun began to tilt down toward the sea, I climbed down from the boat. Though the gangway wasn't particularly steep, the old man came out to escort me. He treated me as though I were still a little girl.

"Take care on the way home."

"I will," I told him. "See you tomorrow."

He stood watching me as I walked away, never moving until I was completely out of sight.

Leaving the harbor behind, my next stop was the observatory at the top of the hill. But I never lingered long. I gazed out at the sea, taking a few deep breaths, and then walked down again.

The Memory Police have done their work here, much as they did in my father's study, leaving it little more than a ruin. Nothing at all remains to remind a visitor that it had once been a place to observe wild birds. The researchers, too, have scattered.

I stood at the window, where I once stood with my father looking out through binoculars, and even now small winged creatures occasionally flitted by, but they were no more than reminders that birds mean nothing at all to me anymore.

As I climbed down the hill and made my way through town, the sun was setting. The island was quieter in the evening. People coming home from work walked with their heads lowered, children hurried along. Even the sputtering engines of market trucks, empty after the day's sales, were muffled and forlorn.

Silence fell around us all, as though we were steeling ourselves for the next disappearance, which would no doubt come— perhaps even tomorrow.

So it was that evening came to the island.

4

On Wednesday afternoon, on my way to take my manuscript to my publisher, I had an encounter with the Memory Police. It was the third time I'd seen them this month, and they seemed to grow a bit more brutal each time.

It occurred to me that it has been fifteen years since they first appeared. In those days, it was just becoming obvious that some people, like my mother, did not lose their memories of the things that had disappeared, and the Memory Police began taking them all away. Though no one had any idea where they were being held.

I had just gotten off the bus and was waiting to cross the street when three of their dark green trucks with canvas covers in back rumbled into the intersection. The cars along the street slowed and pulled to the curb to let them pass. The trucks stopped in front of a building that housed a dentist's office, an insurance company, and a dance studio. Ten men from the Memory Police jumped out and hurried into the building.

The people in the street watched tensely, some ducking into nearby alleys, and they all seemed to hope that the scene unfolding before them would be over before they themselves were pulled into it.

I clutched the envelope that held my manuscript and stood stock-still behind a lamp pole. Several times, as I waited, the traffic light changed from green to yellow to red and back again to green. No one ventured into the crosswalk. The passengers on the streetcar peered out the windows. At some point I realized that my envelope had gotten completely wrinkled.

A short time later, the sound of footsteps could be heard coming from the building—the forceful, rhythmic boots of the Memory Police mixed with quieter, more uncertain steps. Then a line of people emerged: two middle-aged gentlemen, a woman in her thirties with dyed brown hair, and a thin girl barely in her teens.

Though the cold weather had not yet set in, they each wore several layers of shirts, an overcoat each, and mufflers and scarves wrapped around their necks. They held bags and suitcases that were obviously stuffed full. It seemed they had been trying to bring with them as many useful items as they were able to carry.

Judging from the loose buttons, fluttering shoelaces, and bits of clothing protruding from their bags, it was clear that they had been forced to pack quickly. And now they were being marched out of the building with weapons at their backs. Still, their faces were calm and they stared into the distance with eyes as still as a lonely swamp deep in the woods. In those eyes, no doubt, were all sorts of memories that had been lost to us.

As always, the Memory Police, badges glinting from their collars, went about their appointed task with terrible efficiency. The four were led past the spot where I was standing, and I caught just a whiff of an antiseptic smell—perhaps they had come from the dentist's office.

They were loaded, one after another, into the back of one of the trucks, the guns trained on them the entire time. The young girl, who was last in line, carried an orange bag decorated with an appliqué of a bear. She had thrown this into the truck and was attempting to climb up herself, but it was too high and she ended up falling on her back.

I cried out before I could stop myself and dropped my envelope. The pages of my manuscript scattered over the sidewalk, and the other bystanders turned to look disapprovingly. They were afraid of creating a disturbance, of giving the police reason to notice them.

A boy who was standing nearby helped me pick up the pages. Some were damp from falling in puddles and others had been trampled, but we managed to find everything.

"Is that all of them?" the boy whispered in my ear. I nodded and gave him a grateful look.

But this little incident had no effect on the work of the Memory Police. Not one of them had turned to look at us.

The girl had scrambled to her feet, and one of the officers who was already in the truck reached down, caught hold of the girl's hand, and pulled her up. There was still something childish in the small, knobby knees that protruded below her skirt. The canvas cover was lowered over the back of the truck and the engines started.

Even after they were gone, it took a moment before time resumed its normal flow. When the trucks had gone and the sound of their engines had receded in the distance, the streetcar started up again—and only then did I feel sure that the Memory Police had left and would do me no harm. The people on the sidewalk went off in whatever direction they had been heading, and the boy who had helped me crossed the street.

I stood looking at the door to the building, now tightly shut, and wondered how the officer's hand must have felt to the young girl as he pulled her into the truck.

.   .   .

"I saw something terrible on my way here," I told R, my editor, in the lobby of the publishing house.

"The Memory Police?" he asked, lighting a cigarette.

"Yes. They seem worse recently."

"They're awful," he agreed, slowly exhaling a long stream of smoke.

"But today was different somehow. They took four people at once from the center of town, in broad daylight. As far as I know, they've generally acted at night, on the edge of town, taking just one member of a family."

"Those people must have been hidden in a safe house."

"A safe house?" I said, repeating the unfamiliar words, but they died in my throat almost before I'd said them. I'd been told it was best not to talk about such sensitive matters in public. There was no telling whether plainclothes police might be nearby. Rumors about them were rampant on the island.

The lobby was nearly deserted. Just three men in suits near the potted ficus tree, deep in discussion around a thick stack of papers, and a receptionist sitting at the desk looking bored.

"I would guess they had converted one of the rooms in the building into a hiding place. There isn't really much else they can do. I've heard that there's a fairly large underground network that creates these safe houses and then keeps them running. They build the rooms and then provide the occupants with supplies and money. But if the police are starting to raid the safe houses, then there's really no place left to hide . . ."

R seemed to want to add something more, but he fell silent and reached instead for his cup of coffee, his gaze wandering to the garden in the courtyard.

There was a small fountain made of bricks in the garden. A plain, nondescript thing. As the conversation lagged, the sound of the spray could be heard through the window, like soft chords being played on an instrument in the distance.

"It's always struck me as odd that the police can tell who they are," I said, watching him as he looked out at the fountain. "I mean, the people who don't forget after a disappearance. I don't think they have any distinguishing features. They're men and women, all ages, from all different families. So if they're careful and make sure to blend in with everyone else, they should be able to pass. It shouldn't be that hard to play the game, to pretend that the disappearances affect them like they do the rest of us."

"I wonder whether it's really as simple as you make it sound." R thought for a moment. "The conscious mind is embedded in a subconscious that's ten times as powerful, which may make trying to pretend almost impossible. They can't even imagine what these disappearances mean. If it were easy to pretend, they wouldn't be hiding away in these safe houses."

"That's true," I said.

"It's just a rumor, but I've heard they're learning to analyze our genes to find out who has this trait. They're assembling technicians in a secret facility at the university."

"Analyzing genes?" I murmured.

"That's right. There are no visible identifiers that link this group of people together, but the assumption is that there must be something in their genetic makeup. Judging from the behavior of the Memory Police, it seems the research must be fairly advanced."

"But how do they access our genes?" I asked.

"You just drank from this cup, didn't you?" R said, stubbing out his cigarette and lifting my coffee cup to eye level. I nodded.

"They could take this and isolate your genetic material from your saliva. Nothing could be simpler for the Memory Police. They're lurking everywhere—maybe in the back room where they do the dishes. Before we know it, they'll have tested everyone on the island and stored our information in their database, though it's impossible to know how much progress they've made so far. No matter how careful we are, we all leave behind little bits of ourselves as we go about our lives. Hair, sweat, fingernails, tears . . . any of which can be tested. No one can escape."

Slowly he lowered the cup back to the saucer, his eyes looking down at the coffee that remained in the bottom.

The men who had been talking near the ficus tree had finished their conversation. Three cups were left behind on their table. The receptionist began clearing them, her face completely blank.

I waited until she had gone. "But why do they take people away? They haven't done anything wrong."

"The island is run by men who are determined to see things disappear. From their point of view, anything that fails to vanish when they say it should is inconceivable. So they force it to disappear with their own hands."

"Do you think my mother was killed?" I knew it was pointless to ask R, but the question slipped out.

"She was definitely under observation, being studied." R chose his words carefully.

He was quiet for a moment. The only sound was the splashing of water in the fountain. The crumpled envelope lay on the table between us. R pulled it to him and took out the manuscript.

"It seems strange that you can still create something totally new like this—just from words—on an island where everything else is disappearing," he said, brushing a bit of dirt from one of the pages as though he were caressing something precious.

I realized then that we were thinking the same thing. As we

looked into each other's eyes, I felt, once again, the anxiety that had taken root in our hearts a long time ago. The light reflecting from the spray of the fountain lit R's face.

"And what will happen if words disappear?" I whispered to myself, afraid that if I said it too loudly, it might come true.

Autumn passed quickly. The crashing of the waves was sharp and cold, and the wind brought the winter clouds from beyond the mountains.

The old man came from his boat to help me prepare for the cold weather. Together we cleaned the stove, wrapped the pipes, and burned the dead leaves in the garden.

"We haven't had snow in ten years, but we may well this winter," he said as he hung onions on the rack atop the storehouse in my backyard. "It always snows when the onions' skins are deep brown, like these, and thin as butterfly wings."

He peeled off a layer and it made a pleasant crackling sound as he crushed it in his palm.

"Then I might get to see snow for the third time in my life. I'd like that," I said, feeling almost cheerful. "How many times would it make for you?"

"I've never counted. When I ran my ferry in the northern sea, it snowed so much I got sick of it. Though that was long before you were born," he said, going back to hanging the onions.

When we had finished the chores, we lit the stove and ate waffles in the dining room. Perhaps because it had just been cleaned, the stove was slow to start and made a sputtering sound. The vapor trail of a jet was visible in the sky outside the window. A thin pillar of smoke rose from the smoldering leaves.

"Living here alone, I feel a little nervous when winter comes, so I'm truly grateful for your help. Which reminds me, I just finished knitting a sweater and I'd like you to try it on," I said. After my first waffle, I went to get the gray Fair Isle sweater I had made for him. Surprised, he swallowed his tea noisily and reached out to take it with both hands.

"I'm always happy to help, but I've hardly done anything. This is too much, really." But he immediately pulled off the old sweater he was wearing and wadded it up like a used towel. Then he slipped his arms into the new one with infinite care, as if it were delicate and might unravel at the slightest touch. "Oh my, how warm!" he said. "It's so light I feel as though I'm going to float away."

The sleeves were a little long and the collar a bit tight, but he didn't seem to care. He ate another waffle, but he was so taken with the new sweater that he didn't even notice when a bit of cream dribbled on his chin.

After supper, the old man put his pliers and his screwdriver, his sandpaper and his oilcan back in the toolbox attached to his bicycle, and he headed home to the boat.

Winter began in earnest the next day. Suddenly, you needed a coat when you went outside. There was ice on the river behind my house in the morning and fewer kinds of vegetables in the market.

I was hiding away at home, working on my new novel. This one was about a typist who loses her voice. She goes off in search of it, accompanied by her lover, a teacher at the typing school. She consults a speech therapist. Her boyfriend massages her throat and warms her tongue with his lips, and plays songs that the two of them had recorded long before. But her voice doesn't come back. She communicates her feelings to him by typing. The *clack-clack* of the keys flows between them like music, and then . . .

I myself wasn't sure what would happen next. The story

seemed simple and pleasant enough, but I had a feeling it might
take a frightening turn.

. . .

I was still working when, well past midnight, I thought I
heard someone knocking on glass off in the distance. Setting
down my pencil, I listened for a moment, but the only sound
was the wind blowing outside. I went back to my manuscript,
but before I had finished another line, I heard the rattling of glass
again. *Clack, clack, clack . . .* A quiet, rhythmic sound.

I pulled back the curtain and looked out. The houses were
dark and there was no sign of anyone in the street. Closing my
eyes, I tried to hear where the sound was coming from, when I
suddenly realized it was coming from the basement.

Since my mother's death, I had rarely been down to her studio, and I generally kept the door locked. In fact, it had been so
long since I'd needed the key that I'd forgotten exactly where I'd
put it. It took me a few moments to remember, and then there
was considerable rattling as I poked around in a drawer. At last
I found the tin where I kept keys, but there was more noise as
I opened it and located the rusty key on the ring. Somehow I
felt like I should have been doing all this more quietly, but the
knocking from the basement, even and patient, had pushed me
to hurry.

At last I managed to open the door. I went down the stairs
and turned on the light, and when I did I could see someone
standing outside the door that led to the laundry area built out on
the river. It hadn't been used regularly since my grandmother's
time. My mother had occasionally washed her sculpting tools
there, but even that was more than fifteen years ago.

The washing area was little more than a few square feet

YOKO OGAWA

paved in brick, set into the riverbank. It was built up above the basement level, and from there one could walk down a few steps to the glass door at the back of the house. The river itself was only a few yards wide at this point, and my grandfather had built a small wooden bridge to the far bank—though it was now in a state of disrepair.

But why would someone be standing out there?

I turned that question over in my head as I considered what to do. Perhaps it was a burglar. No, a burglar wouldn't knock. The knocking continued, measured and almost polite.

Screwing up my courage, I managed to call out, "Who's there?"

"I'm sorry. I know it's late. It's Inui."

. . .

When I opened the door, I found Professor Inui and his family standing outside. Inui, an old friend of my parents, taught in the dermatology department at the university hospital.

They certainly appeared to be in some kind of difficulty. "What's happened?" I asked, ushering them inside. The sound of the river rushing nearby made the cold even more piercing.

"I'm so sorry to show up like this. I know it's a terrible inconvenience . . ." The professor murmured apologies as they shuffled through the door. His wife wore no makeup, and her face was gaunt. Her eyes were damp, whether from the cold or with tears. Their daughter, who was perhaps fifteen years old, stood with her lips pressed tightly together, while her younger brother, who I remembered was eight, stared curiously around at the room. They clustered together in a group, holding on to one another. Mrs. Inui clutched her husband's arm, which was wrapped around his daughter's shoulders, while the children held hands. To complete the circle, the little boy held the hem of his mother's coat with his other hand.

"It's no trouble, really," I told them. "But I'm amazed you made it across the bridge. Wasn't it a bit scary? It's on its last legs. And I don't understand why you didn't come to the front door. But you're here now, and we should go up to the living room where it's nice and warm."

"You're more than kind, but I'm afraid we have no time. And we should be as discreet as possible. We don't want to attract attention."

The professor sighed, and as if that were a signal, the four of them huddled still closer together.

They were wearing long, well-made coats, and their necks, hands, and feet—anyplace not covered by the coats—were bundled in warm woolens. They carried two bags each, one in each hand, larger or smaller depending on the size of the bearer. The bags appeared to be heavy.

Working quickly, I cleared my mother's table and brought chairs for them to sit on. When their bags were arranged under the table, I waited to hear their story.

"It finally arrived," the professor said, his fingers folded in front of him, as if he hoped to conceal his voice in the semicircle they formed.

"What did?" I asked, urging him on when he paused.

"A summons from the Memory Police." His voice was calm.

"But why?"

"I've been ordered to present myself at the genetic analysis center. Tomorrow—no, this morning it is now—they're coming to escort me there. I've been dismissed from my post at the university, and we've been ordered to vacate our faculty house. Our whole family is to move to the center."

"But where is it?" I asked.

"I have no idea. No one seems to know where it is, what sort of building it's in. But I can guess what they're doing there. Officially, they're conducting medical research, but in reality it's simply a front for the Memory Police. And I suspect they want to use my research to identify people who are able to keep their memories."

I remembered what R had told me. So it wasn't just a rumor.

"The order came three days ago. We had no time to consider what we should do. They're offering to triple my salary, and they apparently have a school for the children. They make special provisions for everything—taxes, insurance, a car, housing. The arrangements are so generous it's frightening."

"Just like the letter for your mother that came fifteen years ago."

His wife spoke up for the first time. The girl listened quietly, her head swiveling toward whoever was speaking. The boy played carefully with the sculpting tools on the table, his hands still in his gloves.

.   .   .

I recalled when my mother was taken away, and how the Inuis had comforted me at the time. I was just a little girl, and their daughter was a baby in her mother's arms.

The order had come in a coarse pale purple envelope. At that point no one had heard of the Memory Police, and neither my parents nor the Inuis saw anything particularly ominous in the letter. They were just a bit anxious because it was unclear why my mother was being called or how long she would be needed.

But I had been fairly certain that it had something to do with the drawers in the chest in the basement. As the adults had stood talking about the envelope, I remembered the quiet sound of my mother's voice as she told me stories about the secret objects—and the troubled look on her face when I had asked her why she remembered these stories and had not forgotten them like everyone else.

The discussion of the letter had ended inconclusively. There was no obvious reason to refuse.

"Everything will be fine. There's no need to be so worried," my mother had said.

"And we'll help look after your house and your little girl, anything at all," said Professor Inui, offering his support to my parents.

The car sent the next morning by the Memory Police was terribly elegant. Jet black and polished to a brilliant shine, it seemed as large as a house. The chrome wheels and door handles and the police insignia on the hood glinted in the sunlight. The leather seats looked so soft I could barely resist hopping in to try them.

The white-gloved driver opened the door for my mother. She gave a few final instructions to the Inuis and to my nurse, kissed my father, and then took my cheeks in her hands.

We were somehow reassured by the opulence of the car and the careful manners of the driver. If she was to be so well taken care of, there was no need to worry.

Mother sank down into the feather-soft seat, and we waved as if she were headed off to receive a prize at a sculpture exhibition.

But that was the last time we ever saw her alive. Her body came back to us a week later, along with her death certificate.

It listed the cause of death as a heart attack. An autopsy was performed at Professor Inui's clinic, but nothing suspicious was found.

"A sudden illness struck her as she was helping with our classified research . . . We would like to offer our sincere condolences in your time of grief . . ."

My father read aloud from the letter the Memory Police had sent, but I understood nothing, as though I were hearing some magic formula uttered in a foreign tongue. I watched, transfixed, as my father's tears made little stains on the lavender paper.

. . .

"The quality of the paper, the font on the typewriter, even the watermark—it was all exactly the same as the one that came for your mother." Mrs. Inui had two scarves around her neck, knotted tightly in front. Her eyelashes fluttered as she spoke.

"Couldn't you refuse?" I asked.

"If I do, they'll just take me away by force," Professor Inui answered without hesitating. "If you don't cooperate, you become their victim. And I doubt they'd spare my family. I have no idea where they take you once they have you. Prison? A labor camp? The gallows? But you can be sure it isn't anyplace pleasant."

"So then you'll go to the research center?"

"No," said the professor, and he and his wife shook their heads in unison. "We're going to a safe house."

"A safe house," I murmured, realizing this wasn't the first time I had heard these words.

"We were lucky enough to find a group that runs them, and they're willing to hide us. We're going there now."

"But you'll be giving up your work, your whole life. Wouldn't it be better to obey their orders? Your children are still so young."

"I don't think we can be sure we'd be safe, locked up in the research center. After all, it's being run by the Memory Police. They can't be trusted. Once I'd outlived my usefulness, I'm sure they'd do anything they felt was necessary to ensure secrecy."

The professor had chosen his words carefully to avoid frightening the children. They were sitting quietly, behaving themselves. The boy was fiddling with a nondescript stone as though it were a toy with some elaborate hidden mechanism. His plain light blue gloves had obviously been knit by hand. They were connected to each other with a strand of yarn, to keep them from becoming separated. I remembered wearing the same kind, long ago, and, in this basement so full of anxiety, they seemed like the lone sign of innocence and peace.

"And besides, we have no intention of helping the Memory Police," added Mrs. Inui.

"But how will you manage in hiding? What will you do for money, food, school for your children? What if one of you gets sick? What will become of you?"

There were so many things I still didn't understand. The genetic code, decryption, the research center, the safe houses, their supporters . . . All these words, not yet properly defined or understood, were buzzing incessantly in my head.

"We don't really know," Mrs. Inui said, tears welling up in her eyes now. I knew somehow that she wasn't actually crying. I knew somehow that she was too sad to cry—her tears were simply drops of liquid appearing of their own accord.

"It all happened so suddenly," she continued. "We had no time. I couldn't think about what to bring, what to leave behind. We have no way of knowing what will happen to us, so it's all we could do to make the most immediate decisions. Should we bring our checkbook? Or did we need cash instead? What clothing should we pack? Did we need to have food? Should we leave behind Mizore, our cat?"

The drops of liquid flowed down her cheeks now without stopping. Her daughter produced a handkerchief from her pocket.

"And we had one more decision to make," said the professor. "We had to figure out what to do with the sculptures your mother gave us. Once we vanish, the Memory Police will search our house. They may destroy much of what we've left behind. Which is why we wanted to protect at least a few of the things we value most—though that could prove dangerous, too. Our secret could get out. We have to limit knowledge of the safe houses to the smallest possible number of people."

I nodded.

"I know it's asking a lot, but we wonder whether you could keep these works your mother gave us. Until we're able to meet again."

As he finished, his daughter reached into the bag at her feet and, almost as if they had rehearsed the moment before showing up on my doorstep, pulled out five small sculptures and lined them up on the table.

"Your mother made this tapir for us as a wedding present. This one she gave us when our daughter was born, and the other three we received the day before she went away with the Memory Police."

My mother had loved to sculpt tapirs, even though she had never seen one in real life. The present to their daughter was a doll with large eyes, carved in oak. I had one just like it. But the other three were different. They were abstract, puzzle-like objects made of both wood and bits of metal. Small enough to fit in the palm of your hand, they were rough to the touch, neither sanded nor varnished. It almost seemed they could be combined to form a single object, and yet the three were distinct and bore no resemblance to one another.

"I had no idea she left these with you before she went away," I said.

"And we had no idea that they would come back to you. But I had the feeling at the time that she must have intended something of the sort. In those last days, she worked down here almost constantly, perhaps wondering when she would be able to sculpt again. When she gave them to us, she said she didn't see any point in just leaving them in the studio."

"And now we'd like to leave them here with you," said Mrs. Inui as she folded the handkerchief.

"And I'm grateful that you've taken such good care of them all this time. I'd be happy to look after them."

"Thank you," said the professor, smiling with relief. "At least they won't get their hands on these."

.   .   .

I understood they needed to hurry, to be gone before dawn, but I wanted to do what I could for them.

I went up to the kitchen, heated some milk, and poured it into mugs. Then I carried them back down to the cellar and we made as if to drink a toast, though we were careful to avoid even the sound of clinking cups. From time to time, one of us would look up as if about to say something, but no words came and we sipped in silence.

The bulb in the lone lamp was covered in dust, and the pale light made the scene in the cellar look like a watercolor. My mother's discarded possessions lay quietly in the shadows—a half-finished stone carving, yellowed sketchbooks, a dry whetstone, a broken camera, a set of pastels, twenty-four colors in all. The smallest movement made the chairs creak on the floor. The sky outside the window was pitch-black, with no sign of a moon.

The little boy, perhaps finding it odd that no one was speaking, peered into our faces one by one. There was a white ring around his mouth. "This is delicious," he said.

"It is," someone murmured, and we nodded at one another. I couldn't imagine the sort of life that might be waiting for them, but at least now, right at this moment, they had good, warm milk to drink.

"Where will you be?" I asked, voicing the question that most concerned me. "Perhaps I could help in some way, bring you things you need or let you know what's going on outside." The Inuis glanced at one another and then their eyes fell back toward their mugs. After a moment, the professor spoke up.

"It's terribly kind of you to be concerned, but I think it would be best not to tell you anything about the safe house. It's not that we're worried you might let something slip—if that were the case, we would never have brought the sculptures here in the first place. But we can't allow ourselves to cause you any more trouble than we already have. The more deeply you become involved, the more danger you'll be in. You can't be forced to reveal what you don't know, but if you do know something, there's no telling what they might do to get it out of you. So I beg of you, please don't ask about the safe house."

"I understand. I'll leave it at that. I may not know where you are, but I'll be praying for your safety. Before you go, is there anything else I can do?" I clutched my empty mug and looked at them.

"Could I trouble you for a nail clipper?" Mrs. Inui murmured. "His fingernails have gotten so long." She took the boy's hand in hers.

"Of course," I said, searching for a clipper in the back of a drawer. When I had found it, I helped the boy remove his gloves. "Hold still now. We'll be done in one second." His fingers were slender and smooth, and spotless, without a single freckle or mole. I crouched down in front of him and gently took hold of his hand. As our eyes met, he gave me a bashful smile. His legs, dangling from the chair, swayed back and forth.

I carefully clipped his nails, starting from the little finger of his left hand. The nails were soft and transparent, and came away with the least effort, fluttering to the floor like flower petals. We listened to the quiet clicking of the clippers, their echoes sealing this moment in the depth of the night.

When I finished, the sky-blue gloves were waiting on the table.

And that is how the Inui family vanished.

6

I climbed the staircase, so narrow I wondered how I'd get past should I meet someone coming down. It was no more than rough boards cobbled together, with no carpet or handrail.

When I find myself here, I always feel as though I'm in a lighthouse. Only once or twice, in my childhood, have I had occasion to visit one, but I have a feeling the smell and the echo of footsteps were quite similar. The dull sound of shoes on board after board, the odor of machine oil.

The lighthouse of my childhood had long ago ceased to give off light, and no adult ventured to visit it. The spit of land on which it stood was overgrown with sharp reeds, and walking to it meant risking scratches on your legs.

I went with an older cousin who licked my cuts one by one.

Next to the staircase was a small room that had once served as a place for the lighthouse keeper to rest. Two chairs and a folding table were left in the room, and, neatly arranged on the table, were a teapot, a sugar bowl, napkins, two teacups, forks, and a cake plate.

Everything was so perfect—the spacing of the dishes, the direction of the cup handles, the shine on the forks—that I felt a shiver of fear, even as I found myself wondering what sort of delicious cake must have been served on such beautiful plates.

The lighthouse keeper had been gone for many years and the light atop the tower was cold and covered with dust, but here in this room it felt as though someone had been taking tea just a few minutes ago. I felt I'd see steam rising from the cups if I stood staring long enough.

Our hearts still racing despite our quick detour into the room, we began to climb the lighthouse steps. I went ahead and my cousin followed. The light was dim and the staircase constantly curved away above, so there was no way to tell how much progress we were making.

I would have been about seven or eight years old, dressed in a pink lace skirt my mother had made for me. It was by then much too short, even when I pulled on the lace, and I remember being terribly worried that my cousin, coming up behind me on the stairs, would be able to see my underwear.

But why were we there in the first place? I can't recall, no matter how hard I try.

Just as I was beginning to feel out of breath, the sound of waves suddenly grew louder and the smell of oil grew stronger—though at the time I was not sure what I was smelling. At first, I thought it might be something poisonous that was floating up through the tower. I pressed my hand over my mouth and held my breath, but that only made matters worse, and soon I was quite dizzy.

There was a sound from below, and it occurred to me that the people who had been eating cake in the little room were climbing the stairs after us. Having skewered the last morsel with a sparkling fork, the lighthouse keeper had let it dissolve on his tongue and was now following me up the tower, crumbs of sponge cake still clinging to his lips.

I wanted to look back at my cousin, hoping he would reassure me, but I was frozen by the fear that I would find the lighthouse keeper instead. In the end, I stopped and crouched down on the stairs, equally unable to face what I might find at the top.

I don't know how long I cowered there. At some point the lighthouse had fallen quiet, above and below, and I could no longer hear the waves.

I listened, but there was no sound. Just an oppressive silence. Working up my courage, I turned at last to look behind me.

But I saw neither my cousin nor the lighthouse keeper . . .

Still, it's strange that this staircase invariably brings to mind that lighthouse. I come here to meet my lover, so you might imagine I would fly up the stairs, nearly tripping with excitement, but for some reason I climb slowly, listening carefully to each step.

I am in the clock tower of a church. The bell rings twice a day, at eleven o'clock in the morning and again at five in the afternoon. The tools for regulating the clock are kept in a small room at the bottom of the tower—exactly the same size as the room at the base of the lighthouse. The clockworks themselves are in a space at the top of the bell tower, but I have never tried climbing up to see them. My lover waits for me in a room halfway up, where they teach typing.

After a certain point in my ascent, the sound of typewriters comes to me, some being pecked hesitantly, others click-clacking away at great speed. I suppose the class has both beginners and more advanced students who will soon be graduating.

Is he standing near one of the beginners, watching carefully as her trembling fingers tap at the keys? When she makes a mistake, does he gently move her finger to the correct spot—as he used to do for me? . . .

.   .   .

Having written this phrase, I set down my pencil. My new novel wasn't going very well. I seemed to be writing in circles, going backward, or running into dead ends, with no idea what should come next. Still, I often encountered this sort of writer's block, and I no longer took much notice of it.

"How are you doing?" R asked each time we met.

"All right," I answered, unsure whether he was asking about my novel or about me personally. But it was always the novel.

"You can't write with your head. I want you to write with your hand," he said. It was rare for him to make a pronouncement like this, so I found myself simply nodding in silence. Then I stretched my hand toward him, fingers extended.

"That's right. That's where the story should come from," he said, but he looked away, as though he had seen into the most vulnerable part of my body.

At any rate, I was ready to give up for today and go to bed. My fingers were tired and stiff. I put my pencil and eraser in my pen box, straightened the manuscript pages, and secured them with a glass paperweight.

In bed, I found myself thinking about the Inui family. Since that night, I had passed the faculty housing at the university any number of times, but from the outside nothing seemed to have changed. The students were sprawled out on the lawn; the elderly man who occupied the guardhouse at the gate was idly reading a book on bonsai trees.

Futons were hung out to air on the balconies of the faculty apartments near the back entrance to the campus. I located the E block and counted the windows from one end to find apartment 619, where the Inuis had lived. The balcony had been cleaned off and was completely empty.

Then I stopped by the dermatology unit waiting room at the university hospital, but the square on the duty chart for Wednesdays, when Professor Inui had done his consultations, was now filled in with the name of an assistant. Nurses were circulating among the rooms with medicine or bandages or charts. Patients were rolling up sleeves or opening shirts to reveal their afflicted skin. No one wondered where the professor had gone or lamented his absence.

The entire Inui family had simply vanished, as though they had melted into thin air.

But I thought about them, wondering whether they were able to eat dinner at a proper table, with all the dishes and glasses they needed, whether they slept in comfortable beds. I had failed to ask them at the time what they had done with their cat. I should have offered to take him, along with the sculptures. Still, if Mizore had been found hanging about my house, I might have come under suspicion. No doubt the Memory Police could have identified him.

No matter how much I tried to sleep, worries seemed to form like so many bubbles, but unlike bubbles they floated about forever in my head, refusing to pop. Could the Inuis really trust their network of support? The professor had not told me much about it. And the most important thing was for the children to stay healthy. Had the little boy's fingernails grown out inside those sky-blue gloves?

. . .

When I opened my eyes the next morning, something else had disappeared.

It had grown colder and there was frost on the garden. Everything in the house—my slippers, the faucet, the heater, the rolls in the bread box—was chilled. At some point, the wind that had blown in the night had fallen still.

I set the pan holding leftover stew on the stove and around it I arranged the rolls, wrapped in aluminum foil. When the water in the kettle boiled, I made tea, which I drank sweetened with honey. I wanted only warm things this morning.

To avoid having to wash dishes, I ate the stew directly from the pan on the stove. Alerted by the odor of toasting bread, I opened the foil and drizzled honey on the rolls.

While I was chewing, I tried to figure out what had disappeared this time. I was certain at least that it wasn't stew or buttered rolls or tea or honey. They all had the same flavor they'd had yesterday.

It's always sad when a food disappears. In the past, the trucks at the market were overflowing with all sorts of things, but now the selection is meager at best. When I was a child, I was fond of a salad with lots of green beans. It had potatoes and boiled eggs and tomatoes, all dressed with mayonnaise and sprinkled with parsley. Mother would ask the man at the market whether he had fresh beans. "Fresh ones, so crisp they break with a snap!" she'd say.

It's been a long while since we stopped eating such a salad, and I can no longer recall how green beans looked or tasted.

When the stew was gone, I put the empty pan in the sink and turned off the stove. Then I drank a second cup of tea, this time with nothing to sweeten it. My fingers were already sticky with honey.

Despite the cold, the river did not seem to be frozen—or at least I thought I could hear the faint sound of flowing water, and above it the sound of footsteps, adults and children together, running toward the alley in back, and the dog next door barking. The unsettled sounds, I knew from experience, of a morning when something had disappeared.

After I'd finished the warm rolls, I followed the sound of the footsteps and opened the window on the north side of the house. There they stood, all in a group: the former hatmaker, the unfriendly couple from next door, the dog with brown spots, and some schoolchildren with their backpacks. They were staring at the river in silence.

Just yesterday, it had been an utterly unremarkable stream where, at most, you might spot the back of a carp from time to time. But now it was far too strange and beautiful to call it simply a river.

I leaned out over the windowsill, blinking again and again. The surface of the river was covered with tiny fragments of . . . something . . . in an indescribable array of hues—reds, pinks, and whites—so thick that not a space was visible between them. Viewed from above, they appeared to be soft, as they collided and merged with one another, flowing along at a pace that seemed more leisurely than the usual current of the river.

I hurried down to the basement and went out to the washing area where I had greeted the Inui family. From there I would be right above the water.

The bricks paving the area were cold and rough, with clover growing between the cracks, and right below me was the miraculous stream. I knelt down and plunged my hands in to scoop up the water. When I held them in front of me, my palms were covered in rose petals.

"Strange, isn't it?" the former hatmaker called from the other bank.

"Strange, indeed," I answered, and there were nods all around. The children took off running along the river, their backpacks rattling behind them.

"Get straight to school!" the former hatmaker called after them.

None of the petals were withered or brown. On the contrary, perhaps because the water was so cold, they seemed fresher and fuller than ever, and their fragrance, mixed with the morning mist from the river, was overpoweringly strong.

Petals covered the surface as far as the eye could see. My hands had cleared a patch of water for a brief moment, but petals soon came flooding in again to fill it, and then they flowed on, almost as if someone had hypnotized each one of them and was drawing them toward the sea.

I wiped my palms together, brushing the petals that had stuck to them back into the stream. Petals with frilled edges, pale ones, vivid ones, petals with the calyx still attached. They all clung for a moment to the bricks of the wash landing, but in no time at all they were caught up in the stream again and melted into the mass.

. . .

I washed my face and rubbed on a little cream. Deciding against spending the time to apply my makeup, I threw on a coat and went out. My plan was to follow the river upstream to the rose garden on the slope of the hill.

A crowd had gathered on the banks, gawking at this beautiful sight, and the Memory Police, too, were out in force, more so than usual. They stood as always, weapons on their hips, faces devoid of expression.

The children, apparently already bored, had begun throwing stones in the water and stirring it up with long poles they had found somewhere. But the current was undeterred by these small disturbances. A sandbar here or stump there proved no impediment to the overwhelming flow of petals. Were you to stretch out in the water, it looked as though the petals would cover you like a soft, comforting blanket.

"Who would have imagined this?" someone murmured.

"It's the most beautiful disappearance ever."

"We should take a picture."

"Better not. What's the use of a picture when something's disappeared?"

"I suppose you're right."

The bystanders discussed the strange sight in low voices, taking care not to attract the attention of the Memory Police.

With the exception of the bakery, none of the stores had opened yet. It occurred to me to go and see what had happened to the roses at the florist, but the shop was still shuttered. The buses and trolleys were mostly empty. The sun was trying to break through the clouds, and the mist had begun to burn off, but the floral fragrance was as strong as ever.

.   .   .

Needless to say, not a single flower was left in the rose garden. The bare stalks, reduced to leaves and thorns, were thrust into the slope like brittle bones. From time to time, a breeze would blow down from the top of the hill—where the observatory had been—pick up the few remaining petals, and carry them away toward the river.

The garden was deserted. The woman with heavy makeup who was usually at the entrance, the caretakers, the visitors— not a soul to be seen. I wondered for a moment whether I still needed to pay the admission fee, but at last I pushed past the gate and walked along the sloping path, following the route marked out by the signs.

The few flowers in the garden other than roses had survived— bellflowers, a couple of spiny cacti, some gentians. They bloomed

discreetly, as though embarrassed to have been spared. The breeze
seemed to discriminate, choosing only the rose petals to scatter.

A rose garden without roses was a meaningless, desolate place, and it was terribly sad to see the trellises and other signs of all the care that had been lavished on the flowers. The murmur of the river did not reach me here and the rich, soft soil made a pleasant sound underfoot. With my hands thrust in my pockets, I wandered across the hill as though walking through a cemetery of unmarked graves.

In years past, I had carefully studied the stems, leaves, and branches and had read the tags that identified the different varieties, but I realized now that I was already unable to remember what this thing called a rose had looked like.

7

Already on the second day, people who had raised roses in their gardens came to the river to lay their petals to rest. They carefully dismantled the flowers, petal by petal, and slipped them quietly into the stream.

At the base of the bridge next to my laundry platform stood an elegantly dressed woman.

"What lovely roses," I told her. Anything I had ever felt about these flowers had already vanished from my heart, but she was plucking the petals from her own blooms with such tenderness that I'd wanted to say something to her. This was the first thing that came to mind.

"Thank you. They won the gold medal at last year's fair, you know." My comment seemed to have pleased her. "They are the last and most beautiful memento I have of my late father." But there was no regret in her voice as she tore apart the petals and sent them fluttering into the water. The polish on her fingernails was nearly the same shade as the flowers. Once her work was done, she turned and, without a glance at the stream, gave me the sort of graceful bow typical of people of her class and left.

In three days' time, the river had returned to normal, with no visible change in the color or level of the water. The carp, too, were swimming again.

Every last petal washed downstream and out to sea. While they had covered the narrow river in impressive fashion, they vanished almost instantly in the vastness of the ocean, sucked under by the waves. The old man and I watched them go from the deck of the boat.

"I wonder how the wind could tell the roses from all the other flowers," I said, as I rubbed my finger along the rail, dislodging some flakes of rust.

"There's no way of knowing," he said. "The only thing we can know for sure is that the roses are gone." He was wearing the sweater I'd knitted for him and his work pants from his days as a mechanic.

"But what's to become of the rose garden?" I wondered aloud.

"That's nothing for you to worry yourself over. Maybe some other flower will bloom there, or they'll plant fruit trees, or turn it into a graveyard. No one knows and no one needs to know. Time is a great healer. It just flows on all of its own accord."

"The hill will be lonely now that the observatory and the rose garden are gone. There's nothing left but the old library."

"That's true. When your father was alive, he often invited me to come to the observatory. If an unusual bird happened by, he would lend me his binoculars. And to thank him, I would make some minor repairs to the plumbing or wiring. I was also friendly with the gardener who looked after the roses, and when some new variety came into bloom, he would let me have the first peek. So you can see why I was constantly going up the hill. But a person like me doesn't have much use for a library. Except when one of your books came out. Then I went to make sure they had put it on the shelf."

"You actually went all the way there just to see my books?"

"And I'd have complained if one had been missing. But they were there."

"I'm glad. Though I can't imagine many people were borrowing them."

"You'd be wrong then. Two people had checked one out: a middle-school girl and a man who worked in an office. I looked at the library card." His nose was red from the cold sea breeze.

A whirlpool of rose petals had formed around the motionless propeller of the boat. They were wilted and wrinkled after traveling downstream to salt water. Their color and luster had faded, and they were now nearly indistinguishable from the seaweed and fish bones and trash. And their fragrance had dissipated.

When a particularly large wave struck the hull, the boat would give a gentle shudder. At such moments, there was a faint grinding noise somewhere in the bowels of the boat. The setting sun struck the lighthouse at the tip of the cape.

"What will your gardener friend do now?" I asked.

"He has already retired. At our age, there's no need to look for another job, so there's nothing to worry about with the Memory Police. He can just forget about tending roses with so many other things to occupy him. Cleaning his grandchildren's ears or plucking fleas from his cat, all sorts of things." He tapped the deck with the toe of his shoe, which was old but sturdy, and so well worn it might almost have been part of the old man himself.

"I worry sometimes," I told him, without looking up. "I don't know what will happen to the island if things continue to disappear."

He put his hand to the stubble on his chin, as if he wasn't quite sure of the meaning of my question. "What will happen?" he murmured.

"I mean, things are disappearing more quickly than they are being created, right?" I asked him.

He nodded and furrowed his brow, like someone suffering from a headache.

"What can the people on this island create?" I went on. "A

few kinds of vegetables, cars that constantly break down, heavy, bulky stoves, some half-starved stock animals, oily cosmetics, babies, the occasional simple play, books no one reads . . . Poor, unreliable things that will never make up for those that are disappearing—and the energy that goes along with them. It's subtle but it seems to be speeding up, and we have to watch out. If it goes on like this and we can't compensate for the things that get lost, the island will soon be nothing but absences and holes, and when it's completely hollowed out, we'll all disappear without a trace. Don't you ever feel that way?"

"I suppose so," he murmured, repeatedly pushing up the sleeves of his sweater and then pulling them back down in a manner that seemed more and more agitated. "Maybe because you write novels, you come up with these extreme ideas . . . No, I'm sorry, that's rude—maybe I should say grand ideas. Isn't that what it means to be a novelist? To come up with grand stories?"

"Well, I suppose so," I mumbled in turn. "But I'm not talking about stories. This is real—"

"Now, don't you worry," he said, cutting me off. "I've lived here three times longer than you have, which means I've lost three times as many things. But I've never really been frightened or particularly missed any of them when they were gone. Even when the ferry was disappeared. It meant you couldn't ride across to the other side to go shopping or see a movie. For me, it meant I lost the fun of getting my hands oily tinkering with the engine. And I lost my salary. But it didn't really matter. I've managed to get by all this time without the ferry. Once you get the hang of being a watchman at a warehouse, it can be pretty interesting, and I've even managed to go on living here on the boat, where I'm most comfortable. I've got nothing to complain about."

"But not one memory of the ferry remains here," I said,

glancing up at him. "It's nothing more than a floating scrap of iron. That doesn't make you sad?"

His lips worked silently as he searched for a response.

"It's true, I know, that there are more gaps in the island than there used to be. When I was a child, the whole place seemed . . . how can I put this? . . . a lot fuller, a lot more real. But as things got thinner, more full of holes, our hearts got thinner, too, diluted somehow. I suppose that kept things in balance. And even when that balance begins to collapse, something remains. Which is why you shouldn't worry."

He nodded again and again as he spoke. I suddenly remembered how, when I was a child, he would answer this same way, mobilizing all the wrinkles on his face when I'd asked him some question—why your fingers turned orange when you ate clementines, or where the stomach and intestines went when you had a baby in your belly.

"I'm sure you're right," I told him. "It'll all be fine."

"It will, I guarantee it. There's nothing too terrible about things disappearing—or forgetting about them. And those Memory Police are only after people who aren't able to forget."

Dusk was falling over the sea, and no matter how long I peered into the distance, I could no longer make out the petals.

It will soon be three months since I lost my voice. Now nothing passes between the two of us except by means of the typewriter. Even when we're making love, it waits quietly by the bed. If I want to tell him something, I reach out for the keys. Typing is much quicker for me than writing by hand.

In the early days of my muteness, I was continually struggling to speak. I tried running my tongue far down my throat, or filling my lungs with air to the point of bursting, or twisting my lips into all sorts of shapes. But once I realized that this was just a waste of energy, I took to relying on the typewriter.

"What should I get you for your birthday?" he asked one day, and I lowered my eyes to my knees, where my typewriter was usually perched.

Tap, tap, tap.

I'd like an ink ribbon.

He cocked his head, resting his hand on my shoulder, and read the words printed on the page.

"An ink ribbon? That's not very romantic," he said, smiling at me.

Tap, tap, tap.

But I'm worried that they'll disappear and we won't be able to talk anymore.

It made me happy to feel the warmth of his shoulder next to mine whenever we were together—so much so, I could almost forget the pain of having lost my voice.

"I understand. I'll go to the stationer's and buy every last one they have."

Tap, tap.

Thank you.

The words lined up on the page felt quite different from those that were spoken.

I can remember the first time he showed me how to change a typewriter ribbon when I was at the school. I was still at the stage in my studies where I was simply practicing typing "it, it, it, it" or "this, this, this" over and over.

"Before you go home today," he told us, "you'll know how to change a typewriter ribbon. Watch carefully."

He gathered the students around a desk in the center of the classroom and opened the cover of the typewriter. It made a soft clicking sound.

The insides of the machine were much more interesting than I had imagined. The levers supporting the letters, the wheel that worked like a pulley, pins of various shapes, and metal rods dark with oil—all brought together in a complex whole.

"You remove the used ribbon like this," he said, sliding it from the bobbin on the right side. The end of the ribbon unspooled through the levers and wheel and pin. "You hold the new ribbon with the inked surface facing up and insert the end into the left roller. The inked surface is the smooth side. Hold the end of the ribbon firmly in your right hand and do not let go of it. The important thing here is the direction and order in which you insert the ribbon. It's like threading a sewing machine. First, you insert the ribbon in this hook-shaped wire; next, through the wheel; then, behind this pin; and finally, you come back a bit to this . . ."

It was, indeed, a complicated procedure. Not something you could remember after one attempt. The other students seemed anxious, too. But his fingers moved nimbly, almost automatically.

"There, all done," he announced.

At the sight of the ribbon snaking through the typewriter from one spool to the other, the students heaved a collective sigh of relief.

"Did you follow that?" he asked, looking around at the class and resting his hands on his hips. They were clean, without a trace of ink or oil, his fingers as beautiful as ever.

I never was able to learn how to change a ribbon in his class. Inevitably it would get tangled and nothing would appear on the paper, no matter how much I typed. I lived in fear of the ribbon breaking in the middle of class while I was typing.

But now I have no trouble. I can actually change a ribbon even more quickly than he can. Since I started using the typewriter in place of my voice, I use up a ribbon in about three days, but I no longer throw away the old ones. Somehow, I have the feeling my voice may come back one day if I study the letters imprinted on the used ribbon.

. . .

I showed R what I'd written. Since there were quite a few pages, he came to my house so I wouldn't have to carry the bulky manuscript.

We went over the work, debating each line. We changed words and added sentences where something was missing. In one place, we cut several dozen lines altogether.

Seated on the sofa, R calmly turned the pages. He treated my manuscripts with the greatest of care. When I watched him working like this, I was always a bit nervous, wondering whether what I'd written was worthy of such consideration.

"Let's stop here for today," he said. The work over, he took his cigarettes and lighter from his pocket while I gathered up the marked pages and clipped them together.

"Would you like some more tea?" I asked when I had finished.

"I'd love a cup, on the strong side."

In the kitchen, I sliced some cake, made tea, and carried everything into the living room.

"Is this your mother?" he asked, pointing to a photograph on the mantel.

"It is."

"She was very beautiful," he said. "And you look a great deal like her."

"No, my father used to say that the only thing I inherited from my mother was my good teeth."

"Teeth are important."

"My mother always kept dried sardines wrapped in newspaper on the desk in her studio, and she would snack on them as she worked. If I got fussy in my playpen, she would slip one in my mouth to quiet me even before I had any teeth. I still remember the way they smelled, mixed with the odors of sawdust and plaster. They were awful, gritty things."

He looked down and smiled, putting his hand to the frames of his glasses.

After that, we ate our cake in silence for a while. When the two of us had spent time discussing my novel, it often happened that we had no idea what else to say. There was nothing at all unpleasant about it, and I would relax, enveloped by his steady, peaceful breathing. And in any case, the only R I knew was the one who read my manuscripts. I knew nothing else about him, not his childhood, nor his family, how he spent his Sundays, his preference in women or his favorite baseball team. When we were together, he did nothing but read my writing.

After what seemed a long while savoring the silence, R spoke up.

"Do you still have many of your mother's works here?"

"Just a few, the ones she gave as presents to my father and me," I answered, looking once more at the picture of my mother. She wore a flowing summer dress and was smiling bashfully as she held me on her lap. Her hands, remarkably strong from handling chisels, hammers, stone, and other heavy objects, caressed my baby legs. "I don't think she liked keeping her work around. But I do have the feeling that there were more sculptures scattered around the studio when I was a child. I think she must have hidden some of them just after she received the summons from the Memory Police. Perhaps she knew something would happen to her. But that was when I was still very young, so I don't really remember."

"Where is her studio?"

"Downstairs. I think she also worked in a small house somewhere up the river, but after I was born, she was always down in the basement." I tapped the floor with the toe of my slipper.

"I didn't realize there was a basement."

"Well, we call it a basement, though it's not exactly underground. The front of the house is along the road to the south, but in back, to the north, it faces the river. The stone foundation was set down into the water, with the house built on top, so the basement is actually below the level of the water."

"That's a bit unusual, isn't it?" he said.

"I think my mother must have loved the sound of water. Not crashing waves but the gentle flowing of the river—which is probably why she also bought the cottage upstream. She needed only three things in her studio to be able to get her sculpting done: the sound of water, my playpen, and dried sardines."

"That, too, is unusual, don't you think?" he said. He turned his lighter over in his palm and then lit a cigarette. "If it's not too much trouble," he said, hesitating a moment, "would you mind showing me the basement?"

"I'd be happy to," I told him.

He slowly exhaled the smoke from his lungs, as if he had at last managed to accomplish something that had long been weighing on his mind.

.   .   .

"It's chilly down here."

"I'll light the heater. It's old and it takes a while to warm the room. I'm sorry."

"No, don't worry. It's cold from the river, so there's something almost pleasant about it."

We were making our way down to the basement, and he gently took my arm on the dark stairs.

"It's bigger than I would have imagined," he said, looking around the room.

"After my mother died, my father couldn't bear to come here, so it's falling apart." I hadn't been down since the Inui family had passed through. "Feel free to look around," I added.

He walked through the room, examining one by one all the objects that had been left behind—odds and ends, cabinets full of my mother's tools, the five sculptures entrusted to me by the Inuis that were lined up on the top shelf, the glass door that led to the washing platform, the wooden chairs. Though there was nothing particularly worth seeing, he spent a long time going around the room, peering into every corner, as though intent on breathing in the ancient chill that permeated the basement.

"You're welcome to open drawers and look at her notebooks and sketches," I told him. He did, and when he turned the pages, he did so with the same sort of care he used with my manuscripts.

As he moved through the room, he sent up clouds of stone dust. Light from a clear blue sky shone in through a window high in the wall. From time to time, we could hear the sound of a boat going by outside.

"What's this?" he asked, coming at last to the cabinet with many small drawers under the staircase.

"It's where my mother once kept secret things."

"Secret things?"

"Yes . . . I'm not quite sure how to explain it. Lots of different things, all unfamiliar to me." I was at a loss for words as he began opening drawers one after another. But they were all empty.

"There's nothing left."

"When I was little, each drawer held one item. When she was taking a break from her work, she would show me the things and tell me stories about them. Strange stories like nothing I had ever read in my picture books."

"I wonder why they're empty now."

"I don't know. But at some point I realized everything was gone. I think it must have happened in the confusion when the Memory Police took her away."

"You think they took these things, too?"

"No, they never came down here. My mother and I were the only ones who knew about this cabinet. We never even told my father. I think she must have found a way to dispose of them between the time they sent her the summons and her surrender. I was barely ten years old, so I had no idea what these things meant, but I think she realized how important they were after she understood what was about to happen. I suspect she managed to hide them or throw them away or leave them in the care of one of her friends."

"I see," R murmured. He stood under the stairs, stooping to avoid hitting his head, and tugged at one of the drawer handles. I worried that he would get his hands dirty from the rusted metal.

"Can you remember what sorts of things were in here?" He peered up at me, the sunlight reflecting from his glasses.

"Sometimes I try to remember—those were precious moments with my mother—but I can't recall the objects. My mother's expression, the sound of her voice, the smell of the basement air—I can remember all that perfectly. But the things in the drawers are vague, as though those memories, and those alone, have dissolved."

"Still, I'd like you to tell me what you can remember, no matter how dim the impression," he said.

"Well . . . ," I murmured, staring at the cabinet. No doubt it had once been a handsome piece of furniture, but it had fallen now into a lamentable state, covered in dust, with its varnish peeling and handles rusted. Here and there, I could see the remains of stickers I had affixed to the drawers when I was young. "The object my mother told me was most precious," I said, after a long pause, "was an heirloom from her own mother that she kept in a drawer in the second row, right about here. A little green stone, tiny and hard, like a baby tooth that had just fallen out. I think I remember it that way because my own baby teeth were falling out about then."

"And the stone was beautiful?" he asked.

"Yes, I suppose so. It must have been, since my mother often took it out and held it up to admire in the moonlight. But nothing about it remains with me—that it was beautiful or dear or that I wanted to have it—nothing. Just the cold sensation when my mother once set it on my palm. When I stand here in front of the cabinet, my heart feels like a silkworm slumbering in its cocoon."

"But that's just the way it is—everyone feels that way about the things that have disappeared." He touched his hand again to the frames of his glasses. "Could the green stone have been called an emerald?" he added.

"Em . . . er . . . ald," I murmured over and over, and as I did I began to sense a faint stirring somewhere deep within. "Of course, that was it . . . em . . . er . . . ald. I'm sure that's right. But how did you know?"

He said nothing for a moment. Instead, he began opening the drawers again one after the other. The handles gave a muffled clank. When he got to the drawer farthest to the left in the fourth row, he stopped and turned toward me.

"This one held perfume," he said. I was about to repeat my question—how had he known?—but stopped myself. "There's still some here," he said, gently pressing on my back to force me closer. "Can you smell it?"

I peered into the little drawer and took a deep breath, recalling suddenly that my mother had made me smell odors this same way. But all that filled my chest was the chill, stale air. The sensation of his hand on my back was much more vivid than the memory of the perfume.

"I'm sorry," I sighed, shaking my head.

"Don't apologize," he said. "It's very hard to recall things that have disappeared." He blinked and closed the "perfume" drawer. "But I remember," he added. "The beauty of the emerald and the smell of perfume. I haven't forgotten anything."

As the winter deepened, the island was blanketed with heavy, stagnant air. The sun shone pale, and the wind blew every afternoon. People walked quickly, shoulders hunched, hands shoved deep in their pockets.

The dark green trucks with canvas covers appeared more often on the streets. Sometimes they would race by, covers rolled up, sirens blaring, and at other times they would trundle heavily along, covers down. In the gap between the canvas and the bed of the truck, you could catch a glimpse of someone's shoe or a suitcase or the hem of a coat.

The methods used by the Memory Police were becoming more and more brutal. No longer were there advance warnings of their visits, like the one my mother had received. Everything happened by surprise, and they now carried heavy battering rams capable of breaking down any door. They invaded houses in search of any space where someone could be hidden—storage rooms, under beds, in the back of closets. If there was enough space for one human body, it was unlikely to escape their attention. They dragged out anyone they found, along with those who had hidden them, and loaded them all in the covered trucks.

There had been no further widespread disappearances since the roses, but it became increasingly common to hear that someone had suddenly vanished—a friend from the next town, an acquaintance from school, a distant relative of the fishmonger. You never knew whether they had been taken away or had been fortunate enough to find a place to hide—or if the place they'd been hiding had been discovered and they'd been arrested.

Nor did anyone try very hard to find out. Regardless of what had happened, it was almost certainly an unfortunate event, and, moreover, simply talking about it could put you in danger. If on occasion a whole household suddenly went missing with no warning at all, the neighbors would simply pass their house with a furtive glance at the windows, hoping that the former inhabitants were safe somewhere. The citizens of the island were by now quite accustomed to these losses.

.   .   .

"If you don't want to hear what I'm about to say, please tell me."

The old man's hand froze as he was about to cut the apple cake, and he let out a little cry. "But how can I answer before you've told me?"

"I'm afraid you'll have to. Once I've told you, it will be too late. What I'm going to tell you must be kept completely secret—and I need you to promise you'll do that. If you'd rather not, it's perfectly fine. I'll simply keep what I know to myself. But I want you to answer me truthfully, without feeling any pressure. Do you want to hear or not?"

He set down the knife and rested his hands on his knees. The water in the kettle on the stove was coming to a boil. A ray of sunlight shining in through a porthole in the first-class cabin fell on the cake. The buttery frosting glittered.

"I want to hear," he said, looking directly at me.

"You realize this could be dangerous?"

"I know."

"It could cost you your life itself."

"The little I have left," he said.

"Are you sure?"

"I am. It's fine. Please tell me." He looked down, hands still on his knees.

"I'd like to try to help someone. To hide him." I studied the old man's face but there was no reaction. He seemed to be waiting for me to continue. "I know what will happen if I'm found out, but if I do nothing, I know I'll lose a person who is important to me. Just like I lost my mother. I can't do this by myself. I need help—someone I can trust completely."

A strong gust of wind made the ferry groan. The cake plates rattled against one another.

"Can I ask you a question?" he said.

"Of course."

"How are you connected to the person you want to help?"

"He's my editor. The first person who reads my work. He's the friend who knows the self that I put in my novels better than anyone else."

"I understand," he said. "And I'll help you."

"Thank you." I folded my hands over his large, wrinkled ones where they lay on his knees.

. . .

After discussing the matter, we decided that the safest option would be the little room where my father used to store his books and documents. It was a space between the ceiling of the first level and the floor of the second that my father had commissioned a carpenter to construct for storage. The only way to access it was through a small hatch in the floor of his office.

The room was long and narrow, about the size of three ta-tami mats in total, and not more than six feet in height. R, who was quite tall, would probably be unable to stand up straight in it. Furthermore, while there was electricity, there was no running water or light from outside.

The basement was much larger and more comfortable, but the neighbors all knew of its existence, and one had only to brave crossing the little crumbling bridge to gain access. If the house was searched, that would be the first place the Memory Police would look. But they had overlooked the storage room even when they'd come to confiscate my father's research materials. If I was going to protect R, I needed a place far removed from the outside world.

On a blank page of his ferry log, the old man wrote down what each of us needed to do.

First, the list for me:

1. *Clear out all books and documents remaining in the room; since they related to birds, they needed to be disposed of carefully.*

2. *Clean and disinfect everything; hygiene will be important since no doctor can come to take care of R if he falls ill.*

3. *Find a rug to conceal the trapdoor; plain and simple, not an elaborate design that might attract attention.*

4. *Assemble basic necessities for R's everyday life: extension cord, lamp, bedding, electric kettle, tea service, etc.; avoid buying everything new—large purchases attract attention.*

5. *Plan a way to get R to my house unnoticed; this is most important and most difficult.*

Next, the list for the old man:

1. *Install ventilation fan; room is too stuffy.*
2. *Install plumbing to provide a minimum amount of running water; find a way somehow.*
3. *Line room with thick paper, to insulate and soundproof.*
4. *Construct toilet; a complicated project but needs to be done discreetly.*
5. *Learn more about R; from now on he won't have contact with anyone except the two of us.*

We discussed everything in detail, going over the plans for preparing the hidden room and hiding R, making sure we had missed nothing. We imagined every possible hitch or obstacle and how we would cope with it. What to do if our truck was stopped for inspection as we were moving construction materials. What if the neighbor's dog caught wind of something. What if the Memory Police took R before we were ready . . . There were any number of causes for worry.

"Let's take a break and have a snack," the old man said at last. He took the kettle from the stove and poured boiling water in the teapot. Then, while the tea was brewing, he went back to cutting the apple cake. "In general," he continued, "most things you worry about end up being no more than that—just worries."

"I suppose so."

"I know so," he said. "Just leave it to me. We'll manage, you'll see."

"I suppose so," I repeated. "I suppose we will."

He put a large slice of cake on my plate. He still thought of me as a young, growing girl and invariably offered me too much to eat. The plate rested on a snow-white paper napkin. The tablecloth was smooth and starched, and in a bud vase at the center was a small branch with red berries from a tree I often saw at the top of the hill.

We reread the notes we had made in the ferry logbook in order to commit everything to memory. Then, to be rid of the evidence, the old man tore out the page and tossed it in the stove. Engulfed in flames, the paper shriveled and dissolved. We stood in silence for a moment, staring into the fire. Horrible things were about to happen, but somehow we felt increasingly calm. The air in the wheelhouse was warm and smelled of cake.

. . .

The work began the next day. I divided the research materials from the storeroom into small batches and burned them in the garden incinerator as though disposing of old magazines. As for the rug, I decided to use one that had been in the living room, and I managed to find all the basic necessities around the house.

But the remodeling of the room proved to be a more difficult problem. It was rumored that all the carpenters on the island had been recruited by the Memory Police and instructed to alert them to any suspicious construction projects. But it would also attract attention if they found out that we were quietly doing the work on our own.

So we were already in a state of nervous exhaustion by the time we had merely assembled the tools and materials. The old man proved his ingenuity in gathering all the things we would need. He slid lengths of pipe and lumber under his sweater, hung bags of nails and hinges and screws around his waist, and stuffed his pockets full of tools. When he finally reached the house for a delivery, the look of relief on his face was obvious. He would laugh and give an odd stretch to his spine, explaining that the clattering sound all around him as he pedaled his bicycle had made him feel as though his bones were coming apart.

It was wonderful to see how he went about his work. He was careful, precise, conscientious, and, on top of all that, quick. From time to time he would study a drawing he had made ahead of time—probably on a page from the logbook as well—then, once he had collected his thoughts, launch into the work without hesitation. Cutting a hole in the wall, he ran a pipe through it and then connected it with another pipe he found running under the ceiling. He spliced an electrical cable, fastened it onto a new out-let, cut a piece of plywood, and affixed it with nails. I helped him as much as I could, taking care not to get in his way.

To cover the noise from the construction, I played records of symphony music in my father's old office. The old man became adept at timing his work with the hammer or saw to correspond to the climax of a piece when all the instruments were playing together. Often we would work straight through the day, without stopping to eat lunch.

The project was finished in the evening on the fourth day. We sat down and looked around at a room that was better than anything we could have imagined. It was simple, neat, and cozy. The beige wallpaper had proven to be a good choice. There was no getting around the lack of space, but we had still managed to provide all the basic necessities in a compact form. There was a bed, a desk, and a chair, and in one corner a toilet concealed behind plywood walls. The new plumbing allowed the water in the plastic tank above the toilet to flush down to the sewer. I could foresee that from now on it would be my task to refill the tank each day.

The old man had come up with the idea of installing a simple system to communicate with the hidden room. He ran a rubber tube from the office to the storeroom below and inserted funnels he had found in the kitchen in either end. By speaking into the funnels, you could talk without actually opening the trapdoor, as though on the telephone.

The freshly washed sheets and blankets were clean and soft. The desk and chair gave off the scent of new wood. The pale orange light of the lamp was enough to illuminate the room. We switched it off, climbed the steps of the ladder, and pushed up the hatch. Negotiating the tight entrance was no mean feat. You had to narrow your shoulders and twist them to one side as you pulled yourself up with both hands. The old man helped me as I struggled through the opening.

I worried that a man as large as R would get stuck somewhere in the middle of this maneuver, but then I realized that he would probably not have many occasions to leave the room once he entered it.

We fit the door back into the opening and covered it with the rug, leaving no sign at all of the room that lay hidden beneath.

"I have a place to hide you. Please come with me."

When we had finished our work, I made this declaration to R, being careful not to change my tone or expression, exactly as though I had been inviting him to dinner.

The lobby of the publishing company was crowded. Here and there, laughter or the clatter of a coffee cup or the ring of a phone could be heard. I needed to explain quickly, using this noise to cover our conversation.

"You'll be safe there, I can assure you. Please get ready as soon as you can."

R set his cigarette down in the ashtray and looked at me without blinking.

"You've found a hiding place for me?"

"For you—of course."

"But how did you find it? It couldn't have been easy."

"That doesn't matter. But we have to hurry, before they decode your genome . . ."

"I've already decided," he said, interrupting me.

"Decided what?" I asked.

"I haven't told my wife anything. She's pregnant, and the baby will be born in a month. I can't go and leave her behind, and I can't take her with me. No one would be willing to hide a pregnant woman."

"You have to hide by yourself. That's the only way to save not just yourself, but your wife and your baby too."

"But what would that change, whether I hide or not? And when would I ever be able to return?" The smoke rising from the ashtray drifted between us. R tapped his lighter three times on the table, as though trying to calm himself.

"No one knows what the future holds. Someday, even the Memory Police are bound to disappear. That's what happens to everything on this island," I said.

"But—I had no idea you were planning this. I'm confused," said R.

"Of course you are. But for the moment, you need to focus on escaping the Memory Police. I know you must be worried about your wife, but those of us who stay behind will find a way to help her. I'll certainly look after her. Your job is to survive, so that one day you'll be reunited with her and your baby. And besides, if you're arrested, what will become of the novel I'm writing?"

Suddenly sensing that my voice had grown louder and louder, I took a deep breath and drank the rest of my coffee.

The fountain in the courtyard of the building had been turned off, and there were leaves floating in the basin. A black cat dozed on the brick wall that surrounded it. The flowers in the beds were withered, and the wind was scattering scraps of paper across the pavement.

"Where is this hiding place?" R asked, his eyes fixed on the lighter in his palm.

"I can't tell you ahead of time," I said, following the script the old man and I had agreed upon. "It could be dangerous if you knew too much. Once you know, there's always the chance that the secret will leak out. The safest thing is for you to simply vanish into thin air, with no preparation, no prior warning. Do you understand?" R nodded. "Then you can trust me. There's nothing to worry about and I'll take care of everything."

"It seems you've got yourself mixed up in something quite dangerous on my account."

My manuscript was still spread out on the table. R's fountain pen and my pencil were lined up next to each other. He stubbed out his cigarette in the ashtray and slowly looked up at me. He didn't seem particularly upset; in fact, the look on his face was almost peaceful. The failing light in the courtyard threw shadows around his eyes that made his expression appear somewhat sad.

"No, it's just that I want to go on writing novels for you for a long time to come, and I need you as my editor." I tried to smile, but my mouth felt numb, so I hurried on with my instructions. "This is the plan. The day after tomorrow, on Wednesday, come to the ticket gate at Central Station at eight o'clock in the morning. I know that doesn't give you much time, but it has to be Wednesday, and there isn't really anything you can do to get ready. You just need to come by yourself, dressed to go to work, and make sure you fit everything you'll need in your briefcase. If there are things you want later, I can always get them from your wife and bring them to you. When you get to the station, I want you to buy the business newspaper at the kiosk and read it in front of the crêpe shop just to your right after you leave the ticket gate. The shop will still be closed at that hour, but don't worry about it. Before long, an old man will approach you. He'll be wearing corduroy pants and a jacket and carrying a paper bag from a bakery. That will be the sign. You shouldn't speak to him, but once you've made eye contact, you should follow him. That's the plan."

.   .   .

It was raining on Wednesday morning. A deluge that seemed to threaten to inundate the whole island and send it spinning down a whirlpool. When I opened the curtains in my room, I could see nothing but the rain splashing against the window.

I didn't know whether the rain would be good or bad for our plan. On the one hand, it might help us evade the eyes of the Memory Police, but I was also worried that it would impede the movement of R and the old man. In either case, there was nothing for me to do but wait.

I turned up the heater and warmed the whole house. Then I boiled a kettle of water. Finally, I took to checking the street every few minutes from the window in the hallway, in order to be prepared to unlock the door as soon as they appeared. Normally, it took about twenty-five minutes to walk from the station, but there was no telling how long it would take in this downpour.

At 8:25, I suddenly began to feel as though the hands of the clock had slowed. I stood in the hallway and looked back and forth between the window and the clock on the wall in the dining room. The windowpane was cloudy with condensation, so from time to time I had to wipe it with the sleeve of my sweater, which soon became damp in turn.

But the only thing I could see were sheets of rain, obscuring everything—the trees in the yard, the fence, the telephone poles, the sky. Thick, suffocating sheets of rain. I prayed that R and the old man would manage to make their way through. It had been a long time since I had prayed for anything.

It was after 8:45 by the time they finally arrived. I unlocked the door and they all but fell into the hallway, soaked to the skin and grasping each other's shoulders. Their hair was plastered to their faces and their clothes were dripping. Their shoes made a squishy sound. I led them into the dining room near the heater.

They were still clutching the business newspaper and the bag from the bakery that had served as their signs, though both were now limp as dishrags. The rolls in the bag had gone soggy and were completely inedible.

R took off his coat, sank into a chair, and closed his eyes. He sat, breathing quietly. The old man, seemingly determined to warm R as quickly as possible, moved the heater closer and went to find a blanket to put around his shoulders. Drops fell to the floor wherever he went, and soon steam was rising from both of their bodies.

We sat for a while, staring at the heater and listening to the sound of the rain. I'm sure we had things we wanted to say, but it seemed as though something weighed on our chests, preventing the words from coming out the moment we opened our mouths. The flickering flame, visible through the round window in the heater, was bright red.

"It all went exactly according to plan," the old man said eventually, as if speaking to himself. "The rain covered everything."

R and I looked up at the same moment.

"I'm so glad you're both safe," I said.

"I was worried we might be followed," said the old man, "so we took the long way around."

"So does this mean that my hiding place is your house?" R asked. "I would never have guessed."

We were all whispering, as though something bad might happen if we disturbed the silence of the room.

"We aren't working with any of the underground organizations. We did this on our own," I said. "Oh, but I should introduce you. This is our collaborator, a friend of my family since long before I was born."

R and the old man reached out from under their blankets and shook hands.

"I don't know how to thank you," R said, but the old man just
shook his head.

"Let me make you something hot to drink," I told them,
going to the kitchen to warm the cups and brew a stronger pot of
tea than usual. We drank slowly, silent again for a time.

Eventually, they began to dry out. R's hair grew soft again,
and the color returned to the old man's cheeks. The rain continued to fall in heavy sheets. When I was sure that all three cups
were empty, I told R it was time to show him to his room.

.   .   .

R let out a little gasp of surprise as I rolled up the carpet and
lifted the trapdoor.

"Like a cave floating in the sky," he murmured.

"It's a bit tight, I know, but at least you'll be safe here. No one
can see you from outside, and there's not much chance of them
hearing you either."

The old man and I climbed down the ladder, followed by R,
and, as we'd foreseen, with three of us in the room, it seemed
quite crowded. R set his heavy, bulging briefcase on the bed.
Under normal circumstances it would have contained manuscripts and galley proofs, but now, I suspected, it contained even
more important papers.

The old man explained how to use the heater, the toilet, our
improvised intercom, and various other features of the room.
R nodded in response to each item.

"I'm afraid it isn't very comfortable, but as long as our friend
is here to help us, everything should be fine. He can make just
about anything you could need." I patted the old man on the
shoulder as I said this.

He blushed and rubbed the stubble of white hair on his head. R simply smiled.

Once these explanations were finished, the old man and I decided to leave R alone in his room. He had been under tremendous strain and needed to rest. I thought as well that he might need time and privacy to process such a sudden separation from his family.

"I'll bring you lunch at noon," I told him, stopping for a moment on the ladder. "But if you need anything in the meantime, just call on the intercom."

"Thank you," he said.

I closed the trapdoor and unrolled the rug, but for a moment I stood there, frozen, staring down at my feet. I recalled the sound of his voice thanking me, a voice that seemed to rise slowly up as though from the depths of a swamp.

Ten days had passed since R had taken refuge, but it was apparent that it would take longer still before we accustomed ourselves to this strange way of living. We needed to decide about each little detail—when to bring more hot water for his thermos bottle, what time to bring meals, how often to change his sheets.

Then, too, when I sat down at my desk to write, I found myself thinking about the hidden room and I made very little progress on my novel. It would occur to me that R might be lonely and want someone to talk to, but then I'd reconsider, still holding the funnel at one end of our intercom, and conclude it would be better to leave him in peace. No matter how hard I listened, there was never any sign of someone living under the floor, and yet this silence made me all the more conscious of his existence.

Eventually, the days came to pass according to a fixed schedule. At nine o'clock, I would bring the tray with his breakfast and a thermos of boiling water and knock on the trapdoor. During that visit, I would retrieve the empty water tank and refill it. Lunch was at one. If R needed anything, he would give me a list and some money, and I would do the shopping when I went out for my walk in the evening. Mostly he asked for books, but there were other requests as well—razor blades, nicotine gum (since the cramped quarters made smoking impossible), notebooks, tonic water. Dinner was at seven. He bathed in the evening every other day, using a basin of hot water to wash himself. After which, he had nothing to do but wait for the long night to pass.

The only time I lingered in his room was when I came to retrieve his dinner tray. If I'd been able to get something good for dessert, we sometimes ate it together. I would put the cookies or pastry on the desk and we would talk at length, reaching out from time to time for another bite.

"Are you feeling a little more settled?" I asked him.

"A bit, thanks to all your kindness," he answered. He was wearing a plain black sweater. Lined up on the shelf that hung on the wall were a mirror, a comb, a tube of ointment, an hourglass, a good-luck charm. Books, all of them old, were stacked high next to his bed—a memoir by a composer who had committed suicide long ago, a treatise on astronomy, a historical novel about the time when the mountains to the north were active volcanoes.

"If something's wrong, please tell me."

"No, everything's fine."

But it seemed that he was not yet completely accustomed to this room. He sat with his back hunched, his hands on his knees, constantly worried that any unguarded movement would mean bumping into the lamp or the shelf or the wall around the toilet. The bed was clearly too narrow, and there was nothing to brighten the room, neither flowers nor music nor anything else. It was as though the air around him and the air in the room had gone stale, having failed to blend together.

"You should eat," I told him, pointing at the cookies on the desk. Food became scarce during the winter, and it was especially difficult to get sweets. The old man had made the cookies from oats he had obtained from a farmer he knew.

"They're delicious," R said, popping one into his mouth.

"The old man could make his living as a cook," I said. There were a half-dozen cookies. R ate two and I ate the rest. He refused a third cookie, saying he had little appetite since he could not move about much.

The electric heater was turned down low, but it was not particularly cold. When the conversation died, I could hear R's breathing. There was no choice here but to sit practically touching each other. When I glanced over at him from time to time, I could see his profile outlined in the orange glow of the lamp.

"May I ask you something?" I said, still looking at him.

"Of course," he answered.

"How does it feel to remember everything? To have everything that the rest of us have lost saved up in your heart?"

"That's a difficult question," he said, using his forefinger to push up the frames of his glasses and then leaving his hand at his throat.

"I'd imagine you'd be uncomfortable, with your heart full of so many forgotten things."

"No, that's not really a problem. A heart has no shape, no limits. That's why you can put almost any kind of thing in it, why it can hold so much. It's much like your memory, in that sense."

"So you have everything inside you that has disappeared from the island?"

"I'm not sure about everything. Memories don't just pile up—they also change over time. And sometimes they fade of their own accord. Though the process, for me, is quite different from what happens to the rest of you when something disappears from the island."

"Different how?" I asked, rubbing my fingernails.

"My memories don't feel as though they've been pulled up by the root. Even if they fade, something remains. Like tiny seeds that might germinate again if the rain falls. And even if a memory disappears completely, the heart retains something. A slight tremor or pain, some bit of joy, a tear."

He chose his words carefully, as though weighing each one on his tongue before pronouncing it.

"I sometimes wonder what I'd see if I could hold your heart in my hands," I told him. "I imagine it fitting perfectly in my palms, soft and slippery, like gelatin that hasn't quite set. It might wobble at the slightest touch, but I sense I'd need to hold it carefully, so it wouldn't slip through my fingers. I also imagine the warmth of the thing. It's usually hidden deep inside, so it's much warmer than the rest of me. I close my eyes and sink into that warmth, and when I do, the sensations of all the things that have disappeared come back to me. I can feel all the things you remember, there in my hands. Doesn't that sound marvelous?"

"Would you really like to remember all the things you've lost?" R asked.

I told him the truth. "I don't know. Because I don't even know what it is I should be remembering. What's gone is gone completely. I have no seeds inside me, waiting to sprout again. I have to make do with a hollow heart full of holes. That's why I'm jealous of your heart, one that offers some resistance, that is tantalizingly transparent and yet not, that seems to change as the light shines on it at different angles."

"When I read your novels, I never imagine that your heart is hollow."

"But you have to admit that it's difficult to be a writer on this island. Words seem to retreat further and further away with each disappearance. I suspect the only reason I've been able to go on writing is that I've had your heart by my side all along."

"If that's true, then I'm glad," R said.

I turned my palms up and held them out. Then we stared at

them for a time, without so much as blinking, as though I were actually holding something in my hands. But no matter how hard we looked, it was painfully clear that they were empty.

. . .

The next day, a call came from the publishing house. From the new editor who had taken over responsibility for my work.

He was short and thin, a few years older than R. His face was so ordinary that it was difficult to make out the expression it wore. On top of that, since he spoke almost in a whisper and mumbled a bit, I missed a good bit of what he had to say.

"When will you be finished with the novel you're working on?"

"I have no idea," I told him, realizing R had never asked me this sort of question.

"The story seems to be reaching a delicate phase, and I think you need to proceed cautiously. Please let me know when you have something more to show me. I'm very anxious to read the next section."

I leaned forward, my elbows on the table.

"By the way," I said, as casually as I could, "what has become of R?"

"Well," he mumbled, and I could hear him picking up his glass and gulping down some water, "he has . . . disappeared."

The last word of this I heard quite clearly.

"Disappeared . . . ," I repeated.

"Yes, that's right. Have you heard anything from him?"

"No, nothing," I answered, shaking my head.

"It was quite sudden," he said, "and everyone is a bit baffled. He simply didn't show up at the office one morning. No message, nothing. Just your novel, sitting out on his desk."

"Really?"

"Yes, that was all. But of course I suppose it's not that unusual nowadays for someone to disappear."

"I hadn't noticed anything out of the ordinary. You don't suppose . . ."

"No, I don't think so."

"I have some records I've borrowed from him. I don't know how I'll be able to return them."

"If you like, I could take them for you. I may get the chance to pass them along to him."

"I'd be grateful," I said. "And if you find out where he is, could you let me know?"

"I will. If I find out," he promised.

.   .   .

We decided it would be the old man's job to be in touch with R's wife. The toolbox on the back of his bicycle let him pass as a repairman, allowing him to visit her without attracting attention.

Soon after R vanished, she went home to her parents' house to deliver the baby, but that plan had been made well in advance and had nothing to do with recent developments. Her parents owned a pharmacy in a town to the north that had once been home to prosperous smelting works, but that was deserted now that the factories had been closed.

We decided to use the abandoned elementary school in the town as our point of contact. On days ending in zero—the tenth, the twentieth, the thirtieth—she would leave things she wanted to send to R in a wooden box in the courtyard that held meteorological instruments used by the children at the school. The old man would go on his bicycle to retrieve them, leaving items R wanted to send to his wife in their place. That was how we had arranged things.

"Everything seems quieter in winter, no matter where you go, but that's the loneliest place I've ever seen," the old man reported after his first trip. "As soon as I got over the hills, a cold wind hit me in the face. That must be right where the north wind starts to blow. The streets were nearly deserted, more cats around than people, and the houses were old and mostly empty. I expect folks moved away when they closed down the smelters, which look pretty spooky just sitting there, like crumbling rides at an amusement park. No matter where you go, there's another one, sad as can be, as though they died, trapped in place by layers and layers of rust."

"I had no idea," I told him, filling his cup with hot cocoa. "When I was little, there was a beautiful orange glow in the night sky that came from just over the hill."

"I remember, too. There was a time when the men who ran those works were respected all over the island. But that's gone now, and lucky for us it is, since the Memory Police don't go there anymore. It's not likely they'll ever suspect us." He took a deep breath and lifted the cup with both hands.

"How is R's wife?" I asked.

"Tired, as you'd expect. She told me she's having trouble understanding what's happened to her, but that's normal enough. Her husband's been snatched away just as she's about to give birth to their first child. But she's smart and tough, and she didn't try to find out where he is or who's hiding him. She just told me to say how grateful she is."

"So she's gone home to her parents to wait for the baby to be born?"

"Yes. But their pharmacy doesn't seem to be doing too well. While I was there they had just one customer, an old woman who'd come for a bottle of Mercurochrome. It's a tiny little place and everything's showing its age—the sliding door, the floorboards, the old glass cases—I almost wanted to get my toolbox and go help fix it up. R's wife works behind the cash register, but I could see her big belly when she moved around the shop." He sipped his cocoa for a while, and then, as if the idea had suddenly occurred to him, he unwound his scarf from his neck and stuffed it in his pants pocket. I refilled the kettle and set it back on the stove. Drops hissed as they fell on the burner.

"And there was no problem with the handoff at the box?"

"Everything worked perfectly. The school is small and there was no one in sight. The whole place seems to have gone cold, with no lingering warmth or smell from the children, not so much as a footprint. It was freezing, like a laboratory of some sort. Not a place I wanted to hang around, so I came straight home."

The old man retrieved the cloth bag that was hidden under his sweater and pulled out a white envelope and a package wrapped in plastic.

"These were in the box," he said.

I took the package from him. It appeared to be several items of carefully folded clothing and a few magazines. The envelope was thick and tightly sealed.

"The box hasn't been used for a while and it's in pretty bad shape," he continued. "The paint is peeling and the latch was so rusted it was tricky to open. But I figured it out. The instruments are all broken—no mercury in the thermometer and a bent needle on the hygrometer—but that means no one else is likely to look inside. R's wife had left the package tucked out of sight in the back, just as we agreed."

"Thank you," I said. "I'm sorry to have put you in so much danger."

"No, that doesn't matter," he said, shaking his head. The cup

was still pressed to his lips and I worried the cocoa would spill.
"The important thing now is to get these things delivered."

"You're right," I said. I clutched the packet and the envelope to my chest and started up the stairs, feeling the warmth of the old man's body still lingering in the objects.

I was a bit surprised when he appeared for the first class I took at the typing school. He did not look anything like a typing teacher. For one thing, for no good reason perhaps, I had it in my head that typing teachers were always women—women of a certain age, with an overly polite way of speaking, heavy makeup, and bony fingers.

But I found, instead, a very young man. One of average build, dressed in well-cut clothing in understated colors. He was not particularly handsome in a classical sense, but each feature—eyelids, eyebrows, lips, jaw—made a strong impression. His expression was calm and thoughtful but tinged with a distinct shadow, something you would notice if you focused solely on his eyebrows, for example.

He looked like a law professor or a preacher—perhaps rightly so, since we were in a church—or an industrial engineer. But he was, in fact, a typing teacher, one who knew just about everything there was to know about typing.

I never once saw him actually using a typewriter, though. He merely circulated among the students, commenting on the position of our fingers or the way we handled the machine and then marking the mistakes on our practice sheets with a red pen.

From time to time, we were tested on the number of words we could type in a given period of time. He would stand in front of the classroom and take a stopwatch from his jacket pocket. We would wait for his signal, fingers poised over the keys, sample text next to the typewriter. I was fairly certain that he had composed the English words on the pages we were to copy, which were usually letters or, occasionally, something that looked like a thesis of some sort.

These tests were not my greatest strength. Even for words I had been able to type quite easily during practice, when it came to the test my fingers suddenly seemed to freeze. I would reverse the letters "g" and "h" or confuse "b" and "v," or, in the worst cases, miss the starting position for my fingers completely and end up typing nonsense.

I was particularly susceptible to that distinct variety of calm that comes before the start of a test. Those few seconds when everyone held his or her breath, when the sounds of prayers and organ music from the church had died away and our senses were concentrated in our fingers—those seconds completely unnerved me.

I was convinced that the calm in the room would assume an almost physical form, like a gas leaking from the stopwatch he held in his hand. The watch was apparently well used, and its thin silver chain was tarnished. The thumb of his right hand would be poised on the button, which he was about to push at any moment. The chain would be draped across his chest.

The gaseous calm, emanating from his hand, crept along the floor of the classroom, accumulating in the corners and eventually coming to rest on my hands. It felt chilly and oppressive. I had the feeling that the least movement of my fingers would rend the membrane of silence and everything would fall to pieces. And my heart would begin to pound.

At the instant my suffering was reaching a peak, when I was unable to stand even another second, he would give the signal to start. His timing was always impeccable—as though the stopwatch had been measuring my heartbeat.

"Begin!"

It was the loudest thing he said in the classroom. Then every typewriter would begin clicking away. Except mine, which remained frozen as though terrified.

For a long time I have wanted to watch him in the act of typing. It must be very beautiful to see. The glittering, carefully maintained machine, the snow-white paper, his perfectly straight back, his expertly placed fingers. The very thought of it makes me sigh. But I've never yet seen him type. Even now that we have become lovers. He never types in front of other people.

It happened about three months after I'd started attending the typing classes. A heavy snow had fallen that day—the most I'd ever seen. The buses and trains were stopped and the whole town was buried.

I left the house early, walking to the church in order to be on time for a three o'clock class. On the way, I fell several times and the cloth bag I used to carry my books had gotten wet. Even the top of the steeple was covered in snow.

In the end, I was the only one who made it to class that day.

"It's good of you to have come in such weather," he said. As usual, his clothes were perfectly pressed, without a stain or wet spot from the snow. "I thought no one would show up."

"If I skip a single day, my fingers get stiff," I told him, taking my textbook out of the damp bag.

It was particularly quiet that day, perhaps because of the snow. I sat down at the fourth typewriter from the window. We had a rule that the first to arrive could choose any machine she wanted, since each had its idiosyncrasies—sticky keys or worn-out letters. Usually he would sit at his desk near the blackboard, but that day he stood near me.

First I typed a business letter, a request for an advance copy of an instruction manual for a recently imported machine for manufacturing jam. He stared at my hands the whole time I typed.

As soon as my eyes strayed the least bit from the text, some portion of him appeared in my field of vision—shoes, pants, belt, cuff links.

It's difficult to type a letter, with all the rules concerning the line spacing and layout. I'd always had trouble, even under normal circumstances, but with the teacher observing me so closely, I grew more and more tense and made one mistake after another.

Nor did he miss a single one of them. He would bend over, bringing his face close to the typewriter, and point to each error. It wasn't done in the spirit of reproach, but nevertheless, I felt increasingly oppressed, as though I were being backed into a corner by a powerful force.

"You need to press harder with the middle finger of your left hand. That's why the top of the 'e' is always missing." After pointing out the faulty "e," he took hold of my finger. "None of your other fingers are bent this way at the tip."

"No, that's right. I jammed this one playing basketball when I was a little girl." I could tell that my voice sounded a bit hoarse.

"It will work better if you strike the key straight down," he said, holding my finger and tapping several times as he pulled up on the curved joint.

eeeeeeeeee

He had taken hold of the barest tip of my finger, but I was as overwhelmed as if he had taken me in his arms. His hand was cold and hard. I don't believe that he held me with unusual force, but I felt an inescapable sense of oppression, as though the skin of his hand had attached itself to my finger, which continued to tap at the key.

His shoulder, his elbow and hip were just there, next to me. He seemed to have no intention of releasing my finger, which continued to tap at the key.

eeeeeeeeee . . .

The tapping of the key striking the paper was the only sound in the room. Snow had begun to fall again, covering the tracks I had made between the gate of the church and the clock tower. He continued to hold me tighter and tighter. The stopwatch slipped from his breast pocket, turning over once in the air as it fell to the floor. I wondered whether it had broken. It seemed strange that I would be preoccupied with the stopwatch when I should have been worrying about what he was trying to do to me.

The bell in the clock tower began to chime. Five o'clock. The vibration came from far above, rattling the window glass and passing through our bodies, before being absorbed by the snow below. The only motion was the falling of the snowflakes. I held my breath, unable to move, as though locked inside the typewriter.

.   .   .

From that point on, I decided to have R read my manuscript before showing it to the new editor. Needless to say, he could no longer write comments in the margins, but we discussed every detail of the work as we always had, there in the secret room. Since there was just one chair, we would sit next to each other on the bed, using the back cover of a sketchbook as a makeshift table for the manuscript.

It was better for him, too, to have work to do. The healthiest way of living in the secret room was to wake in the morning thinking about the things that had to be done during the day; then, at night before going to bed, to check that everything had been accomplished, whether satisfactorily or not. Moreover, the morning agenda needed to be as concrete as possible, and the tasks ideally involved some sort of reward, no matter how small. Finally, the day's work needed to tire him out in both body and spirit.

"If it wouldn't be too much trouble," R began rather guardedly one evening as he received his dinner tray halfway up the ladder, "would you mind finding me some sort of work to do? I'd like to contribute what I can—and besides, it would help me pass the time."

"You mean something other than reading my novel?" I looked down at him through the trapdoor.

"I do. I know I can't be very useful working here in this room, but any sort of trivial task will do. It may be difficult for you to find something, but I'd be truly grateful. I feel so useless."

He held the tray in both hands and looked down at the food arranged on it. As he spoke, little ripples ran across the surface of the potato soup.

"It won't be difficult at all. I have all kinds of little chores. By tomorrow morning I'll find something. It's an excellent idea, killing two creatures with one stone. So eat your dinner while it's still warm. I'm sorry that it's the same soup day after day, but the harvest was terrible this year, and there are no vegetables other than last year's potatoes and onions."

"Not at all. It's delicious."

"That's the first time anyone has ever complimented my cooking. Thank you."

"And my thanks to you for finding me something to do."

"Not at all. Good night then."

"Until tomorrow."

Standing on the narrow ladder, his hands encumbered by the tray, R simply nodded his good-bye. Once I was sure he had reached the floor, I closed the trapdoor.

Thus it was that supplying him with work came to be added to my daily tasks. They were all simple jobs—organizing receipts, sharpening pencils, recopying my address book, putting page numbers on my manuscripts—but he eagerly took them all on. And by the next morning everything had been finished in the most precise manner possible.

In this way we managed to live in relative security. Everything went according to plan, and we seemed to have solutions for any problems that did occur. The old man did much to help us, and R did his best to adjust quickly to the secret room.

But quite apart from the small satisfactions we enjoyed, the world outside was deteriorating day by day. The disappearances, which had slowed down after the roses, returned with two in quick succession: first, photographs, and then fruits of all sorts.

As I was gathering all the albums and photos in the house—including the portrait of my mother on the mantelpiece—to burn them in the garden incinerator, R made a desperate effort to stop me.

"Photographs are precious. They preserve memories. If you burn them, there's no getting them back. You mustn't do this. Absolutely not."

"But what can I do? The time has come for them to disappear," I told him.

"If their photographs are gone, how will you remember your parents' faces?" he asked, looking deeply troubled.

"It's their photographs that will disappear, not my mother and father," I said. "I'll never forget their faces."

"They may be nothing more than scraps of paper, but they capture something profound. Light and wind and air, the tenderness or joy of the photographer, the bashfulness or pleasure of the subject. You have to guard these things forever in your heart. That's why photographs are taken in the first place."

"Yes, I know, and that's why I've always been very careful with them. They brought back wonderful memories every time I looked at them, memories that made my heart ache. As

I wander through my sparse forest of memories, photographs have been my most reliable compass. But it's time to move on. It's terrible to lose a compass, but I have no strength to resist the disappearances."

"But even if you can't resist them, you don't have to burn your photographs. Important things remain important things, no matter how much the world changes," said R. "Their essence doesn't change. If you keep them, they're bound to bring you something in return. I don't want to see any more of your memories lost."

"No," I said, shaking my head wearily. "Nothing comes back now when I see a photograph. No memories, no response. They're nothing more than pieces of paper. A new hole has opened in my heart, and there's no way to fill it up again. That's how it is when something disappears, though I suppose you can't understand . . ."

He looked down, his eyes sad.

"The new cavities in my heart search for things to burn. They drive me to burn things and I can stop only when everything is in ashes. Why would I keep them when I don't think I will be able to recall the meaning of the word 'photograph' much longer, not to mention the danger if the Memory Police find them. They're even more vigilant after a disappearance, and if they suspect me, that will put you in danger."

He said nothing more. Taking off his glasses, he pressed his fingers to his temples and heaved a deep sigh. I took the paper bag full of photographs that I'd been holding to the incinerator at the back of the garden.

The disappearance of fruit was much simpler. When we woke in the morning, fruit of every sort was falling from trees all over the island. A pattering sound could be heard everywhere, and in the northern hills and the forest park, fruit came down like a hailstorm. Some were as big as baseballs, some small as beans, some covered in shells, some brightly colored—fruits of all kinds. Though the morning was perfectly still, fruit fell from the branches one after the other.

They fell on your head if you walked outdoors, and if you failed to watch your step, you trampled them underfoot. Then, before long, the snow began to fall, covering all the fruit.

It was the first time in ages that snow had fallen. When it started, it had seemed as though white sand was being blown in with the wind, but gradually the flakes grew larger, and in no time the whole countryside was covered. Snow collected on the tiniest leaves on the trees, on the streetlights, on the window frames—and it stayed there for a very long time.

The hunt for memories became a daily activity in the midst of the snowstorm. The Memory Police roamed the town in trench coats and boots. The coats were made of material that looked soft and warm, and the collars and cuffs were trimmed in fur that had been dyed deep green. You could have searched every clothing store on the island and never have found such elegant coats— which made them stand out immediately in any crowd.

Sometimes the Memory Police would appear in the middle of the night, completely surrounding a whole block with their trucks, and search every house without exception. At times these searches would yield results, but at other times they came up empty. No one knew which block would be chosen next. I began waking at night at the slightest sound. My eyes focused on the pattern in the carpet, floating up out of the darkness, while my thoughts turned to R, holding his breath below. I prayed he would pass the night in safety.

The townspeople avoided going out any more than neces- sary, and on weekends they stayed home and shoveled the snow.

They closed their curtains at dusk and lived as quietly as possible. It was as though the snow had frozen their hearts.

Nor did the secret we harbored escape the influence of the island's oppressive atmosphere. One day, out of the blue, the old man was taken by the Memory Police.

.   .   .

I raised the trapdoor and called, "They must have learned something! What should we do?"

I was trembling so hard it was difficult to climb down the ladder, and when I reached the floor, I collapsed on the bed.

"I'm sure they'll be coming soon. We've got to hide you somewhere safer, but where? We should hurry before it's too late. What about going to your wife's family? But I suppose that's the first place they'd look. No, I know. What about the abandoned school where we leave her messages? There must be plenty of rooms you could use: the teachers' lounge or a laboratory, the library or the cafeteria. That would be the perfect place to hide. I'll go to prepare it right away."

R sat down next to me and put his arm around my shoulders. As the warmth of his hand worked its way into my skin, I trembled harder and harder, unable to stop myself—even though I knew he meant his touch to soothe me.

"The first thing we need to do is calm down." He spoke slowly as he loosened my fingers from his knee one by one. "If they knew about this place, they wouldn't have arrested him, they would have come straight here. So there's nothing to worry about for the present—they haven't found us out. But they might, if we make a careless mistake. More than likely, they are looking elsewhere."

"But why did they take the old man?" I asked.

"You can't think of any reason? Had he been stopped on the street while he was carrying something suspicious? Or had the Memory Police come to search the old boat?"

"No, nothing like that," I said, staring at the tips of my fingers, which were still numb despite his gentle care.

"So then don't worry. The investigation probably has nothing to do with me. They're always gathering information. They round up anyone and question him or her about anything at all. A neighbor raising roses in his greenhouse; someone buying slightly more bread than strictly necessary for the number of people in their family; suspicious shadows on the window curtains—things like that. At any rate, we should wait here as quietly as we can. That's the best plan."

"Yes, I suppose you're right," I said, taking a deep breath. "I just hope nothing terrible has happened to him."

"What could have happened?"

"They could have tortured him. There's no knowing what they're capable of. And then even if he didn't want to, he might break down and tell them about this place."

"You mustn't let yourself worry so much." R hugged my shoulder tightly. The electric coils of the space heater lit our faces from below, and the fan continued to rotate with a creaking noise, like the whimper of some small animal.

"If you tell me you need me to leave here, I'll go," he said, his voice low and calm.

"No, of course not. I wouldn't dream of it. I'm not afraid of being arrested. I'm afraid that you'll disappear. That's why I'm trembling like this."

I shook my head as I said this, my hair brushing against his sweater. He held me in his arms for a long while, though there was no way to measure the flow of time in this room where the sun never entered.

I wondered how long we sat there. As the heat of his body warmed me, the trembling gradually subsided. Finally, I pulled free of his embrace and stood up.

"I'm sorry to have lost my nerve," I said.

"There's no need to apologize. The old man is our friend." He looked down at his lap.

"I suppose all I can do is pray," I said.

"I'll pray, too."

I climbed the ladder and released the latch. Then I pushed open the trapdoor. When I turned to look back, R was still sitting on the bed, staring at the coil in the heater.

. . .

The next day, without consulting R, I decided to pay a visit to the headquarters of the Memory Police. I knew that he would have been opposed if I had so much as mentioned this plan, and it was true that nothing good was likely to come from intentionally entering their stronghold. But I couldn't sit by and do nothing. Even if I couldn't get in to see the old man, I would probably be able to learn something about his situation and perhaps even send something to him in his cell. I wanted to help him in any way I could.

The sun was shining weakly that morning, but on the sidewalks, the snow was still piled up, fluffy and new, and it came up to my ankles with each step I took. The Memory Police wore snow boots, but the townspeople had great difficulty making their way through the streets. With their backs bent and their bags clutched to their chests, they pushed ahead step by careful step, like so many animals trudging along, lost in thought.

The snow poured down into my shoes as I walked, and before long my socks were soaking wet. In my bag, I had brought some extra clothes, a blanket, a hand warmer, a tin of hard candies, and five rolls I had baked earlier that morning. On the avenue where the tramway ran, an old theater had been renovated to serve as the Memory Police headquarters. The main entrance was reached by climbing a flight of wide stone steps flanked on either side by ornate pillars. The flag of the Memory Police hung limply atop the building in the still morning air.

Guards were posted on either side of the entrance, their legs slightly apart, hands crossed behind their backs, eyes staring straight ahead. I hesitated, unsure whether I should announce my business to them or try to enter without saying anything. The wooden door ahead of me was thick and heavy, and I wasn't sure whether I would be able to open it by myself. But the guards continued to ignore me, as though they were under orders not to speak.

"I wonder if I could ask a question." Having summoned my courage, I addressed the guard on the right. "I've come to see someone and deliver a few things to him, and I'd like to know where I should go."

The guard continued looking straight ahead and never batted an eyelash. He was pale and much younger than I was, just a boy. The fur trim at his collar looked damp, as though snow had melted on it.

"Then may I go inside?" I said, this time addressing the guard on the left. But the result was the same. So, having no other choice, I put my hand on the knob and tried to pull the door open. As I'd imagined, it was extremely heavy, but by hitching my bag over my shoulder and tugging with both hands, I was at last able to move it little by little. Needless to say, neither young man made any move to help me.

Inside, the hall was dim, with an enormously high ceiling. A number of officers dressed in the familiar uniforms paced back and forth across the room. There were also a few outsiders hurrying along with tense looks on their faces, but no voices could be heard, no sound of laughter. Nor was there any music playing. Just the ringing of heels against the hard floor.

Facing me was a gently curving stairway leading to a mezzanine lobby, and behind that an elaborate elevator left over from the days when the building had been a theater. To my left were a massive antique desk and chair. An enormous chandelier hung from the ceiling, but the glass around the electric bulbs was cloudy and it cast much less light than one would have imagined. And every available space—next to the elevator buttons, over the telephone on the wall, on the pillars under the staircase—was hung with pennants emblazoned with the insignia of the Memory Police.

An officer was seated at the desk, utterly absorbed in something he was writing. Deciding this must be the reception area, I took a deep breath and approached him.

"I have a package I'd like to have delivered to an acquaintance . . ." My voice trailed off, echoing from the ceiling before being lost in the vastness of the hall.

"Package?" He paused, twirling his pen in his fingers, and repeated the word as though trying to recall the meaning of some rarely used philosophical term.

"Yes," I said, thinking this was at least an improvement from the stony guards outside. "Just a few things I thought he could use, some clothes and food."

The man replaced the cap on his pen with a loud click and then cleared away the pages he had been working on to make space on the desk, where he then rested his folded hands. Finally, he looked up at me with a blank expression on his face.

"Actually, I'd like to see him in person, if that's possible."

Since I was getting barely any response at all, I decided to throw
caution to the wind and add this request.

"And whom would you like to visit?" he said, his words quite
polite but his tone so flat that it was difficult to read. I said the old
man's name and then repeated it a second time.

"I'm afraid he's not here," he said.

"But how can you be sure if you haven't even checked?" I
answered.

"There's no need to check. I know the names of everyone
who is being held here."

"But they bring in new people every day. Do you mean to say
you memorize the names of every one of them?"

"That's right. That's my job, you see."

"My friend was just brought in yesterday. I'd be very grateful if you could check to see whether he's here. He must be listed
somewhere."

"I'm afraid that would be useless."

"Then where is he?"

"This is our headquarters, but we have branch offices in
many other places. The only thing I can tell you is that the person
you are looking for is not here."

"So he's being held in one of your other offices. Could you tell
me which one?"

"Our work is divided up into a number of divisions, and the
structure is complex. It's not as simple as you might imagine."

"I never said it was simple. I just want to get this package to
my friend."

The man's brow knit with frustration. The brightly polished
desk lamp illuminated his folded hands, highlighting the bulging
veins. His papers were thickly covered with numbers and letters
in a script I did not understand. The rest of the tools of his trade

were close at hand—files and cards, a bottle of correction fluid, a letter opener, a stapler.

"You don't seem to understand how it works," he murmured, glancing at someone or something behind me. It was the subtlest of gestures, but in an instant two officers appeared and stood on either side of me. These men wore fewer badges on their chests, so I assumed they must be of lower rank than the officer at the desk.

After that, things moved along in silence. Orders were unnecessary, since the procedure had apparently been decided in advance. I was hurried into the elevator, an officer on either side, and then guided through a maze of corridors and into a room at the heart of the building.

As I looked about me, I was puzzled by the unexpected luxury of the furnishings: elegant leather couches, Gobelins tapestries on the walls, a crystal chandelier, and heavy curtains on the windows. There was even a maid who brought in tea. I wondered what they had in store for me. But when I recalled the fancy limousine that had come to take away my mother, I knew I had to be on my guard. I sat down on the couch and set my bag on my lap.

"I'm sorry you've gone to the trouble of coming all this way through the snow, but both visits and packages are forbidden."

The man who had come to sit across from me was short and slender, but the elaborate insignias and medals on his chest seemed to indicate he was quite important. His large eyes made it easier to read his expression. The guards who had brought me to the room stood at the door.

"But why is that?" I said, though I was conscious that I had done nothing but ask questions since I'd arrived at the headquarters.

"Because those are the rules," the man replied, his eyebrows raised.

"There's nothing dangerous here, you can see for yourself," I said, turning over my bag and emptying the contents onto the table between us. The candy tin and the hand warmer rattled noisily as they tumbled out.

"You have no need to worry. Your friend has plenty to eat and a warm room to sleep in," the man said, ignoring my offerings.

"He's an old man whose memories disappear right on schedule. He spends his days doing almost nothing at all. Surely you can't have any reason to keep him here."

"That's for us to determine."

"Then can you tell me what you've decided?"

"You have a talent for asking the impossible, young lady." The man pressed his fingers against his temples. "Most of what we do here must be kept secret. That's the nature of our work," he added.

"Then can you at least tell me whether he's being kept safe somewhere?"

"I can assure you he's perfectly safe. And haven't you just told me there's no need to interrogate him? Or is there something that causes you to worry that he might come to harm?"

I told him no, that there was nothing, and reminded myself that I mustn't get drawn into this sort of exchange.

"Then you have nothing to worry about. We are asking only for his cooperation. He's being served three meals a day, as much as he can eat, and the chefs who work for us come from first-class restaurants. Even if we were to send him that," he said, casting a disdainful glance at the objects on the table, "I suspect he wouldn't want to eat any of it."

"I suppose your rules also prevent you from telling me when he'll be able to go home?"

"Indeed they do," the man said, smiling and recrossing his legs. "You catch on quickly." The tassel from one of the medals on his chest shook. "Our primary function here is to assure that there are no delays in the process and that useless memories disappear quickly and easily. I'm sure you'd agree that there's no point in holding on to them. If your big toe becomes infected with gangrene, you cut it off as soon as you can. If you do nothing, you end up losing the whole leg. The principle is the same. The only difference is that you can't touch or see memories, or get inside the hearts they're kept in. Each one of us hides them away in secret. So, since our adversary is invisible, we are forced to use our intuition. It is extremely delicate work. In order to unmask these invisible secrets, to analyze and sort and dispose of them, we must work in secret, to protect ourselves. I think you can understand." He stopped his monologue here and began tapping the table with his fingers.

I could see the streetcar running outside the window. As it turned the corner, a layer of snow slid from the roof. However weakly, the sun was shining for the first time in many days, and the glare from the snow was blinding. Outside the entrance to the bank across the way, people were lined up to withdraw money. As they waited, they rubbed their hands together and hunched their shoulders against the cold.

Inside, the temperature was comfortable. It was silent, except for the tapping of the man's fingers. The guards continued to stand quietly by the door. I looked down at my muddy shoes, realizing that my stockings had dried at some point.

I came to the conclusion that it would be useless to inquire further about the old man. Thinking back over everything that had been said since I'd entered the building, I realized I had no idea what had become of him. I gathered the items on the table and returned them to my bag. The rolls, which had been warm when I'd left home, were completely cold.

"Now then," said the man, taking a sheet of paper from a

drawer in the table, "it's my turn to ask you some questions." The paper, gray and shiny, contained boxes with endless categories: name, address, and occupation, of course, but also academic history, medical history, religious affiliation, employment experience, height, weight, shoe size, hair color, blood type, and on and on. "Please fill this out," he said, taking a pen from his pocket and setting it in front of me.

That was the moment I began to regret having come. The more information I provided, the closer they would be to R. I should have realized that beforehand. Still, it was even more dangerous to hesitate. Given their history with my mother, it was more than likely they already knew all the information they were asking me to write down. They weren't interested in my name and address; they were testing me. So the important thing was to remain calm, to act naturally.

Telling myself exactly that, I looked the man in the eye as I picked up the pen. The questions weren't particularly difficult, but in order to avoid trembling, I moved my hand more slowly than usual across the paper. The pen glided smoothly, and I could tell it must be expensive.

"Please," said the man, nodding at the tea. "Before it gets cold."

"Thank you," I murmured, but at the first sip I knew it wasn't tea I was drinking. The smell and flavor were subtly different, like nothing I'd ever consumed. A mixture of bitter and sour, as though brewed from dried leaves piled up on a forest floor. The taste was bearable, but it took considerable courage to swallow that first sip, since I was all but certain it was drugged. Was it a potion to make me sleep so they could extract my secrets, or a solution that would allow them to analyze my genes? Or who knew what else?

The man stared at me from across the table, and I could

feel the eyes of the men by the door as well. I drained the cup in silence and then handed him the completed form.

"Excellent," he said, glancing down at the page with a slight smile as he returned the pen to his pocket. The tassel on his medal brushed back and forth.

. . .

It snowed again that night. I found I wasn't at all sleepy, wired from the stress of the afternoon and the strange drink. I took out my manuscript, thinking I would make some progress on my novel, but not a single word came to mind. In the end, I sat by the window and watched the snow through the gap in the curtains.

After some time, I moved aside the dictionary and thesaurus on my desk and pulled out the funnel hidden behind them that we had rigged as a speaker.

"Are you asleep yet?" I asked, my voice hesitant and quiet.

"No, not yet," R answered, and I could hear the mattress springs squeaking. The funnel in the hidden room was mounted on the wall next to his bed. "What's happening?"

"Nothing in particular," I said. "I just can't sleep."

The funnel was made of aluminum, dented and quite old. Though I had washed it carefully, it retained a faint odor of spices from its days in the kitchen.

"It's snowing again," I told him.

"Is that so? It must be getting deep."

"It is," I said. "This is an unusual year."

"It's hard to believe it's snowing just outside the wall here."

I liked the sound of R's voice through the makeshift speakers. Like a spring bubbling up from far below me. As it traversed the long rubber tube between the two funnels, all unnecessary sounds faded away, leaving only the soft, transparent liquid of his voice. I pressed my ear against the funnel, unwilling to waste even a single drop.

"Sometimes I put my hand on the wall and try to imagine what's going on outside. It almost seems as though I can sense it—the direction of the wind, the cold, the damp, where you are, the sound of the river, all the vague signs. But in the end, it never works. The wall is just a wall. There's nothing on the other side, no connection to anything else. This room is completely closed off. All my effort only serves to convince me that I'm living in a cave, suspended in the middle of nothingness."

"Everything outside is completely different from when you came here. The snow has changed everything."

"Changed how?"

"Well, it's difficult to describe. For one thing, the world is completely buried. The snow is so deep that the sun barely starts to melt it when it does come out. It rounds everything, makes it look lumpy, and it somehow makes everything seem much smaller—the sky and sea, the hills and the forest and the river. And we all go around with our shoulders hunched over."

"Is that so?" he said, and I could hear the springs squeaking again. Perhaps he had stretched out on the bed as we talked.

"Right now, the flakes are quite large, as though all the stars are falling out of the sky. They dance in the shadows and glint in the streetlights and bump into one another. Can you picture it?"

"I'm not sure I can. It's almost too beautiful to imagine."

"It's truly lovely," I said. "But I suppose that even on a night like this, the Memory Police are out there hunting. Perhaps some memories never perish, even in this cold."

"I suspect you're right. And I doubt the cold has any effect. Memories are a lot tougher than you might think. Just like the hearts that hold them."

"Is that so?"

"You sound as though that's a bad thing."

"It's just that you have to hide here because of those memories. If you could let yours fade away like the rest of us, there'd be no need."

"Oh, I see." The words were half murmur, half sigh.

When we talked using this makeshift system, we were forced to move the funnel back and forth from our ears to our mouths, leaving a brief silence between each utterance. And thanks to these pauses, the most mundane conversation sounded quite important.

"If it keeps up like this, I'll have to shovel the walk tomorrow morning," I said, reaching out to part the curtains a bit wider. "Trucks from the town hall come every Monday and Thursday to collect the snow. They dump it into the sea at the harbor near the old man's boat. It gets terribly dirty and sad on the way, and you can hear the sound when it gets sucked into the water, as though the sea were swallowing it down its enormous throat."

"They throw it into the sea? I didn't know that."

"It's the perfect place. But I've watched from the wheelhouse on the boat, and I always wonder what happens to it after it vanishes into the waves."

"I suspect it melts almost immediately," R said. "Melts and mixes with the salt water, and then onto the fishes and the seaweed."

"I suppose so. Or the whales drink it in, release it to the tides."

I switched the funnel to my right ear and rested my elbow on the desk.

"At any rate, it's gone without a trace," I added.

"Yes, I suppose it is." He took a breath.

The windows were dark in the neighboring houses, and no noise reached me, no sirens, no cars, not even the wind. The whole town slept, and the only waking sound was the voice coming to me through the funnel.

Though the old man had done a wonderful job of constructing our listening system, it was still extremely rudimentary, and the slightest twist of the tube or tilting of the funnel made our voices seem distant and weak. Nor did it do much good to speak louder. I put my mouth into the funnel and let my words tumble down the tube.

"When I was a child, I was drawn to the mystery of sleep. I imagined it as a land with no homework, no bad meals, no organ lessons, no pain or self-denial or tears. When I was eight years old, I was thinking of running away from home. I no longer remember why. The reason was probably something insignificant—a bad grade on a test or the fact that I was the only one in the class who couldn't do a pull-up. I decided to run away in search of the land of sleep."

"That was quite a plan for an eight-year-old."

"I put it into effect one Sunday when my parents were away at a wedding. My nanny was in the hospital for gallbladder surgery. I found a bottle of sleeping pills in a drawer in my father's desk. I had seen him take a pill every night before he went to bed. I don't remember how many I took that day. I certainly intended to take as many as possible, but it was probably just four or five. But soon I started to feel sleepy, and I let myself drift off, satisfied that I'd taken enough to ensure that I would be going to the land of sleep and would never return."

"So what happened?" R asked, his tone careful.

"Nothing, really. I slept, of course, but there was no world of sleep. Just darkness stretching out in every direction. No, that doesn't quite capture it. It wasn't even darkness. There was nothing, nothing at all, no air or noise or gravity—not even me to experience them. Just overwhelming nothingness. It was evening when I woke again. I looked around, wondering how long I'd slept. Five days? A month? A year? The windows were dyed with the colors of the sunset. But I realized almost immediately that it was the evening of that same day. My parents had come home from the wedding, but neither of them seemed to realize that I'd slept the entire day. They were animated and wanted me to taste the cake they had brought home from the reception."

"The pills didn't make you sick?"

"On the contrary, I felt refreshed after so much sleep. Which made the whole thing worse. Perhaps they weren't sleeping pills at all, but just vitamins or something. In any case, I never made it to the land of sleep or anywhere else—like the snow vanishing into the sea."

The night had deepened and my hand had grown cold holding the funnel. The flame in the stove was wavering, the fuel having run low.

"Would you like me to hold the funnel by the window so you can hear the snow falling?"

I stood up to open the window. The cold was sharper than I'd imagined, and it stung my cheeks. The tube was not long enough, but I pulled it out as far as it would go to bring the outside air to R. As I opened the window, the snow swirled upward for a moment, then quickly settled back into its quiet pattern.

"How is that?" I asked. The snow falling into the room collected on my hair.

"Aah, I can feel it. I can feel the snow."

His quiet words were absorbed into the night.

The old man was released three days later. I had stopped by to check on the boat during my usual evening walk and found him stretched out on the bed in the first-class cabin he used as his room.

"When did you get back?" I asked him, kneeling by the bed.

"This morning," he answered, his voice hoarse and weak. His face was pale, his beard had grown out, and his lips were covered with scabs.

"I'm so glad you're safe," I said, stroking his hair and cheeks.

"I'm sorry I worried you."

"That doesn't matter. How are you feeling? Are you injured? Should I take you to the hospital?"

"No, I'm fine. I'm just a little tired, so I've been lying down."

"Are you sure? Then you must be hungry. Hold on a minute. I'll make you something." I patted his chest through the blanket.

During his absence, everything in the refrigerator had gone limp and stale. But it hardly seemed the moment to worry about it, so I made soup out of every vegetable I could find and then made some tea. Propping him up in the bed, I tucked a napkin around his neck and spooned the soup into his mouth. After a moment, when I thought he seemed to have recovered a bit, I began to question him.

"But what did they do to you?"

"Don't worry. They don't know anything about the room.

I'm sure of that at least. Their attention is focused on a smuggling incident."

"Smuggling?"

"At the end of last month, some men took a boat and escaped from the cape by the lighthouse. They were fleeing the Memory Police."

"But how? I thought the boats were useless. They disappeared years ago. Your ferry doesn't work, does it? And no one would remember how to sail it anyway."

"No, the people who they were hunting haven't forgotten anything—the sound of the engine, the smell of the fuel, the shape of the waves as the boat glides through them." He wiped his mouth with the napkin and coughed before continuing. "There must have been someone in the group who was a naval architect or a navigator, someone who still knew about boats. That must be why they were able to do the impossible—smuggle themselves off the island. Up until now, everyone has been focused on trying to hide. No one even imagined he could get away by crossing the sea. Even the Memory Police seemed caught off guard."

"Did they think you had helped them somehow?"

"Yes. It seems they brought in everyone who knew anything about boats. They questioned me over and over, about everything. Showed me pictures of people I didn't know, took my fingerprints, made me go back over the past few months and tell them where I'd been and what I'd done. It was an impressive interrogation. But I didn't tell them anything about the room, and they were too focused on boats to be suspicious."

I stirred the soup, scooping up some parsley and a piece of carrot, and fed them to the old man. With each bite, he bowed his head, as though excusing himself again for the trouble he was causing.

"But it's too terrible, doing all that to someone who wasn't involved with the escape."

"No, no, it wasn't so bad. Since I had nothing to hide as far as the boat was concerned, their questions didn't really bother me. I just wish I'd been able to put up a bit more of a fight."

"But how did they manage to get the boat ready without the Memory Police finding out?"

"I don't know the details, but I think they must have secretly repaired a boat that was left in the shipyard. They wouldn't have had the right tools or parts. The Memory Police stripped out all the engines when the boats disappeared, broke them in pieces and threw them in the sea. They probably had to make do with all sorts of improvised parts—that's what the police were asking me about, technical things about ships. But of course I didn't help them, since I don't remember anything at all."

"Of course," I said, pouring some tea and passing it to the old man. The air outside the window was still, but the sea had worked up a considerable swell. Strands of seaweed floated in the waves. Evening was creeping over the horizon. The old man took his cup in both hands, peered into it for a moment, and then drained it in one gulp. "But it must have been terrifying—heading out to sea like that in the middle of the night." I shuddered.

"I'm sure it was. Especially since the boat would have been patched together from whatever they could find," said the old man.

"How many do you think there were?"

"I don't really know. But I'm sure it was more than the boat was intended to hold. There must be more than one boatload of people trying to get off the island."

I looked out the porthole again, trying to imagine it—a little wooden boat like the fishermen used, with a flimsy little roof, floating on the sea. The paint peeling away, the hull covered in barnacles and seaweed, the engine puttering softly. And the people crowded together on the deck.

The lighthouse had, of course, long since ceased working, so the only light would have come from the moon, making it difficult to see the expressions on their faces. But perhaps it had been snowing and even the moon had failed to shine, leaving them no more than a black lump huddled close in the bottom of the boat. So tightly packed that the slightest loss of balance threatened to tip them into the sea like so many kernels of popcorn scattering from a pan.

The overloaded boat would have had difficulty working up speed. Nor could they have opened the throttle completely, since the noise would have alerted the Memory Police. That was their greatest fear, a fear that would have forced them to make their way toward the horizon at only the slowest of speeds. Every soul aboard keeping one hand firmly on the rail, the other pressed to his or her chest, praying continually that the boat would clear the cape and find its way to the open sea.

When I blinked my eyes, I realized that the only things floating on the water outside the porthole were the plumes of seaweed. It had been years since I'd seen a boat moving across the horizon. The day they had disappeared, my memories of them had been fixed in place and had sunk into the bottomless swamp of my soul—so that now it was hard work indeed to imagine these people who had gone off over the water.

"I wonder if they got away safely," I said.

"I'm sure that they managed to get off the island. But the seas are rough in winter. It's possible they vanished without a trace."

He set his cup on the table next to the bed and then wiped his mouth with the napkin.

"But where do you think they were going? You can't see anything beyond the horizon," I said, pointing out at the sea.

"I don't know. Maybe there's a place out there where people
whose hearts aren't empty can go on living."

He folded the napkin and set it on the blanket.

.   .   .

In addition to the old man's return, there was another happy
event to celebrate: R's child was born. A baby boy, six and a half
pounds.

Since the old man had not completely recovered, I was making his regular trip to the elementary school myself. The snow
was too deep to go by bike, and I didn't have the money to hire a
driver, so I had to walk all the way to the north of the hill.

Once you turned the corner at the far end of the cape, the
smelting works came into view and all you had to do was continue straight on. The iron tower rose beyond the shuttered cafeteria, the cluster of company apartments, the gas station, the
withered fields. Just as I'd been told, it looked like a great iron
mummy of a corpse that had died of exhaustion.

The streets were unplowed, with only a few tracks from
those who had already passed in the same direction, so I had
trouble walking. Any number of times I lost my footing and fell
to the ground. Only occasionally did I meet another traveler—an
old woman shrouded under her scarf, a single sputtering motor-
bike, a mangy cat.

It was long past noon by the time I reached the school.
The playground was an untouched field of snow. On my right
were a horizontal bar, a seesaw, and a basketball hoop. On the
left, several hutches that must have held rabbits or some other
animal, but which were empty now, of course. Ahead of me

was the school building, three stories high with evenly spaced windows.

Nothing moved in this little tableau—no wind, no sign of life—with the sole exception of my breath, which labored quietly in the cold. Everything that had lost its purpose seemed to have been gathered together right here.

Blowing on my fingers through my gloves, I crossed the schoolyard, heading for the meteorological box. The snow was so perfect and untouched that it was almost frightening to disturb it, and I found myself unable to resist turning around to see whether my footsteps were following me as I made my way across the field of white.

A round cap of snow was perched atop the box. Just as the old man had advised, I pulled on the door while lifting it up just a bit, and it opened with a creak. A spider's web was draped across the dim interior, and I could see the objects behind the thermometer and the hygrometer. A neat package, bound in twine, small enough to fit in my two palms—underwear, some paperbacks, a small box of candy—and tucked on top, a picture of a baby.

Who could have drawn it? I picked it up and studied it. A portrait of a baby with its eyes closed, drawn in colored pencil on a heavy piece of paper the size of a postcard. His hair was soft and brown, his ears perfectly formed, his eyes clearly outlined. Wrapped around him was a pale blue crocheted blanket. The drawing wasn't particularly skillful, but it was clear that tremendous care had been taken in rendering each strand of hair, each stitch in the blanket.

A note from R's wife was written on the back: "The baby was born on the twelfth at 4:46 a.m. The midwife said that it was the easiest birth she'd assisted with in her entire career. He's doing fine. He peed almost as soon as they set him down on my belly. I bought both pink and blue buttons for his clothes, and today I

sewed the blue ones on everything. Please don't worry about us.
We're waiting, hoping for the day when you'll be able to take him in your arms. Please take care of yourself."

I read these words over three times, then tucked the picture back under the twine and closed the door of the box. The snow piled on top broke into pieces and fell at my feet.

.   .   .

I opened the trapdoor to the hidden room without knocking. R was busy at his desk and seemed not to notice as he continued to work on the task I had given him the day before: polishing all the silver in the house.

I watched him from behind for a few moments. Was it an illusion, or had his body actually begun to shrink since he'd hidden himself away here? He had definitely grown pale, without any contact with sunlight, and his appetite was poor, so he'd lost weight, but what I sensed was not that sort of tangible change but some more abstract transformation. Every time I saw him, I could feel the outline of his body blurring, his blood thinning, his muscles withering.

Perhaps this was just evidence that his body was adapting to the secret room. Perhaps it was necessary to rid oneself of everything that was superfluous in order to immerse completely in this airless, soundproof, narrow space shrouded in the fear of discovery and arrest. In recompense for a mind that was able to retain everything, every memory, perhaps it was necessary that the body gradually fade away.

I recalled a circus freak show I'd once seen profiled on television. There was a shot of a wooden box that held a young girl who had been sold to the show. Her head protruded from a hole, but her arms and legs must have been folded tightly inside. She had been forced to pass months and then years in that state, never released even to eat or sleep. In time, her arms and legs would have frozen in place, and she was exhibited to the public as a kind of deformed human insect.

For some reason, as I stared at R's back, this young girl came to mind, her withered limbs and knobby joints, her protruding ribs, filthy hair, downcast eyes.

Still unaware of my presence, R continued his polishing. His back was bent as though in prayer, and he spent a long time rubbing the cloth between each tine of the fork in his hand, each groove in the design. The pieces that did not fit on the desk were lined up on sheets of newspaper he had spread on the floor—the sugar bowl, the cake server, some finger bowls and soup spoons.

My mother used to bring out the silver for special guests. It had been part of her trousseau. But it had been years since anyone had last used it; it had been hidden away in the back of the cupboard in the dining room. No matter how carefully R polished it, I knew it was unlikely I would ever have occasion to use it again. Never again would there be guests, nor parties to invite them to, nor was my grandmother alive to prepare food worthy of these elegant utensils.

It had been harder than I'd imagined to find tasks to distract R that could be done in the hidden room but weren't too tiring. Whether they were truly useful or not was beside the point. Among the chores I had come up with, polishing silver proved to be the one best suited for R.

"Do you plan to go on polishing that fork when the Memory Police come barging in?" At the sound of my voice, R started and turned. He let out a quiet cry, the fork still clutched in his hand. "I'm sorry," I added quickly, "I didn't mean to startle you."

"No, it's fine. But I really didn't notice you," he said, setting the polishing cloth on the table.

"You were so absorbed in what you were doing, I didn't want to interrupt you."

"I suppose I was, though I can't imagine what was so interesting." Embarrassed, he took off his glasses and set them next to the polishing cloth.

"Can I bother you for a few minutes?" I asked him.

"Of course," he replied. "Come and sit with me here." I tiptoed through the silver on the floor and sat down on the bed. "There are some valuable pieces here," he said. "Things you could never find now." He made a half turn in his chair to face me.

"Do you think so? My mother loved them at any rate."

"They're certainly worth the effort it takes to keep them polished. The more care you take with them, the more gratifying they are."

"Gratifying? How so?"

"The film of age gets peeled away and their luster returns—it isn't grand, but something humble, even solitary. When you hold them in your hands, it seems as though you're holding light itself. I feel they're telling me a story."

"I'd never realized silver could have that effect," I said, glancing at the dark blue polishing cloth crumpled in a ball on the desk. He opened and closed his hands to stretch his tired fingers. "I've heard that wealthy families used to employ whole teams of servants just to keep the silver polished," I continued. "I imagine them working day and night in a stone building off a courtyard, with no other job than polishing. There would have been a long, narrow table in the middle of the room, and the servants sat there on both sides of it with their daily quota of polishing stacked in front of them. They were strictly forbidden to speak, lest their breath cloud the silver, so the work took place in absolute silence. The room was always chilly, and even in the middle of the day, the sun never shone in, meaning that the sole source

of light was a single sputtering lamp. Apparently it was only possible to tell that the silver had been properly polished by viewing
it in the lowest of lights. A servant of slightly higher rank—the
one responsible for kitchen utensils—would carefully check
everything as it was finished. He would hold up each piece under
the lamp, with the stone wall in the background, and examine
it from every angle. The slightest smudge would mean starting
over from the beginning—and a doubling of the next day's quota
for the servant, which would keep him polishing through the
next night. So the servants sat, heads bowed in fear, as the inspection was taking place . . . But I'm sorry, this isn't the right time or
place for this story."

I realized I'd said too much on the subject of silver polishing.

"No, not at all," he said.

"I'm afraid I've bored you."

"Anything but," he said, shaking his head.

Up close, I could see even more clearly how frail R had
grown. When I'd known him in the outside world, he had been
much sturdier, more balanced. Each part of his body had played
its proper role, giving the whole a sense of cohesion. There had
been no chinks in his armor. But now it seemed that the smallest
tap of my finger on his chest would have sent him collapsing into
pieces, like a marionette whose strings had been cut.

"The thing that I found most surprising," I said, taking up the
story, "was that over time, the servants who did this work lost the
power of speech. After many long days, dawn to dusk, rubbing
their cloths in that stone room, they actually became mute. They
had no fear of clouding the silver with their words, for even after
they finished work and left the room, they could no longer recall
the sound of their own voices. But these were poor, uneducated
people who were unlikely to find work elsewhere, so they continued polishing year after year, willing to sacrifice their voices for a

steady income. And the room became quieter and quieter as one after another lost the power of speech, with nothing to be heard but the muffled sound of cloth on silver. But I wonder how it got to that point."

I picked up a large dessert plate that had been sitting on the floor and set it on my lap. It was one my mother had used at parties to serve chocolate, something I was never allowed to eat. My nanny had told me that bugs came to infect the chests of children who ate chocolate. The border around the edge of the plate had a raised design of grapes—which R had apparently not yet polished, since the grooves were dark and tarnished.

"I suppose it's hard to know," R said after a pause. His voice sounded weak, as though he had nothing more to say.

The funnel that served as the speaker on his intercom had rolled out by his pillow. The bedcover was freshly washed and starched. X's had been drawn on the calendar on the wall to mark the passing days. I had the impression that the shelves by the bed, which had been empty when R moved into the room, were gradually filling each time I saw them.

"There's no need to hurry with the polishing, you know," I said, after I'd looked around the room for a moment. "You can take your time."

"Thanks, I understand," he said.

"And it would be terrible if you lost your voice."

"No danger there," he replied. "You forget, I'm the one who never loses anything."

"I see what you mean," I said. Our eyes met and we smiled.

When it was time to leave, I gave him the things his wife had left in the box at the school. He looked at the baby's picture in silence. I thought I should say something, but I couldn't think what it would be.

But he didn't seem to be overly emotional. He simply sat qui-

124 etly, his eyes lowered, just as he did when reading my manuscript or polishing silver.

"Congratulations," I said at last, unable to stand the silence.

"Of course, photographs have already disappeared," he murmured.

"Photographs?" I said, not understanding what he meant. Then, after repeating the word to myself, I finally realized I had a vague memory that there had once been smooth pieces of paper that captured someone's image. "Yes, now that you mention it, they must have disappeared."

He turned over the card and began reading the note.

"He's beautiful," I said, when I thought he had finished reading. "The photographs are all gone, but there must still be some frames somewhere. I'll find you one." I rested my foot at the bottom of the ladder.

"Thank you," he said, without looking up.

Something annoying happened. One morning, my typewriter suddenly broke. No matter how hard I tapped the keys, the levers wouldn't move to strike the paper. They just vibrated slightly, like the twitch of a cicada's leg. From A to Z, from 1 to 0, none of them worked, not the comma nor the period nor the question mark.

Up until I'd typed "Good night" to him the night before, the typewriter had functioned normally, and I hadn't dropped or bumped it in the interim. How could it be that I was now unable to type a single character? Of course, I'd had minor repairs done in the past—straightening a bent key or oiling the rollers—but it had always been a sturdy, reliable machine.

So, thinking I might still be able to fix it, I rested the typewriter on my lap and started pressing each key with as much force as I could manage. He knelt next to me, watching as I hit the keys . . . A, S, D, F, G, H, J, K. As I reached L, he wrapped his arm around my shoulders.

"You'll just make it worse, treating it like that," he said, taking the typewriter from me. "Let me have a look." He opened the cover and gently prodded and pulled on various parts.

"Is it broken?" I wanted to ask, but my voice was as frozen as the keys. Only my fingers continued to tap into space as though I were still a typing student.

"It's serious," he said. "It might need major repairs."

What should I do? my look said to him.

"We need to take it up to the room in the steeple. The church lets me use it as a repair shop. I've got the right tools there, and if we can't fix it we can always get you another machine from the school. Don't worry, they have plenty of extras."

.   .   .

I'd had no idea that the space above the classroom was being used for repairs. It had housed the works for the clock-tower bell that struck twice a day, at eleven in the morning and five in the afternoon, but I'd never actually been up there.

To tell the truth, the sound of the bell had terrified me ever since I was a little girl. It reminded me of the groans of a dying man. No matter where I was or what I was doing, if the bell began to ring, my body would suddenly go stiff and my heart would pound in my chest. So it had never occurred to me to want to climb to the top of the tower.

The door to the room was locked, but he reached into his jacket pocket, pulled out a ring of keys, and without hesitating fit the right one into the door. As he did, I caught a glimpse of the stopwatch he kept in the same pocket.

The room was somewhat different from what I had imagined. Behind the face of the clock, there were, of course, gears and pulleys and springs all moving in unison, but the whole of this mechanism took up only a small part of the room. The remaining space was dominated by a mountain of typewriters.

I stood in the doorway for a moment and stared at the sight, shocked that the room could have been hiding so many machines.

"Come on," he said, taking my hand and gently leading me inside. The door clicked shut behind us.

The ceiling was low and there were no windows except for a

circle of glass at the very top of the steeple—all in all, it was a cold and dusty room. The floorboards creaked, and from time to time my heel got caught in the space between them. The sole source of light was a single bulb that hung from the ceiling, too weak to illuminate the whole space. There was no wind, but it swung slightly on its cord nonetheless.

First, I went over to examine the clock. It seemed much larger here than it appeared when seen from below. There was a space between the face and the mechanism so that it was possible to touch the arrow-shaped hands—hands so sturdy I couldn't have moved them had I wrapped my legs around them to weigh them down.

The churchyard below looked tiny, and I felt dizzy realizing the distance to the ground. The clockworks clicked relentlessly; the smell of oil filled the room.

"Have a seat over here," he said, indicating a table and chair in the middle of the room. They were the sole furnishings, old and plain but carefully maintained.

"How do you like it?" he said, looking around at the room as he unceremoniously added my broken typewriter to the pile.

He seemed to be in a good mood, looking perhaps happier than I had ever seen him.

"Well?" He was determined to get my opinion of the room, but I could manage nothing more than a smile and a nod as I stared at him. "I was sure you'd like it," he said, manifestly pleased.

I am unable to relax if I don't have a typewriter. Things seem out of balance. I was obviously upset when I first realized I'd lost my voice, but my anxiety was even greater now at having lost my typewriter.

Why doesn't he start repairing it? I said to myself. But I had no way of communicating the thought. I looked around for my pad and pen, but there was nothing. I regretted having left them at home, but he had taken them from my pocket as we were leaving.

"You won't be needing these," he'd said. "I'll have it fixed in no time."

I gave him a tap on the shoulder and pointed to my typewriter, sitting atop the heap. But he paid no attention and instead took out his stopwatch and began polishing it with a scrap of velvet. I wasn't sure whether he'd failed to understand what I was asking or whether he was trying to signal that the repairs could be done quickly so there was no need to hurry.

We heard voices talking below us, and the sound of children's laughter. People were apparently beginning to gather in the church. Choir practice perhaps, or a bazaar. Though the church was right beneath us, the sounds that came from inside might have been coming from some distant quarter of the town.

He seemed to be content to go on polishing the stopwatch no matter how long I waited, and I found myself amazed that he could spend so much time on such a small object. Nothing escaped his attention as his fingers found their way into each groove in the crown, each link in the chain, each line in the mark engraved on the back of the case.

"The intermediate class has a test today, so I have to give this a good polishing. Come to think of it, you weren't very fast on the speed tests when you first started. You turned in some awful manuscripts," he said, without looking up. If he would not look at me, it was pointless to shake my head or point my finger or bite my lips or even smile, so I sat there with a blank expression.

I looked around the room again. The space that was not occupied by the clockworks was filled with typewriters stacked as high as my head. How many were there? I had no idea. But I was certain I had never seen so many in one place before.

They came in all shapes and sizes—some looked massive and heavy, while others appeared to be as fragile as toys. Some had square keys, others round ones. A few were attached to wooden bases. Some were obviously expensive models, while others appeared to be cheaply made. They were stacked helter-skelter, one pressing tightly against the next. The ones at the bottom of the stack were half crushed, with keys and levers bent out of shape, and even the ones that had escaped this fate were badly rusted.

Were they all waiting here to be repaired? But there were too many. It would be better to get rid of those that were no longer usable. Or so I thought as I rose and moved toward the pile—and as I did, I suddenly realized something. I wondered why I hadn't noticed it before. I was not myself perhaps, stunned at the sight of so many typewriters. Of course! I could simply use one of these machines, and then I would be able to talk with him as I always had.

I chose the newest, least damaged one I could find, but no matter how hard I pressed the keys, they would not move. The ink ribbon on the one next to it was crumpled and twisted, half of the levers on the one after that were broken, and the roller had come off the one after that one. No matter how many typewriters I tried, it was always the same. None was in working order. Still, refusing to give up, I tried to pull a likely looking machine from the middle of the pile, but as soon as I did, the whole mountain began to creak and threatened to collapse.

"They're all useless," he said, still staring at the stopwatch. "Every last one of them."

At that moment I noticed something that should have been quite obvious: there was no paper anywhere in the room. Not a single sheet of typing paper, nor even a scrap fit for a note. There was no point in hunting for a working typewriter if there was nothing to type on.

Once I realized there was no means to get them out, words seemed to proliferate wildly inside me, filling my chest and suffocating me.

Fix one, quickly!

Unconsciously, my fingers began to move as though tapping

out these words. But with nothing to strike, they just fluttered in the air. I went to the pile, retrieved my broken typewriter, and placed it in front of him again, unable to stand the trapped feeling a moment longer.

Why won't you fix it? What's wrong with it? I can't stand it if I can't talk to you.

I held tight to his shoulder, trying with all my might to convey this feeling to him through the expression on my face.

His hands stopped moving and he let out a long sigh. Then he wrapped the stopwatch in the velvet cloth and set it on the table.

"Your voice will never come back."

I had no idea why he was telling me this. The problem now was not my voice but the typewriter.

You can't repair it?

I tapped at the keys at random, but the levers still refused to move.

"Your voice is trapped inside this machine. It's not broken, it's just been sealed off now that it no longer has a purpose."

Sealed . . . sealed . . . sealed . . . The word spun meaninglessly in my head.

"It's an extraordinary sight, don't you think?" he said. "Every one of these is a voice. A mountain of voices wasting away here, never again able to make the air tremble. And today, yours joins them." He picked up my typewriter with one hand and tossed it back where it had been resting. It sounded like a heavy door slamming shut—closing off my voice.

Why? Why are you doing this?

My lips moved but no sound emerged.

"You don't seem to understand. There's no point in trying to talk anymore."

He put his hand over my mouth. His palm was cool and smelled vaguely of metal, no doubt from the stopwatch.

"You'll forget you ever had a voice," he continued. "You may find it annoying at first, until you get used to it. You'll move your lips as you just did, go looking for a typewriter, a notepad. But soon enough you'll see how pointless it is. You have no need to talk, no need to utter a single word. There's nothing to worry about, nothing to fear. Then, at last, you'll be all mine."

The hand that had been resting over my mouth slid down to my chin and then to my throat, where he took his time caressing every hollow, as though making sure that the voice that had once been there was, in fact, gone for good.

I wanted to cry out as loudly as I could, to push him away and run from the room. But I simply stood still, tensing my body. The sensation of his fingers on my throat was like a strand of wire being wrapped around me again and again.

"Do you know why I became a typing teacher?" he asked, his hand still at my neck.

I don't know. I don't understand anything.

I shook my head back and forth, but his hand stayed in place.

"And you don't need a voice to type," he said, closing his hand more tightly around my throat. The tips of his fingers sank into my skin. Perhaps he was trying to wring out any last bit of my voice that remained.

"In the classroom, you were all silent. Not one word while you were typing, while every nerve was concentrated in your fingers. There are rules to govern the fingers, but not the voice. That was the one thing that bothered me. But the fingers! They moved with nothing but the sound of tapping to accompany them, according to my instruction, rapidly and precisely. Glorious, wasn't it? The end of the hour always came too soon. The fingers were lifted from the keys. And then you would begin to talk about anything you wanted to. Someone wants to eat cake on the way home. Someone else knows a good bakery. By the way, are you free on Saturday? What about a movie? It's been ages. How utterly boring. And the fingers that had been obedient a moment before have lost their coherence, are reduced now to fastening a purse or fixing a hairdo or clinging to my arm."

But what could be more natural? I say what I want to say, move my fingers as I want to move them. You only give orders in the class.

"I was glad that I was able to erase your voice. Did you know that an insect will fall silent if you cut off its antennae? It will just sit there, as if frozen, and even refuse to eat. The same as you, really. When you lost your voice, you lost the ability to make sense of yourself. But don't worry. You'll be staying right here. You'll live among the fading voices trapped in these typewriters, and I'll be here with you, giving you instructions. Nothing too difficult. In fact, it will be a bit like learning to type."

He released me at last. I sat down, rested my head on the table, and drew in a deep breath. My throat throbbed.

"The intermediate class is about to begin. I'd better be going down." He slipped the stopwatch into his inner pocket. "The test today involves typing a medical article. Quite difficult, in fact, which should make it fun. But you wait here and keep quiet."

He closed the door behind him. I could hear the sound of a heavy lock turning and his footsteps receding. Then I was alone . . .

.   .   .

I realized that the woman in my novel had also become trapped in a tight place. At this point, I gathered up the pages I'd written that day, secured them under a paperweight, and turned off my desk light. I had imagined that the two of them, bound by a warmer and more ordinary affection, would wander off to search for her voice at a typewriter factory or in a lighthouse at the end of a cape or in a morgue or in the storage room of a stationer's, but somehow things had ended up like this. It happened quite often that my writing went far astray from what I'd imagined before I started, so I went to sleep without worrying any more about it.

The next morning, when I woke up, the calendars had disappeared.

. . .

There were only three or four of them in the house, and they were all advertisements, so I was hardly attached to them. Nor was R as upset over calendars as he had been about photographs. Of course, the loss would cause some inconvenience to begin with, but one could always find other ways to count the days.

I burned them in the little incinerator in the garden. They caught fire easily, and they left behind just the wire spirals that had bound the pages.

The bottom of the incinerator was filled with ashes. They formed a soft mass, which, when nudged with the poker, rose up in a cloud. As I watched the ashes, it occurred to me that the disappearances were perhaps not as important as the Memory Police wanted us to believe. Most things would disappear like this when set on fire, and they could be blown away on the wind with very little regard for what they might once have been.

Smoke rose from the gardens of the houses nearby and was soon absorbed into the low-hanging clouds. The snow had stopped, but the morning was cold as usual. The children wore their school backpacks over heavy winter coats. The neighbor's dog studied the scene from his doghouse with sleepy eyes, only his muzzle protruding out into the snow. People had gathered in the street and were talking in small groups.

"I haven't seen your old friend recently." The man who had once made hats spoke to me over the fence. "Is he all right?"

"He was ill for a while, but he's feeling much better," I told him. For a moment I worried that he knew the old man had been picked up by the Memory Police, but I quickly realized that did not seem to be the case.

"Who wouldn't be under the weather with the cold going on and on like this?"

"Not to mention the fact that there's almost nothing in the market to buy, and you have to wait in long lines for the little they do have." The woman from a house across the street had joined us. "A half hour out shopping in the snow chills you to the bone."

"A few days ago my grandson said he wanted some custard to soothe his swollen tonsils, but I couldn't find any no matter how hard I looked." This was the man who worked at the town hall and lived in the house next to mine.

"Custard is a luxury nowadays. You need eggs, and the chickens won't lay because of the cold. I waited an hour the other day and they would sell me only four eggs."

"I went to five different grocers before I could find a head of cauliflower, but the only one they had left was brown and shriveled."

"And the butcher shops get a little emptier every time you go in. In the old days, you could barely see the ceiling for all the sausages they had hanging there, but now it's just one or two scrawny things and they sell those by half past ten."

Each one in turn told of his or her trials finding enough to eat.

"But it's not just food. Fuel for the stove is getting scarce, too. The other night I ran out completely and it was so cold I couldn't stand it. My knee has started to ache as well, so I knocked on a neighbor's door to ask if she could put me up, just for the night, but she turned me away without so much as an excuse." This was the woman two houses down from mine.

"You can't expect anything from them. They act as though they've never seen you when you pass in the street, and they're rude when you go to collect for the neighborhood association. You can never tell what they're thinking."

They were talking about the house next to mine where they kept a dog. I didn't know much more myself, except that the owners were a young couple in their thirties who both worked and apparently had no children.

Since the topic had shifted to complaining about these neighbors, I wanted to go back inside but, lacking an excuse to leave, I occupied myself by knocking the snow from the top of the wall with the fire poker and nodding. The dog barked, as though he'd realized that they were speaking ill of his masters.

"Still," began the ex-hatmaker. "I wonder if spring will ever come."

The rest of them nodded in agreement.

"Perhaps it never will again," murmured the woman with bad knees.

The former hatmaker zipped up his jacket as far as it would go. I continued my work with the poker.

"In any normal year, the winds would have shifted by now and trees would be budding out. The color of the sea would be lightening. It seems strange to have so much snow on the ground this late."

"Though perhaps not all that strange—we get these odd years now and then."

"But it's not that simple. Think about it. With the calendars gone, no matter how long we wait, we'll never get to a new month . . . so spring will never come."

The old woman rubbed her knees through her woolen leggings.

"Then what's going to happen?"

YOKO OGAWA

"If spring never comes, does that mean summer won't either? How will the crops grow when the fields are covered with snow?"

"I'm not sure I could stand cold like this going on forever. We're already low on fuel."

And so the complaints circled back to the beginning. One after the other, we let our anxieties bubble up. An even colder wind blew down the street as a muddy car rumbled past.

"Don't worry. It's no good overthinking this. Calendars are just scraps of paper. Be patient. It will all work itself out." The former hatmaker seemed to be reassuring himself as much as the rest of us. But we nodded in agreement.

. . .

In the end, however, it was the old woman's prediction that turned out to be accurate. No matter how long we waited, spring never came, and we lay buried under the snow along with the ashes of the calendars.

We decided to celebrate the old man's birthday in the secret room.

"Now that the calendars are gone, there's no way to know when it really is, so please don't make a fuss," he told us. But birthday parties have been a tradition in this house since long before I was born, and even if we couldn't recall the exact date, I knew that his came around every year just as the cherry blossoms were budding out. I was quite certain that time was fast approaching. I also thought that a party would be good for R, who had spent so many dull days hidden away.

I went to the market every day for a week in order to assemble the ingredients for the festivities. As the neighbors had said, the shelves in the stores were poorly stocked, there were lines here and there, and it was particularly difficult to get anything of good quality or a bit out of the ordinary. Still, I patiently made the rounds to every corner of the market.

A sign was posted in front of the greengrocers: "Tomorrow morning, 9:00 a.m., we expect a shipment of fifty pounds of tomatoes and thirty pounds of asparagus." It had been months since we'd seen any sign of either, but if I could buy some, I could make a fresh salad for the party. The next morning I showed up at the store two hours early, but there was already a long line. As I waited, I anxiously counted and recounted the number of people ahead of me, and when it was finally my turn, there was almost nothing left on the shelf. What's more, the tomatoes were green and small, and the asparagus tips were broken off. Still, I was luckier than those behind me who had waited almost as long but came away empty-handed.

A circuit of all the other grocers in the market yielded a small bunch of parsley to decorate the dishes, a few spindly mushrooms of indeterminate variety, a handful of worm-eaten beans, three red and three green peppers each, and a withered head of celery.

And I ended up giving the celery to an old beggar woman.

"Excuse me, young lady. Would that possibly be celery I see peeking from your sack? If it's not too much to ask, I wonder if you'd mind sharing a bit of it with me." Her tone was extremely polite as she approached. "I took a fall in the street from all the snow and I must have dropped my wallet. I don't know what to do. This weather is awful for an old woman like me. You can see that my basket is empty."

She held a plastic shopping basket in front of me, which was, as she'd said, quite empty. I could have passed by without stopping, but for some reason the void in the basket struck me as so sad that I filled it with the celery.

The next day and the day after that I saw the same old woman holding her empty basket in front of someone in the market. I looked for more celery, but there was none to be had anywhere.

The market itself was crowded with people at all hours of the day. Snow had been pushed up in the alleys between the stalls, covering piles of vegetable scraps and fish scales, bottle caps and plastic bags. Shoppers wandered between the stalls, clutching the things they had managed to buy, looking around eagerly for something more interesting. The sounds of laughter or a minor dispute could be heard here and there among the shops.

There were still all sorts of things I wanted to buy. Butter for a cake, wine, spices, fruit for a punch, flowers, a lace tablecloth, new napkins. But I knew I would not be able to get even half of these, since I had to keep some money in reserve for the most important thing: the present.

Buying meat and fish was relatively easy. The shop owners were both friends of the old man.

"I put aside the most tender chicken I had," said the butcher, bringing out a package that had been tied up like a present with a proper bow.

The fishmonger let me choose from a bucket full of live fish. After hesitating for several minutes, I finally selected one that was more than a foot long with spots on its back.

"You have a good eye," said the fishmonger. "This one will be delicious, with nice firm flesh. You're lucky—we don't catch many of these." As he spoke, he snatched up the fish and slapped it down on his cutting board. After striking it once with a heavy stick shaped like a pestle, he scaled and gutted it in the wink of an eye. Clutching the package carefully to my chest, I set off home.

.   .   .

The old man showed up precisely on time that day, dressed in his only suit and wearing a striped tie. His hair had been neatly slicked back.

"Come in!" I told him. "I'm so glad you came."

He bowed as he passed through the door, holding his hand to his throat as if self-conscious about his tie.

He let out a cry as he reached the bottom of the ladder in the secret room.

"How magnificent!"

"It may be a bit crowded, but the decorations dress it up nicely, don't you think? R helped me with everything," I said, feeling rather proud.

We had put things not related to the party away, and then we'd set up a long, narrow folding table for us to sit around—which took up nearly every inch of available space.

Steam rose from the platters of food that had already been set out. The spaces between the dishes were decorated with dried herbs and wildflowers. Since the tablecloth was old and well used, I had set out as many platters as possible in order to cover up the stains, and I had arranged the knives and forks, the glasses and napkins to look as nice as possible.

"Sit down," I told him. "You're right here."

It was quite complicated for the three of us just to take our seats. We had to move on tiptoe in the narrow space, taking care not to bump into the plates or flowers. R took each of us by the hand, helping us to reach the bed, before he maneuvered himself into the lone chair.

Then he opened the wine, which looked more like soapy water, put up as it was in an old, scratched bottle. It had come from the hardware store where they produced it clandestinely in the yard out back, but it was the only thing I could find. Still, I was relieved to see that when it had been poured into our glasses it glowed a lovely pale pink under the lamp.

"A toast!" I said, and we had only to raise our glasses slightly from the crowded table to bring them together.

"Happy birthday!" R and I cried.

"To your health," the old man added, as the glasses clinked softly.

It had been a long time since any of us had been so jolly. R was much more talkative than usual, and the old man's eyes wrinkled with pleasure. As for me, after just one sip of wine my face was glowing and I felt utterly happy. It was as though we had forgotten where we were. Still, from time to time, after a particularly loud burst of laughter, we would cover our mouths and look around sheepishly at one another.

The serving of the fish was an event in itself. It had been steamed in sake and was set on a platter decorated with greens.

"I don't think I can do this," I told them. "I'm sure it will end up a mess. Would one of you do it instead?"

"Don't be silly! It's the hostess's duty to serve the main dish," R said.

"And such a beautiful fish it is!" added the old man.

"I suppose it is," I admitted, "though it lost the lovely spots on the back when I cooked it."

"There's a little cavity here on the head," R said.

"That's where the fishmonger hit it to knock it out. It was swimming around until just a short while ago, so it should be delicious, though it would have been even better if I'd had some celery to flavor it," I said.

"Give our guest of honor some of the meat from the back, where it's most tender," said R.

"Of course," I replied. "But watch out for the bones."

The conversation flowed on without pause. Our voices, the clattering of dishes, the sound of wine flowing into glasses, the creaking of the bed, all blending together with nowhere to go in the tiny, hidden room.

In addition to the fish, we had pea soup, salad, sautéed mushrooms, and pilaf with chicken—all quite simple and in small quantities. R and I tried to make sure that the old man's plate was never empty and that we found the tastiest bites from each dish to serve him. And he, in turn, ate slowly and gratefully.

When everything had been consumed, we stored the plates under the table in order to make room for the cake.

"I'm sorry I couldn't manage to bake something grander," I said, as I pushed it toward him. It really was rather pitiful—barely enough to cover my palm, without whipped cream or chocolate or strawberries to decorate it.

"Don't be ridiculous!" said the old man, turning the plate to admire it from all sides. "I doubt there's a more beautiful cake in the whole wide world."

"I nearly forgot!" said R, taking a packet of thin candles from his pocket and pushing them gingerly into the top of the cake. Anything less gentle would no doubt have reduced the whole thing to crumbs, since I'd been forced to use fewer eggs and far less butter and milk than called for in the recipe, which had yielded a fragile, flaky mass.

"And we won't need this," R added, reaching out to turn off the lamp once his match had lit all the candles. We huddled still closer together as it grew dark, and I could feel the heat of the little flames on my cheeks.

Darkness spread out behind, like a soft veil of shadows shrouding the three of us and keeping out the noise and cold and wind, all trace of the outside world. In here, there was only our breath and the gently flickering flames.

"Well then, blow them out," I said.

The old man nodded and blew ever so carefully in short puffs, as if afraid that he would send cake and candles flying across the room.

"Happy birthday!" R and I shouted again, applauding the old man's efforts.

"I have something for you," I said. As R turned on the light, I reached under the bedspread and pulled out the present I had hidden there: a porcelain shaving set I'd found at the notions store that also had a place for a bar of soap and a pot of talcum powder.

"You really shouldn't have done all this. I don't know what to say."

As he always did when I gave him something, the old man held out both hands to receive it, as he might have when making an offering at the household altar.

"You'll be quite the man of fashion," said R, nodding approval at my choice.

"Why don't you put it in the bathroom on the boat? It will make me happy to think of you using it every morning."

"I certainly will. The pleasure will be mine. But could I ask what I would do with this?" he said, holding up the puff that was meant for applying the talcum powder and eyeing it dubiously.

"It prevents razor burn. Like this," I said, taking it and brushing it lightly against his jaw. He closed his eyes tightly and pursed his lips, as if I were tickling him.

"That feels wonderful!" he said, stroking his cheek. R laughed as he pulled the candles out of the cake.

"I have a present for you, too," said R. We had finished the cake, barely three bites each, and were sipping our tea, one cup each.

"I wish you wouldn't worry about an old man like this, when you've got so much to worry about yourself." He seemed overwhelmed.

"Don't be silly," R said. "I wanted to show my gratitude for everything you've done, though I'm afraid it's not much of a present." He turned in his chair, opened the desk drawer, and brought out a wooden box that was about the same size as the cake I had baked. The old man let out a muffled cry as we stared at the object that had been set in front of us.

The box was stained a dark brown and carved with a geometric pattern of diamond shapes. Four small legs resembling cat's paws were attached to the bottom. A blue glass bead was set in the lid, which was attached with small hinges, and the color seemed to change as the angle of the light shifted. The design wasn't particularly unusual, but something about the look of it made you want to hold it in your hand and open the lid.

"I've used it for a long time, for tiepins and cuff links. I'm sorry it's secondhand, but I don't think you'll find anything like it in the stores now. I suppose you could say it's from another time." R opened the lid, and as he did it almost seemed to me that warm rays of light came from his hands. The old man and I looked at each other and held our breath. There was a quiet creak from the hinges and then we heard a sound coming from inside the box.

The box was lined with felt and a mirror was affixed to the inside of the lid, but beyond that there was apparently nothing else inside. No record spinning, no hidden instrument, and yet a melody was coming from it.

It might have been a lullaby, or a song from an old film, or a hymn. I had a feeling it was something my mother had hummed from time to time, but I couldn't quite remember. The sound was like nothing I'd ever heard before, unlike any stringed instrument or woodwind. It was simple but with a certain sense of style, soft as a murmur and yet in no way weak. As I listened, transfixed, I felt the same slow, spinning sensation that I felt every time something disappeared.

"Where is it coming from?" the old man asked before I could say anything. We were both clearly puzzled.

"The box is playing the song," said R.

"But it's just a box. No one's touching it, and nothing's moving. How can that be? Is it a trick of some kind?" I asked. R smiled but said nothing more.

Before long the song began to slow and the notes seemed to blur and tumble hesitatingly one after the other. The old man cocked his head and peeked anxiously into the mirror. Suddenly, a final note sounded in midtune, and silence returned to the hidden room.

"Is it broken?" the old man murmured, clearly upset.

"No, not at all," said R. He picked up the box and gave three turns to a key attached to the bottom. No sooner had he done so than the music resumed, louder and more cheerful than ever.

"Oh!" the two of us cried together.

"It's like magic!" added the old man. "I don't know how I can accept a gift like this." He reached out toward the box several times only to drop his hands to his knees again, as if afraid he might destroy the magic by touching it.

"It's not really magic," R said. "It's an *orugōru*."

"*Oru* . . ."

". . . *gōru*."

The old man and I divided the word between us.

"That's right."

"What a beautiful word."

"Like the name of a rare animal or flower," said the old man.

We whispered it to ourselves again and again in order to commit it to memory.

"It's a music box. It plays music all by itself thanks to an internal mechanism. You don't remember? Even when you're looking at one? You probably had a few here in this house, somewhere on a shelf or in a drawer. From time to time, when the thought occurred, you would have picked it up and wound the mechanism, to hear a familiar old tune."

I desperately wanted to be able to tell R that I remembered, but no matter how hard I concentrated, the object sitting before me did not trigger a single memory. "So this is something that has already disappeared?" asked the old man.

"That's right," R replied. "A very long time ago. I'm not quite sure when I realized that the disappearances weren't affecting me, but I think it must have been about the time the *orugōru* disappeared. I told no one. I knew instinctively that I had to keep silent. But that was also when I decided to begin hiding as many of the objects that disappeared as I could. It was impossible for me to simply discard them the way everyone else did. Touching them became a way of confirming that I was still whole. This box was the first thing I ever hid. I unraveled a seam in the bottom of my gym bag and sewed the box inside." He pushed his glasses up on his nose.

"Which is why I can't possibly accept something so precious."

"Not at all. The best gift I can give you is one of the things I've been hiding. Of course I know something so insignificant can never make up for all the risks you've taken on my behalf. But I'll be happy if I can help delay or stop this decay in your hearts even in some small way. I'm not sure how to do that, but I think there might be some benefit from holding these forgotten objects in your hands, feeling their weight, smelling them, listening to them."

R turned the box over and wound the key. The melody started again from the beginning. I could see the knot of the old man's necktie and my left ear reflected in the mirror.

I looked over at R. "So you really think our hearts are decaying?"

"I don't know whether that's the right word, but I do know that you're changing, and not in a way that can be easily reversed or undone. It seems to be leading to an end that frightens me a great deal." As he spoke, he swiveled the handle of his teacup back and forth. The old man continued to stare at the music box.

"An end," I murmured to myself. It was not as though I had never thought about this. End ... conclusion ... limit—how many times had I tried to imagine where I was headed, using words like these? But I'd never managed to get very far. It was impossible to consider the problem for very long, before my senses froze and I felt myself suffocating. Nor was it helpful to talk about this with the old man, since he simply repeated over and over that everything would be all right.

"It feels terribly odd to have something that has disappeared right here before my eyes," I said. "After all, this is something that supposedly no longer exists. Yet here we are looking at this box and listening to the music and pronouncing the name . . . *o* . . . *ru* . . . *gō* . . . *ru*. Doesn't that seem strange to you?"

"Not strange at all. The box exists without any doubt and it's right in front of us. The music continues to play, before the disappearance and after. It plays on faithfully, as long as the key is wound. That's its role, now and forever. The only thing that's different is the hearts of those who once heard it."

"I understand," I said. "It's not the box's fault that it disappeared. But what can we do? It's disturbing to see things that have disappeared, like tossing something hard and thorny into a peaceful pond. It sets up ripples, stirs up a whirlpool below, throws up mud from the bottom. So we have no choice, really, but to burn them or bury them or send them floating down the river, anything to push them as far away as possible."

"Is the music from the box that painful?" R asked, bending over and crossing his hands on his knees.

"No, not at all. I don't think so at all," the old man hurried to put in.

"In any case, I suspect the feeling would go away once you got used to it," said R. "In fact, the sound of a music box is particularly soothing. Which is why you should wind it up once a day, in the quietest place on the boat, where no one is likely to hear. I'm sure you'll be able to get the effect of the sound before long. Nothing would make me happier," he added, lowering his forehead to his folded hands.

"Of course!" said the old man. "I'll be very careful with it. I'll put it in the cupboard in the bathroom where I keep the tooth powder and hair tonic and soap, so there'll be nothing suspicious about having a box like this mixed in, and then I'll open it in the morning while I'm shaving with this beautiful set you've given me and in the evening when I'm brushing my teeth. How elegant I'll feel, listening to music while I'm doing my little rituals, and how lucky I feel today, being here with you and celebrating a birthday at my age."

His face was so covered in wrinkles that it was impossible to tell from his expression whether he was laughing or crying. I pressed my hand against his back.

"It was a wonderful party," I said.

"Indeed it was," said R. "The best birthday party I can remember." He reached out to slide the music box toward the old man. The tune danced around us, echoing off the walls of the room. Using both hands, the old man gently closed the lid, as if determined to show how terrible it would be to break it. The hinges creaked and the music died.

At that very instant, the front doorbell gave a shrill ring.

I froze, instinctively grabbing the old man's arm. He held the music box on his lap with one hand, but the other arm he put around my shoulders. R had not flinched, but his eyes stayed fixed on the ceiling.

The bell continued to ring, and we could hear a fist pounding on the door.

"The Memory Police," I whispered, though my voice trembled so much I hardly recognized it.

"Is the door locked?" asked the old man.

"Yes."

"Then we should go and let them in."

"Wouldn't it be better to pretend I'm not home?"

"No. They'll just break down the door and come in anyway. And they'll be all the more suspicious. We need to ask them in as if we couldn't care less and let them search to their heart's content. Don't worry, it'll be fine." He took my hand and together we stumbled the few steps from the table to the bottom of the ladder.

"No need to worry." The old man turned and spoke to R from halfway up the ladder. "I'll be back soon for my wonderful birthday present." R just nodded.

We closed the trapdoor, praying as we did that it would never be opened by anyone other than the two of us.

.   .   .

"Memory Police. Put your hands behind your head. Don't touch anything. Don't talk until we are finished. If you do not comply, you'll immediately be placed under arrest."

There were five or six of them, and they must have been accustomed to giving this speech on doorsteps all over town. After one of them had delivered these lines, they all made their way quickly into the house.

It was snowing hard outside, but I could see that dark green trucks were stationed in front of other houses in the neighborhood. The tension felt palpable in the still of the night.

Their operation proceeded as it always did. Efficiently, thoroughly, systematically, and without any trace of emotion. One after the other, they searched the kitchen, the dining room, the living room, the bath, the basement. They wore their boots and coats throughout. As though their roles had been assigned in advance, some of them moved furniture while others tapped on the walls or rifled drawers. Spots formed on the floor as the snow melted from their boots.

We stood with our backs against a pillar in the hallway and our hands behind our heads, as ordered. They appeared to be focused on their work, but at the same time they never took their eyes off the old man and me, making it impossible for us to move closer together or even so much as exchange looks. The old man's tie was crooked, probably because we had left the hidden room in such a hurry, but his eyes remained fixed straight ahead. To calm myself, I tried to recall the song from the music box, and though it had played only a few times, I was able to remember the whole tune from beginning to end.

"Who are you and why are you here?" A man who appeared to be the leader of the group pointed at the old man and barked his question.

"I've been doing odd jobs here for a long time, so I'm sort of part of the family," said the old man firmly, after first pausing to take a breath.

"The sink is full of dishes. Were you cooking?" The man who had been searching the kitchen turned back to question us.

He had seen the pile of dirty pots and pans and bowls and utensils from the party preparations—clearly a bigger mess than one woman living alone was likely to make—and there was not a single dirty dish in the pile, since we had not started clearing the ones we'd taken to the hidden room. Nor did the dinner table show any sign that we'd eaten there. Perhaps they had sensed that something was strange. The melody inside me played faster and faster.

"Yes."

I had meant to answer clearly, but nothing more than a weak sigh slipped out. The old man took a half step toward me.

"I cook enough for a week and then freeze it," I added, surprised that such nonsense was coming out of my mouth. But of course! I suddenly realized it would have been even more suspicious if there had been three sets of plates in the sink. I told myself I should calm down and be grateful for this stroke of good luck.

The man picked up the pot I'd used to boil the vegetables and the bowl in which I'd mixed the cake batter and studied them for a moment before returning them to the sink and moving off to search the cupboard. I swallowed with relief.

"Move on," the man in charge told the others. "Upstairs." The men filed up the staircase and we followed behind.

I wondered whether their footsteps and the noise from the search had reached R in the hidden room. Was he clutching his knees, his back rounded into a ball, trying to make himself smaller? He was probably sitting on the floor, since the bed and chair tended to squeak, and no doubt he was barely breathing for fear of being heard. And through it all, the music box was watching over him.

There were fewer rooms on the second floor, but the search was even more thorough. The Memory Police rattled about noisily, held things up to the light to examine them, fidgeted with their guns. Each activity seemed to have some hidden meaning, which made the process all the more oppressive.

We were standing against the windows along the hallway on the north side of the house. My arms, still crossed behind my head, grew heavier and heavier. The river flowing beneath the windows had vanished into the night. Lights were on in the neighboring houses, which were probably being searched as well. The old man coughed quietly.

We could see what was happening in the office through the half-open door. One of the men had taken all of the books from the bookshelf and was shining a flashlight into the space between the shelf and the wall. Another had pulled the mattress from the bed and was removing its cover, and a third was glancing through manuscript pages he had found in the desk drawers. Their long, carefully tailored coats made the men seem terribly tall, as though they were looking down menacingly on everything around them.

"What's this?" the man who had been going through the desk asked. He had a wad of pages in his hand. The fact that he'd taken an interest in the desk was, in itself, dangerous, since the speaker for our makeshift intercom was concealed behind the dictionaries.

"A novel," I replied, speaking in the direction of the door.

"A novel?" he repeated, as though the word was somehow vulgar. Then he threw the papers on the floor with a snort, scattering them about the room. More than likely he was the sort of person who had never read a novel in his life. Which was, in fact, a stroke of good luck. As soon as he lost interest in the manuscript, he turned away from the dictionaries as well.

Their boots crisscrossed the rug on the floor of the office, heavy-looking boots that had been carefully greased and polished, that must have been difficult to pull off at the end of the day. As I watched them, I realized something important. One corner of the rug was ever so slightly turned up.

I had been the last one to close the trapdoor and replace the rug. Even in such a rush, how could I have failed to do it more carefully? If one of them noticed and pulled up the rug even a bit, the entrance to the secret room would be discovered instantly.

Once I'd noticed it, I was unable to take my eyes off the turned-up corner. I knew I might be drawing their attention to it, but I couldn't help myself. I glanced to the side, wondering whether the old man had noticed, but his eyes seemed to be focused on some point deep in the distant night.

The boots moved back and forth across the rug. The turned-up corner was barely an inch in length and under normal circumstances would hardly have attracted notice, but now it seemed to fill my entire field of vision.

"What's this?" one of the men said. I immediately thought he must have noticed the rug, and my hands came reflexively to cover my mouth. "What is this?" he repeated, coming toward us with long strides. I repeated a phrase from the music box melody to myself, trying to keep from screaming. "Keep your hands behind your head," he ordered in a deep voice.

I slipped my hands behind my head and clasped them together to keep them from trembling.

"Why is this still here?" he said, holding a small rectangular object in front of my face. I blinked and stared at a pocket date-book that had been in my handbag.

"No particular reason," I said, trying to stop the tune from the music box that was still playing in my head. "I just forgot about it because I hardly ever used it."

He was interested in the datebook and had not noticed the rug—or so I told myself. And the datebook presented no real problem. Nothing important was written in it, at most the date the dry cleaning would be ready or the schedule for street sweeping in the town or an appointment with the dentist.

"The disappearance of the calendars means that we no longer have any use for days and dates. You know what happens if we keep things around us that should have gone away." He flipped through the pages at random but apparently had no interest in what was written on them. "We need to get rid of this right away."

He took a lighter out of his coat pocket, lit the pages of the book, and tossed it out the window. I could see the rug in the space between his widespread legs. The book tumbled through the air, sending off sparks like tiny fireworks. There was a splash, and the sparks lingered briefly in the darkness before being sucked into the river below the window.

At that moment, as though the sound were a prearranged signal, the leader of the group called out, "Stop!" The men left what they were doing, quickly formed a line, and marched down-stairs. Then they walked out the front door, their guns clattering at their belts, without so much as a word to us or any attempt to close the drawers and cupboards they had left in disarray. When they were gone, I collapsed against the old man's chest.

"It's all right now," he murmured, smiling down at me. The corner of the rug had escaped their notice.

. . .

Outside, having completed their search, the Memory Police climbed into their trucks and prepared to depart. The neighbors watched the scene from the shadows of their gates. Cold snow fell against their cheeks and necks and hands, but they didn't seem to feel it. Tension and fear lingered in their bodies, leaving no room for other sensations.

The headlights of the trucks mixed with the streetlights and the white of the snow and chased away the darkness. Though there were now many people gathered in the street, it was so quiet you might almost have heard the snow pressing against the night air.

Just then, three shadows emerged from the house to the east of mine. It was too dark to distinguish their features, but they walked wearily through the snow, backs bent, the Memory Police pushing them from behind, the light glinting cruelly off their guns.

Snatches of my neighbors' voices could be heard in the dark.

"I had no idea they were hiding people in there," said the former hatmaker. "Who would have thought it?"

"Seems as though both the husband and wife were in a secret group that helps folks like that."

"I guess that's why they didn't get to know anyone in the neighborhood."

"Look at him. He's just a child."

"Poor thing."

The old man and I held hands and watched as the Memory Police forced them into the covered back of one of the trucks. We could see a boy of fifteen or sixteen being held on either side by the couple. He looked sturdy enough, but the pom-poms decorating the fringe of his scarf made it clear he was still young.

The canvas cover was lowered and the line of trucks drove away. The neighbors retreated to their houses. Alone now in the street, the old man and I squeezed our hands more tightly and stared into the darkness for a long time. The dog from the house next door, left to his own devices, was rubbing his snout in the snow and snorting.

.   .   .

That night, I wept in the hidden room. Never in my life had I cried for so long without stopping. I knew, of course, that I should be happy that nothing had happened to R, but for some reason I was unable to control my emotions and they were swept away in a direction I hadn't anticipated.

But I'm not sure the word "crying" did justice to what I was experiencing. Clearly, it was not a matter of being sad. Nor was it just relief from the tension I had felt. It was simply that all the thoughts that had floated through my mind since I'd first taken R into my care had been changed into tears and come flooding out. And there was no way to stop them. I clenched my teeth, telling myself that I shouldn't let him see me in such a pitiful state, but despite his attempts to comfort me with gentle reassurances, it was useless. I could do nothing but sit very still, eyes downcast, in the company of my flowing tears.

"I never thought I'd be happy that this room is so small," I murmured, turning to sprawl facedown on the bed.

"And why is that?" He was sitting next to me, stroking my hair and back, trying as best he could to calm me.

"Because the smaller it is, the closer we feel. On a night like this, when I couldn't stand to be alone, it's peaceful to be in such a tiny space."

The quilt was warm and damp against my cheek. The folding table and dishes from the party had been put away and the room was back to normal. I thought I detected the slightly sweet smell of the cake, the only sign of our celebration.

"You can stay here as long as you want to. I don't think they'll be coming back again tonight." As he spoke, he bent toward me as though trying to read my expression.

"Forgive me," I said. "The truth is, I should be comforting you."

"Don't be silly. Your night was much more frightening than mine. All I had to do was stay here and keep quiet."

"They walked back and forth, back and forth, right above you. You must have heard them."

"Of course," he said, nodding.

"The corner of the rug was turned up ever so slightly. We were hurrying when we left you and I didn't put it back quite the right way. I knew it would be the end if they noticed it. It felt terrible that your fate depended on something as insignificant as the corner of a rug. I wanted to run over and stomp it down, stomp it until the rug melted into the floor—but I knew I couldn't. I could only stand there trembling like a frightened rabbit."

My tears had continued to flow the whole time I was speaking, and it seemed strange that I was able to express myself so clearly while I was crying. My feelings and tears and words all seemed to flow from a place I could not reach.

"I'm sorry you were suffering so much on my account."

He looked down at the electric heater at his feet.

"I'm not crying about that. Believe me, if I were so afraid of the Memory Police I never would have agreed to hide you in the first place. I don't really know why I'm crying. I can't explain it myself, much less stop it."

I raised my head from the quilt and brushed the hair out of my eyes.

"There's no need to look for an explanation for something that has none. What matters now is that I've put you and the old man in danger," said R.

"No, it's not that. I think all this crying must be proof that my heart is so weak that I don't know how to help myself."

"But I'd say it's just the opposite. Your heart is doing everything it can to preserve its existence. No matter how many memories these men take away, they'll never reduce it to nothing."

"I hope that's true."

I looked at R. I needed only to lean slightly in his direction for us to be touching. He raised his hand and brushed away a tear at the corner of my eye with his fingers. They were warm. I watched as my tears fell on his hand. And then he took me in his arms.

The silence of the night had returned. It suddenly seemed unbelievable that less than an hour ago the doorbell had rung and boots had stomped across the floor above this room. Now I could feel nothing but the beating of his heart through his sweater.

He embraced me gently, his hands encircling my back as though holding a cloud, and at last my tears stopped. Everything that had happened—shopping in the market, the death of the fish, lighting the candles on the cake, opening the music box, the burning of the datebook—seemed like memories from the distant past. We were entirely in the present. *There, behind your heartbeat, have you stored up all my lost memories?* I thought this to myself, cheek pressed against R's chest. If I could, I would have liked to take them out and line them up in front of me one by one. I was sure that any memories that remained inside him would be very much alive, so different from my own, which were few in number and very pale—sodden flower petals sinking into the waves or the ashes at the bottom of the incinerator.

I closed my eyes. My eyelashes touched the wool of his sweater.

"The people in the house next door were loaded into a truck and taken away," I murmured. "They were hiding an innocent boy. I wonder how long he'd been there. It seems strange to think that I had no idea there was someone nearby who was going through exactly the same thing you are."

"Where do you suppose they took him?" He breathed the words into my hair.

"I watched for a long time in the dark after the truck had gone, wondering the same thing. I didn't even notice that I wasn't wearing a coat or gloves, that the snow was hitting my face. I stood there hoping that if I waited long enough I might discover where my memories have gone."

R took my shoulders in his hands and gazed into the space between our bodies.

I wanted to tell him that I knew I'd never learn anything, no matter how long I waited, but he had covered my lips with his and I could say nothing more.

I wonder how many days I've been stuck here, in the clock tower. I have no way of knowing.

Of course, with this enormous clock right here, you can always find out what time it is. There's even a bell that rings twice a day, at eleven in the morning and again at five in the afternoon. In the beginning, to count the passing days, I made a mark with my fingernail each morning on the leg of the chair. But I've long since lost track. The chair was scarred to begin with and it eventually became impossible to tell which marks were ones I'd made.

Time passes like a long, frigid stream, without my knowing the month or date or day of the week. But I suppose it's enough to be imprisoned here just as he wants me to be, surrounded by innumerable voices of the dead. What good would it do me to know the day or the date?

At first I could see only the typewriters and the mechanism of the clock, but after a time, I began to notice other details about the room.

Near the center of the wall to the west, the mountain of typewriters dropped off precipitously. I had only to climb over a few machines to reach a door, through which I found a simple bathroom. There was a small window above the sink, and from time to time I would climb up on the sink, open the window, and stare at the scene outside. I could see the roofs of houses, fields, a stream, a park. The clock tower is the tallest building in the town, so there was nothing

above me as I looked out, just the sky stretching in every direction.
It felt good to breathe fresh air like this. It soon became apparent
that the sink was not strong enough to support my weight, and water
began seeping from a spot where the pipe must have pulled away
from the porcelain and the tiles.

Another revelation came from the contents of the drawer in the
table, though it contained nothing as interesting as a hammer that I
might have used to smash the lock on the door. What I did find was
a puzzle made of bent wire, some thumbtacks, a tube of menthol-
scented cream, an empty box of chocolates, a pack of cigarettes,
toothpicks, a shell, finger cots, a thermometer, a glasses case . . . that
sort of thing. Not much, but better than nothing. Things to add a little
flavor to my life of captivity.

I tried to imagine how all these things had come to be in the
drawer. In the days before the mechanism had been automated,
an attendant must have lived in this room to look after the clock.
Wind the spring, oil the gears, ring the bell at the appointed
hours—a regular sort of job. He had probably helped out around the
church when he had free time. A serious, taciturn old man without
attachments. The cigarettes and glasses case must have been his.
The cigarette pack was an old-fashioned design, and though there
were still a few cigarettes left, they no longer smelled of tobacco. The
case, made of cloth, was quite ragged. It seemed entirely possible
that the old man had lived and died in this room.

At least I could pass the time playing with the wire puzzle. I
made my mind go blank and stared at the ball of silver wires. Come
what may, manipulating something with my fingers was always good
for my mental state, and when I remembered how anxious I'd been
when I'd first taken up the typewriter, the puzzle seemed rather nice
by comparison. Still, as my fingers became accustomed to the way
the wires fit together, I began to worry that it would not take me long
to solve.

The menthol cream was also useful. I could rub it on my temples, under my nose, along my neck. I knew that the sharp odor would improve my spirits as soon as I smelled it. Not that it stimulated me; rather, it felt like a cool breeze blowing over my body and calming my nerves. The feeling lasted a long while, until the menthol evaporated. The tube was already half empty, so I would have to use it infrequently, in small quantities.

The bed was another thing that altered my impression of the room. He had brought it up himself, and it was just a simple folding sofa, but still it must have been extremely difficult to carry up the winding stairway. I had never seen him look tired before. He had always seemed completely in control. His clothes, his hair, the movement of his fingers, the words he spoke—everything had been subject to his will, and I was certain now that he had not willingly shown me his sweaty brow.

Still, it had apparently been worth the effort it had cost him to move the bed, since he did all sorts of things to me on it.

.   .   .

The ringing of the bell is more frightening here than it was in town, which makes sense since it's so close I can almost touch it. As eleven and five o'clock approach, I cower in a corner of the room and rest my head on my knees. I close my eyes and hold my breath, hoping to block the sound and minimize the shock. But as the last second ticks away and the clapper of the bell begins to swing back and forth, I realize how meaningless my feeble resistance will be.

The sound of the clock flows along the ceiling, strikes the wall, shakes the floor, and, having nowhere to go, rattles about the room for a long time. It washes over me like a crushing wave, and though I steel myself in an attempt to push it away, it's no use.

On the first day I was brought here, when the bell rang at

five o'clock, I had the feeling that the typewriters were crying out together, as though the voices locked in them had been released all at once. In reality, if all the keys on all the typewriters were struck at the same time, that would be an even more dreadful noise than the bell itself.

I can no longer tell which of them was mine. At first it seemed newer than the rest, with shiny levers and a brightly painted cover. But gradually the dust clogged the keys and the paint faded, so that it was impossible to tell it from the others, and now it has simply melted into the mountain of machines.

I wonder if what he says is true, that someone's voice is trapped in every typewriter here. If voices, like bodies, decline and decay, then most of these, crushed under this mountain, have been choked off and are hardened and useless.

At some point I realized that I could no longer recall the sound of my own voice, and the thought dumbfounded me. How could I have so easily forgotten something I'd heard for so many years, a sound that had been silenced only for a fraction of that time?

But in a world turned upside down, things I thought were mine and mine alone can be taken away much more easily than I would have imagined. If my body were cut up in pieces and those pieces mixed with those of other bodies, and then if someone told me, "Find your left eye," I suppose it would be difficult to do so.

. . .

He treats me just as he pleases.

He brings me my meals. It seems he prepares them in the little room at the back of the typing classroom where there's a burner to heat water. They are far from gourmet, but they are perfectly acceptable. For the most part, he brings soft, liquid things that have been stewed or simmered.

He sets the tray on the table, sits down across from me, rests his chin in the palm of his hand, and stares at me. He never takes a bite. I'm left to dine alone.

I have never been able to get used to eating this way. It wears on my nerves to have to swallow each bite under his unwavering gaze, without music or laughter or conversation. I have no appetite, picturing as I do the morsels of food falling down my throat, scraping past my ribs, and finally making their way to my stomach. When I'm barely half finished, I've had enough, but I force myself to eat everything—because I'm afraid to imagine what he might do with anything left over.

"You have some sauce on your lip," he'll say to me from time to time. I'll hurry to lick it off, since there's never a napkin. "More to your right," he'll say, forcing me to lick my lips from one side to the other. Then he'll tell me to go on eating.

He has the mannerisms of a waiter in a fancy restaurant. And I eat slowly, ripping off small pieces of bread, cutting my meat into tiny bites, sipping my water, and glancing up at him from time to time.

At night, he strips me, makes me stand under the light, and then washes my body. The water he brings in a bucket is very hot, and steam floats around the room. But he takes so long and washes me so carefully that it has all dissipated by the time he's finished. He moves his hands much as he does when he polishes the stopwatch.

As he works, I find myself surprised by the sheer number of parts that make up a human body. The job seems almost endless. Eyelids, scalp, behind the ears, collarbone, armpits, nipples, belly, the hipbone cavity, thighs, calves, between the fingers. Nothing is neglected, not the tiniest part. He works tirelessly, wiping every inch of my body, without seeming to strain himself, without so much as a change of expression.

When he's done, it's up to him, of course, to choose the clothes

I put on, and his choices are always odd, unlike anything I have
seen in the stores. So odd, indeed, it's unclear they should be called
"clothes" at all.

First of all, the materials themselves are strange: vinyl, paper,
metal, leaves, fruit peels. When they're handled roughly, they tear
away from the body or cut the skin or tighten around the chest.
Which is why the garments have to be put on slowly, with great care.

One day he confessed that he had made the clothes himself. An
image would come to him, he would sketch it, make a pattern, and
then gather the materials from here and there. As he told me this, the
most absurd, inexplicable realization came to me: I was absolutely
certain that his fingers were terribly beautiful as they fashioned
these clothes. That's what I thought. To imagine his fingers as they
threaded a needle or cut the peel from a piece of fruit held the same
charm as imagining them as they typed out words on a page.

He stands smiling with satisfaction as I hunch my shoulders
and bend my legs and wriggle my hips in order to force myself into
the strangely shaped garments. The light from the lamp overhead
is reflected in the bucket of water, which is by now quite cool.
By morning, the clothes will be crumpled on the floor like a
worn-out rag.

. . .

Needless to say, my nerves are frayed. But it is the inability to
speak that confines me much more than being shut up in the room.
As he'd said, to be deprived of one's voice is much the same as
having one's body go to pieces.

From time to time he gives me an icy stare and asks whether I
want to speak.

I shake my head violently from side to side, knowing full well
that nothing will come from nodding.

In the past few days I've begun to feel my body growing more distant from my soul. It's as though my head and arms, my breasts and torso and legs are all floating somewhere just out of reach, and I can only watch as he plays with them. And that, too, is because I have lost my voice. When the voice that links the body to the soul vanishes, there is no way to put into words one's feelings or will. I am reduced to pieces in no time at all.

I wonder if there is any way out of here. Of course I think about the possibility. At the instant he opens the door, I could push past him and run down the stairs. I could beat on the floor with a typewriter to alert the students in the classroom below, or take one apart and throw the pieces out the window. But these ideas all seem useless, and besides, even if I found my way outside again, I wonder whether I would be able to reassemble the pieces of myself.

While he's busy teaching the typing students downstairs, I peek out from behind the face of the clock and look at the scene below. The church garden is carefully tended, with some flower always in bloom. People often gather here, chatting in the shade of the trees, sitting on the benches to read. Children play badminton, the typing students pass through on bicycles. Occasionally someone will look up at the clock on the tower to check the time, but of course no one notices me.

If I listen, I can hear the sound of their voices, but I can't understand what they are saying. At first I thought it was because they were too far away. But that wasn't really the reason. It's simply that I can't comprehend the words.

One day I saw him laughing and chatting with some of his students in the garden. From a distance, he looked stylish, intelligent, and distinguished, and the students seemed quite taken with him. I am the only one who knows what he becomes here at the top of the tower.

"No matter how much you're tempted, you mustn't look at the keyboard. That's the secret to improvement. You find the keys with your fingers, not your eyes."

They seemed to be talking about typing. I could hear his voice quite clearly, as though the wind bore it up through the crack in the clock face and into my ears. But then one of the students, a woman with short hair and dangly earrings, turned and said something to him.

I could hear the sound of her voice, but not her words. The wind seemed to carry her words past the clock and off into the sky.

"Close your eyes and let your fingers feel the typewriter. The position of the keys, of course, but also the shape of the levers, the thickness of the roller—learn all of it with your fingers."

I had heard the same instructions when I was his student, and I could hear each word he spoke now.

The young women around him spoke one after the other, but nothing they said meant anything to me.

"From now on, if you look at the keyboard during class, I'll be handing out a punishment. So that's clear? We'll start tomorrow."

He clapped his hands, and the girls recoiled, letting out a sound that was neither laugh nor scream.

It was then I realized that I could no longer understand anyone but him. Any words but his, coming from the outside, sounded to me like the random squeaking of an out-of-tune instrument.

Even if I were able to escape now, I realized it was too late. My degeneration was already too far advanced. If I took one step outside, my body would dissolve into a million pieces.

He was the only thing holding me together now. Only his fingers. And so, again this evening, I wait for the sound of his footsteps as he climbs the tower.

. . .

I did not venture back down to the hidden room again after the Memory Police came to search the house. As before, when I took R his meals, we would still exchange a few meaningless words. I would cast about for plausible excuses to climb down the ladder, but in the end I closed the trapdoor without voicing any of them.

The shock of that evening seemed to sink in gradually. R smiled only rarely now and often left food on his plate. Perhaps because the invasion by the Memory Police had upset me so much, he had missed the opportunity to express his own feelings—which seemed now to be festering like a wound. As I would turn to go, I would stop in midmotion and hold the heavy trapdoor for a moment, peeking inside and thinking I would give him a chance to say something more before we parted. But I invariably found him at the desk, his back turned, or already burrowing his way into the covers on the bed.

It was too painful to realize that there was no chance he would open the interior latch, lift the door, crawl out from under the rug, and come to me. I knew, of course, that his situation was complicated, but no matter how often I reminded myself of this, I still worried that he was simply avoiding me.

The more I thought back over the events of that night, the more they seemed to retreat, one by one, from reality. The various dishes we had prepared, the cake, the pile of dirty pots and pans, the presents, the wine, the boots, the burned datebook, the turned-up corner of the rug, the three figures in the distance, the covered truck, the tears . . . I had trouble believing that all of this could have happened to me in one evening. But I knew that sleeping with R had been the only way to survive that horrible night. In order to protect each other, we had simply taken refuge in the only safe place left to us. Or so I said, to comfort myself.

. . .

I put aside the manuscript pages I'd written that day, took the speaker from its hiding place behind the dictionary, and held it to my ear. At first I couldn't hear anything, but as I continued to listen, I gradually began to make out the quiet sounds from the hidden room.

First came the sound of water. Then coughing, the rustling of cloth, the motor of the ventilation fan. I gripped the funnel and pressed it harder against my ear.

He was washing himself. That evening, I'd brought him the usual items: washbasin, pot of hot water, plastic sheet, towel.

"Ah, it's bath day, is it?" he said as I handed all this down to him. "I'd forgotten."

"I'm sorry it's such a poor excuse for a real bath," I told him, gently bumping the bottom of the basin against the handrail.

"Not at all," he said, gathering all the items in his arms. "I'm grateful that you manage to remember the schedule even without a calendar."

The sound of water came to me intermittently like a soft murmur. Of course I had never seen how he managed to wash himself, but as I listened I felt as though his movements were coming to me through the funnel.

First, he spread out the plastic sheet to keep the floor from getting wet. Then he undressed and sat down on it with his legs crossed under him. His neatly folded clothes were stacked on the bed. Working quickly, before the water cooled, he wet the towel, wrung it out, and then carefully washed his neck, his back, his shoulders, his arms. When the towel was no longer wet enough, he dipped it in the basin again. His skin, so far removed from air and sunlight, was pale and soft, and the towel left red marks if he

170 rubbed too hard. His face expressionless, he moved his hands in silence. Drops of water sparkled on the plastic sheet. I was able to trace the contours of his body, able to recall the movement of each muscle, the angle of each joint, the pattern of each vein showing through his white skin. Even though the sounds coming through the funnel were barely audible, as they came to my ears and to my memory, the sensation became clearer and clearer.

The curtains on the window by the desk were parted slightly, and I could see stars in the night sky—a rare enough sight in recent days. The darkness had painted black the snow that blanketed the town. The wind rattled the windowpane from time to time. I untangled the rubber tube that ran down to the floor. The funnel had warmed in my hand. The pages of my manuscript were neatly stacked and secured under a paperweight on the desk. To me, they seemed the only ticket I could use for admittance to the hidden room below me.

I could hear a thin stream of water being slowly poured into the basin.

Several weeks had passed since the old man's birthday party. During that time, a few incidents occurred, though nothing to compare with the visit from the Memory Police.

One of these was a chance encounter with an old woman during a walk one evening. She had come in from a farm somewhere and set out a mat along the road to sell vegetables. The selection was small, but her prices were cheaper than those at the markets in town, so I happily filled a bag with a cauliflower, bean sprouts, and some green peppers. But as I was handing over the money, she suddenly leaned in close to my face.

"Do you know a safe hiding place?" she whispered. I was so startled I nearly dropped the coins.

"What?" I blurted out, thinking I might have misunderstood.

"I'm looking for someone who can hide me," she said clearly. But she did not glance at me as she slipped the money into a bag hanging from her belt. I looked around but saw no one except a few children playing in the park across the way.

"Are the Memory Police looking for you?" I asked, trying to appear as though we were simply chatting after my purchase. She said nothing more, perhaps afraid she'd already said too much.

I looked at her again. She seemed solidly built, but her clothes were threadbare. Her work pants, which had probably been fashioned out of material from an old kimono, were tattered, and the shawl she had wrapped around her shoulders was pilling. There were holes at the toes of her tennis shoes. The corners of her eyes were crusty with sleep, and her hands were chapped and swollen. But no matter how long I stared at her face, I had no recollection of having seen her before.

But then why had she made such an important request of someone she had never met? I found the whole thing puzzling. How did she know that I wouldn't denounce her to the Memory Police? Was she really in such danger that she had no other choice? If so, I felt I wanted to do something to help her even if I couldn't give her a place to hide. But then again it was also possible that this was some sort of trap laid by the Memory Police, as that was just the sort of trick to be expected from them. Or then again, perhaps this old woman already knew that I was hiding someone in my house, and she'd approached me because she wanted to be hidden as well. But that seemed unlikely. There was no way our secret had gotten out—not if the Memory Police themselves had been unable to discover it.

My mind was racing, but I found I couldn't say a thing for a moment.

"I'm afraid I can't help you," I said finally, picking up the bag. The old woman said nothing more. Her expression was blank as she went back to arranging her vegetables, the coins clinking at her hip. "I'm sorry," I said and hurried away.

Later, I was saddened at the thought of her red, swollen hands, but I knew there was nothing I could have done, given the situation. A careless move would have put R in danger. Still, I couldn't get the woman out of my mind and for the next week, when I went out for my walk, I would find myself at her make-shift vegetable stand. Sometimes I would buy something, and other days I would pass by in silence. She always had the same modest assortment on offer, but she never seemed to give a sign that we'd met before and she never mentioned her need of a refuge again. Perhaps the enormity of her problem had caused her to completely forget my face, or the request she had made of me.

A week later, she suddenly vanished, and I had no way of knowing whether she had run out of vegetables to sell, or had moved on to a different spot, or had found a place to hide—or if she had been caught by the Memory Police.

Another significant incident that took place was that the former hatmaker and his wife who lived in the house across the way came to stay with me for the night. They were having their whole house painted and asked whether I could put them up just until the smell dissipated.

Needless to say, I offered them the Japanese-style room on the first floor, as far as possible from the hidden room. Though it caused both R and me no end of anxiety for the whole time they were there, refusing them would have been even more awkward.

"I'm sorry to put you out," the hatmaker had said, "but it will take at least a day or two for the paint to dry, and we couldn't really sleep with the windows open in this cold."

"You're more than welcome," I told him, smiling as warmly as I could. "There's plenty of room."

That day, I got up well before they were due to arrive and made lots of sandwiches and tea and took them to the hidden room.

"I'm afraid you'll have to make do with this today," I told R. He nodded silently, apparently a bit nervous himself. "And no footsteps, or running water for the toilet." I repeated my cautions and then carefully closed the trapdoor, which would not open again until the following day.

The hatmaker and his wife were simple, honest people, not the type to poke around my house or ask question about my private life. She made herself at home in the Japanese-style room and occupied herself with her knitting much of the day. When the hatmaker got back from work, the three of us ate dinner and then chatted for a while in front of the television. Shortly after nine o'clock, they were ready for bed.

But the whole time they were there, my mind was focused on the second floor. Every sound frightened me, even those that had nothing to do with R—the distant moaning of the sea, honking horns, the wind—and I found myself studying their faces intently. But they showed no signs of suspicion. In fact, at times I myself felt that the hidden room must have emerged from a fevered dream and that my preoccupation with it was nothing more than some sort of hallucination.

The next day, when the paint had dried, they returned to their house. By way of thanking me, they sent a sack of flour, a can of sardines in oil, and a sturdy black umbrella that the hatmaker had made himself.

Also during this period I began taking care of the dog that had belonged to the neighbors to my east. The day after the family had been taken away, the Memory Police sent a truck to remove all the furniture from the house, but for some reason they had left the dog. For several days I fed him scraps or bowls of milk through the fence, but when it became clear that no one was coming for him, I consulted with the head of the neighborhood association and finally decided to adopt him.

The old man helped me move the doghouse into my garden, and then we drove a stake into the ground to secure his chain. We brought his dish, which had been covered in the snow, over from next door. The name "Don" was written on the roof of his house, so that is what I called him. I wasn't sure whether this referred to Don Juan or Don Quixote, but he was, at any rate, a docile and obedient animal. He very quickly grew accustomed to the old man and me. He was a mutt, with brown patches on his coat and

a slight crimp in his left ear. Though it was rather odd for a dog,
his favorite food was whitefish; he had a habit of licking the links
of his chain.

So it was that a walk with Don during the warmest part of
the day became one of my regular duties. Since the nights were
cold, I made him a bed from an old blanket and let him sleep in a
corner of the entry hall. It occurred to me that I was giving Don
all the love and care I wished I could give to the couple who had
been his owners, the boy who had been hidden in their house, the
Inui family, and Mizore, their cat.

. . .

After these relatively uneventful weeks, another disappearance occurred. I thought I'd become accustomed to them, but
this one was more complicated: this time novels disappeared.

. . .

As usual, it started during the night, but this time it developed more slowly. Throughout the morning, there was no apparent change in the town.

"We didn't have a single novel in the house, so this one was
easy. But it must be horrible for you as a writer. If there's anything
I can do to help, just let me know. Books are heavy things."

I was standing in the street in front of the house when the
former hatmaker came over to offer his condolences.

"Thanks," I said, my voice barely audible.

Needless to say, R was violently opposed to losing our collection of novels.

"You've got to bring them all here," he said, "including your
manuscript."

"If I do, the room will be buried in books, with no place for you to live." I shook my head.

"Don't worry about that, I don't need much space. If we hide them here, they'll never find them."

"But then what happens to them? What's the point of storing away books that have disappeared?"

He sighed and pressed his fingers to his temples—as he always did when we talked about the disappearances. Try as we might to understand each other, nothing changed for either of us. The more we talked, the sadder we became.

"You write novels. You of all people must know that you cannot choose between them, divide them into categories. They are all useful in their own way."

"Yes, I know. Or at least I did until yesterday. But that's all changed now. My soul seems to be breaking down." I said those last words cautiously, as though I were handing over a fragile object. "Losing novels is hard for me," I said. "It's as though an important bond between the two of us is being cut."

I stared at him for a moment.

"You mustn't burn your manuscript. You must go on writing novels. That way, the bond will remain."

"But that's impossible. Novels have disappeared. Even if we keep the manuscripts and the books, they're nothing more than empty boxes. Boxes with nothing inside. You can peer into them, listen carefully, sniff the contents, but they signify nothing. So what could I possibly write?"

"Don't be impatient. You have to take your time and try to remember. Where did all those words come from? How did you find them?"

"I'm afraid I've lost my nerve. The word 'novel' itself is getting harder to pronounce. That's how you know the disappear-

ance is taking hold. It won't be long now until I'll have forgotten
everything. Remembering is impossible."

I lowered my head and ran my fingers through my hair.
R leaned over to look up at me and rested his hands on my knees.

"No, it will be all right. You may think that the memories
themselves vanish every time there's a disappearance, but that's
not true. They're just floating in a pool where the sunlight never
reaches. All you have to do is plunge your hand in and you're
bound to find something. Something to bring back into the
light. You have to try. I can't just stand by watching as your soul
withers."

He took my hands in his, warming each finger.

"If I go on writing stories, will those memories protect me?"

"I know they will." He nodded and I could feel his breath on
my hands.

. . .

By evening, the disappearance was settling in more rapidly. People were bringing books to burn in fires that had been
started in parks and fields and vacant lots. From the window of
my study, I could see smoke and flames rising all over the island,
being absorbed into the heavy, gray clouds that covered everything. The snow had turned filthy with soot.

In the end, I chose a dozen books from my shelves and took
them to R for safekeeping, along with the manuscript I was writing. I asked the old man to help me pile the rest in the back of
my bicycle cart, and we took them to burn at one of the fires. It
would have been impossible to hide all of them, and furthermore
I knew it would seem suspicious if I, as a writer, had nothing to
destroy.

It was difficult to decide which books to keep and which to part with. Even as I picked up each volume, I realized I could no longer remember what it had been about. But I knew I couldn't linger over these decisions, since it was quite possible the Memory Police would be around to check on my progress. In the end, I decided to keep books that had been given to me by dear friends and those with beautiful covers.

At five thirty, as dusk was falling, the old man and I set off, pulling the cart behind us.

Don came running, apparently eager to join us.

"We're not going for a walk this time," I told him. "We have important work to do. You keep guard at home." He went to lie down on the blanket in the entranceway.

We passed several other people carrying heavy paper bags or bundles. The street was icy in places and there were snowdrifts, making it difficult to pull the cart. My books, which had been loaded in neat bundles, were soon reduced to a jumble in the cart, but since we were taking them to be burned, it didn't seem to matter.

"If you get tired, you can climb on the cart and take a rest," said the old man.

"Thanks, but I'm fine," I told him.

We made our way along the main street, skirted the market, and arrived at last at the park in the center of town. The whole area was filled with light and heat. A great mountain of books was already burning, sending sparks high into the night sky. A crowd had gathered around the fire, and Memory Police officers could be seen standing among the trees just outside the circle.

"What an incredible sight . . . ," the old man murmured.

The flames, like some enormous living creature, shot up to the sky, higher than the streetlights, higher than the telephone poles. When the wind blew, a great mass of burning pages danced into the air. The snow had melted all around and the mud sucked at your shoes with each step. An orange light illuminated the slide, the seesaw, the park benches, the walls of the restroom building. The moon and the stars were nowhere to be seen, as though they had been scattered by the brilliance of the flames, and only the corpses of burned books lit the sky.

The people in the crowd, cheeks blazing with the fire, stared, openmouthed, at the spectacle before them. Stunned and silent, as if attending a solemn ceremony, they made no move to brush away the sparks that rained down on them.

The pile of books was taller than I was. Some had not yet caught fire, but it was impossible to read the titles. I squinted at the spines, though it would have made no difference had I been able to recognize them. Still, by watching them until the moment they disappeared, I hoped to preserve in my memory something from their pages.

There were books of all sorts—some in slipcases, some bound in leather, weighty tomes and slender novellas—piled together awaiting their turn in the flames. From time to time, the mountain would collapse with a muffled whoosh, the flames would shoot up, and the heat would grow more intense.

After one of these moments, a young woman suddenly moved out of the circle of onlookers, climbed up on a bench, and began to shout something. Startled, the old man and I exchanged a nervous glance. Others in the crowd turned to look at her.

She was screaming so frantically that it was impossible to understand what she was saying. Arms flailing, saliva flying, she was clearly agitated, but it was hard to tell whether she was angry or just distraught.

She was dressed in a shabby overcoat and checked pants, and her long hair was tied up in a braid. On top of her head, perched at a jaunty angle, she wore an odd thing made of soft material. As she rocked violently to and fro, I found myself fearing it would come tumbling off.

"Do you think she's mad?" I whispered to the old man.

"I wonder," he answered, crossing his arms. "She seems to want them to put out the fire."

"But why?"

"To stop the novels from disappearing, I suppose."

"Do you mean, she's—"

"—unable to rid herself of her memories. Poor thing."

Her cries gradually rose to something close to a scream, but of course no one made a move to extinguish the enormous mountain of flames. The people nearby just watched her with pitying looks.

"They'll take her if she goes on like that," I said, starting toward the bench. "She's got to get away, we've got to do something."

"I'm afraid it's too late," said the old man, catching hold of me before I could move.

Three members of the Memory Police had appeared from the woods and were already pulling on her arms. She tried to resist, clinging to the bench, but it was hopeless. The thing on her head fell into the mud.

"No one can erase the stories!" The last words she said as they dragged her away were the only ones I was able to understand clearly.

I heard sighs from the people around us as they turned back to stare at the fire. I looked down at the thing she had left on the ground, which was now even more limp and filthy than it had been. Her words continued to ring in my ears—"No one can erase the stories."

"Of course! A hat!" I was suddenly able to remember. "The man who lives across the street used to make them, but they disappeared years ago. You wore them on your head—the way she did—didn't you?"

I looked up at the old man, but he just seemed puzzled.

At that moment someone moved out of the crowd, picked up the hat, and, without a word, tossed it into the fire. It spun as it flew and then fell among the flames.

"Well then, we should be getting on with it," the old man said.

"You're right," I said, looking up from the spot where the hat lay burning.

We left the cart near the fountain and walked toward the fire, our arms filled with books. But as we approached, the heat grew more fierce and sparks threatened to burn our clothes and hair, so we could not get very close.

"You should keep back," the old man said, as always worried for my safety. "I can manage."

"No, it's fine. We can't get closer anyway. Why don't we just throw them from here?"

I took a book with a pea-green cover decorated with a picture of fruit and tossed it toward the fire. I'd thrown it as hard as I could, but it barely reached the edge of the pile. The next one, thrown by the old man, made it a little farther up the side. The people around us glanced in our direction, but they said nothing and their faces remained expressionless.

We continued throwing the books, one after the other, without flipping through the pages or so much as glancing at the covers. We repeated the movements almost automatically, as if performing some solemn duty. Still, as each volume left my hand, I felt a slight twinge, as though the hollow place in my memory were being enlarged book by book.

"I had no idea books burned so well," I said.

"I suppose it's because they pack so much paper into such

a small object," said the old man, as he continued tossing them into the fire.

"It may take a long time for every word to disappear."

"I wouldn't worry, they'll be nothing but ashes by tomorrow morning," he said. Pulling a towel from his pocket, he wiped the sweat and soot from his face.

When we'd burned about half the books, we left the park and once again began wheeling the cart through the town. Working so close to the heat of the enormous blaze had tired us out, so we were looking for a smaller fire to finish the job.

The town was quiet. I could sense the roughness in the air that I'd felt after other disappearances, but somehow people seemed calmer. There were almost no cars on the streets, with the exception of the Memory Police trucks, and though the crowds were thick, no one seemed to be stopping to talk. The only sound was that of burning books.

We walked aimlessly, and the cart was easier to pull now that our load was lighter. We turned north, along the street where the streetcar ran, cut through the parking lot at city hall, and made our way along a street lined with houses. From time to time we came upon a vacant lot where a small fire was burning.

"Would you mind if we joined you?" the old man asked the people standing around, and we would stop to warm our hands and burn an armful of books. We might have burned the rest of the cartload at any of these fires, but we worried about the danger of the fires spreading, so we repeated the process: burning some books, pulling the cart farther along, finding another fire. The night was deepening but fires continued to burn. I would have thought the number of novels on the island was relatively small, but pillars of smoke rose in many places with no sign of stopping.

We passed the community center, a gas station, the cannery,

a company dormitory, and arrived at last at the sea. Following the coast road, we came upon groups of people gathered around fires on the sand. The sea had dissolved into the darkness. No more than a few books remained in the cart, but we walked on.

The hill came into view. A fire was raging halfway up the slope.

"The library," I murmured.

"I'm afraid you're right," said the old man, holding up his hands to shade his eyes and squinting at the flames.

The road up the hill was steep and narrow, so we left the cart and decided to carry the rest of the books in our arms. Under normal circumstances, it would have been too dark to walk this way at night, but thanks to the fire above us, it was nearly as light as day. Partway up, we came upon the garden, though there were no longer any flowers to be seen. Just the occasional bare, withering stalk, above which sparks danced like glittering flower petals.

The library was completely engulfed in flames. Never before had I seen anything burn as brightly or as beautifully, and the intense light and heat chased away all traces of the fear and sadness I had been feeling. The things about which R had been trying to persuade me, the words the woman had screamed into the fire—everything seemed to recede into the distance.

People had gathered to watch the fire, and we could hear them talking.

"I don't know why they had to burn the whole building."

"But there's nothing but books inside, so it's simpler to just do it all at once."

"I wonder what they'll do with the land when it's gone."

"I suppose they'll leave it, the way they did with the garden. But I heard they'll build a headquarters for the Memory Police someday."

We climbed a bit farther up the hill to the observatory and found it deserted. The last time I had stopped in on a walk during the day, I had thought it seemed largely unchanged, but now, at night, I realized that it was practically in ruins. The windows were broken and covered with cobwebs. Cabinets and desks had been overturned. And the floor was strewn with trash of all sorts—old mugs, pencil holders, blankets, shredded documents. We made our way across the room, and I set the remaining books by the window where my father and I had watched the birds through his binoculars.

"There could be broken glass, be careful," said the old man. I nodded as I leaned against the window frame.

The library was visible down the slope, through a thick tangle of underbrush. It seemed so close you could reach out and touch it and, at the same time unreal, like an image on a movie screen. In the darkness, only the flames appeared to move. We held our breath, just as the trees below us and the sea beyond seemed to, as though fearful of disturbing this beautiful scene.

"I remember hearing a saying long ago: 'Men who start by burning books end by burning other men,'" I said.

"Who said that?" asked the old man, speaking softly and bringing his hand to his chin.

"I've forgotten, though I'm sure it was someone important. But I wonder if that's where we're headed."

"I wonder," echoed the old man. "It's hard to say." He looked up at the ceiling, blinked, and rubbed his chin again. "But there's nothing to be done. It's not as though they're burning every printed word. It's just the novels, so there's no reason to think they'll go further anytime soon."

"But what if human beings themselves disappear?" I asked.

This was the question that had been on my mind. The old man swallowed and blinked again.

"You have to stop worrying about things like that. The disappearances are beyond our control. They have nothing to do with us. We're all going to die anyway, someday, so what's the difference? We simply have to leave things to fate."

. . .

The library continued to burn. I picked up one of the books from the pile at my feet and threw it out the window. It opened as it flew through the air, cleared the underbrush, and fell gently into the flames. The pages had caught the breeze, and it fluttered as it flew, as if dancing on air.

Next it was the old man's turn. He chose a thinner, lighter volume, so it floated even more gracefully before vanishing in the flames.

We repeated this ritual over and over, handling each book with great care.

When the wind changed, a current of warm air came blowing in the window. Our feet were frozen from walking the snowy streets, but our cheeks were warm.

"How did it feel when the ferry was disappeared?" I asked him.

"It's so long ago I don't really remember."

"Did you worry about how you would make a living?" I picked up a thick, heavy book with a brown paper cover.

"I suppose I did. It was upsetting at first. But don't worry. You'll find something else to do, and eventually you won't even remember that you used to write novels." He stared out the window into the distance.

"But I'm going to go on writing them in secret," I told him.

He let out a little gasp and turned to look at me. I threw the thick volume into the air with both hands. The paper wrapper made a sound that was almost a sob.

"Do you think you'll be able to?"

"I don't know, but R told me that I had to, that my soul would die if I didn't."

"He did, did he? . . ." The old man's chin came to rest on his hand again, and a thoughtful look settled over his wrinkled face. "I've been doing what he told me to do," he said. "I've been listening to the music box every day, but I don't feel any different. My lost memories aren't coming back, and I don't feel any stronger. All I hear is a lot of strange sounds."

"I know it may not do any good, but I've hidden the manuscript I'm working on. I know it's dangerous, but I don't want to disappoint R. I don't know that I'll feel any different if my soul withers away, but I don't think I could stand to see him looking so sad."

"And I'll keep listening to the music box. What else would I do with such a wonderful present?" As he spoke, the old man brushed away some ash that had landed on my hair. "You should take care not to tire yourself, and you must tell me if there's ever anything I can do to help."

"Thank you," I said.

The last book had finally been tossed out the window. The library building was beginning to collapse in upon itself. From time to time, a portion of the roof or a section of wall would come down with a crash. The circulation desk and the chairs in the reading room could be seen burning in the ruins.

I followed the arc of the last book as it tumbled through the air—and suddenly I realized that, long ago, I had stood at this same window with my father and looked out at a similar sight.

I took a deep breath and felt a slight pain, as though a spark had found its way into the bottomless swamp of my heart.

"A bird."

I remembered. The pages of the book had opened and fluttered through the air just the way birds had once spread their wings and flown off to distant places. But this memory, too, was soon erased by the flames, leaving behind nothing but the burning night.

As the old man had predicted, I soon found another job. The head of the neighborhood association made an introduction for me at a trading company run by an acquaintance.

"They sell spices in bulk. It's not a large firm, but the owner is an interesting man and the offices are nice enough. He's apparently looking for a typist."

"A typist?" I said.

"That doesn't interest you?"

"I don't have much experience, just a bit when I was at school. I'm not sure I'd be good enough . . ."

I repeated the word "typist" silently to myself several times. It seemed to have a special significance.

"Not to worry," he said. "You can learn as you go. The owner said as much. At any rate, I'm sure you'll have various other duties to start."

"I'm very grateful, and I apologize for putting you to so much trouble." I bowed, but all the while the word "typist" repeated itself in my head. I tried to recover my faded memory, but it remained distant and vague.

"Not at all! Don't mention it. I was just connecting the dots. We all have to pull together after a disappearance." He smiled with satisfaction.

And so I came to work at a spice company, and the rhythm of my days changed drastically. I woke early in the morning, prepared the food, water, and other things R would need during the day, and carried them all to the hidden room. In the evening, when I got home from work, I would check to see that R was all right before taking Don for a walk. After that, I would start making dinner. At first, it bothered me to be away from the house for ten hours a day. Inevitably, I imagined the worst happening while I was gone, a fire or a robbery or R suddenly falling ill—or another visit from the Memory Police—and besides that, I was much busier now than I'd been before. It proved to be fairly difficult to juggle my job, watching over R, caring for Don, and managing the house, and I rarely had time to visit the old man on the boat. But the days passed without any major problems.

The spice company was a pleasant, almost homey place. My duties included dusting, answering the phone, and some basic filing. And I was lent a portable typewriter and a typing manual and asked to practice at home. It was the first time I had worked outside the house, but it seemed as though I would manage well enough. The one thing that bothered me, however, was the strong smell of the spices that came from the warehouse behind the office. The bitter, medicinal odor clung to me like the stench of rotting fruit.

On the other hand, one of the perks of the job was that I received gifts of food from some of our clients, like sausage and cheese and corned beef, which had long since vanished from the markets and were an enormous treat for the old man, R, and me.

. . .

I understood why I had reacted so strongly to the word "typist" when I reread the manuscript I'd given to R for safekeeping, though in point of fact I was no longer capable of reading a novel, much less writing one. I could read the words out loud,

190 but I could no longer understand them as parts of a coherent story with a plot to connect them. They were just characters on the manuscript page, and they evoked in me no feeling or atmosphere, no recognizable scene.

As I traced the words one by one and came at last to that word, I remembered that my novel was about a typist. But the discovery only made it clearer that writing the rest would not be as easy as R had suggested.

On Friday and Saturday evenings, I sat down at my desk. Putting aside the paperweight, I carefully examined the manuscript, beginning from the first page. But the work never went smoothly. I tried various strategies—reading the same line several times, staring at a single word, running my eyes over the words at a steady speed—but nothing seemed to help. By the fifth or sixth page, I had invariably lost the will to continue. Then I would flip through the pages until I came upon a section that looked promising and try the same thing again, but the results were always the same. In the end, I was so weary that the mere sight of the lines on the paper made me dizzy.

But if continuing what I'd already written was impossible, it occurred to me that perhaps I could write something new, and so I took out a fresh sheet of paper. To warm up my fingers, I tried writing *a, i, u, e, o*. Then, taking care to match the size of the characters to the lines on the paper, I continued with *ka, ki, ku, ke, ko*. And as I wrote these meaningless characters, I began to feel a certain satisfaction in the knowledge that I was fulfilling R's hopes for me, even in the tiniest way. But when I erased the characters and the blank lines spread out in front of me, my fingers grew numb and my anxiety returned with the realization that I had no idea what to write.

What *had* I written? I asked myself. At night, I would try to recall anything at all about those moments, seated at my desk, when I had been searching for words. The typewriter had sat at the edge of the desk, watching me in silence. Fortunately, my coworkers at the spice company had not said much about my typing practice, since I was making little progress. I would tap the keys at random, producing a stream of metallic clicks. In these moments, I would suddenly have the feeling that a story was coming back to me and I would reach out instinctively to seize it. But there was nothing for me to hold. When I could no longer stand to stare at the blank page, I would type *a, i, u, e, o,* and then, imagining that I would now be able to write something, I would erase them again. But of course nothing came to me, and I would return to *a, i, u, e, o.* And the process would repeat itself. In the end, all that was left was a torn page, from the many times I'd erased what I'd written.

. . .

"You shouldn't force the memories. Just try to untangle them slowly," R told me. I had apologized for handing him a blank sheet of paper, but his response was encouraging and showed no sign of disappointment.

"I've tried, but I'm afraid it's useless."

"You shouldn't say that. You're the same person now that you were when you wrote novels. The only thing that's changed is that the books have been burned. But even if paper itself disappears, words will remain. It will be all right, you'll see. We haven't lost the stories."

He took me in his arms, as he always did now. The bed was soft and warm. His skin was growing whiter and whiter, and his muscles seemed more visible than ever. His hair had grown out and hung down over his eyes.

"The flames burned all night. So long that I thought the night itself might never end. And everyone stayed on to stare at the fire, even after they'd burned all their books. The sound of burning paper filled the air, and yet, for some reason, I felt as though I were surrounded by total silence. As though my eardrums were frozen. This was the first time a disappearance seemed like a solemn ceremony. The old man and I just stood there holding hands, because it felt as though I would be sucked into the flames if someone didn't hold me back."

I told R every detail of what had happened that night. Once I opened my mouth, things came tumbling out one after the other and I couldn't stop myself. The difficulty we'd had pulling the cart, the red glow on the playground equipment in the park, the *hat* that had fallen in the mud, the ruined library, the *bird* . . . But no matter how long I talked, I couldn't help feeling that I was leaving out the most important thing—whatever that was. He listened attentively to every word.

When at last I grew tired of talking, I heaved a deep sigh and looked up. He seemed to be staring far into the distance. Behind him I could see the empty plate that had held his dinner, with a single pea remaining in the middle. The books that had escaped the flames were neatly arranged on the shelf above.

"I suppose a great deal has changed in the outside world since I've been here," he said as he gently stroked my hair. I could feel his voice filling the space between our bodies.

"Does my hair have an odd smell?" I asked him.

"Odd how?"

"Like spices."

"No, it has a wonderful smell, like shampoo." He ran his fingers through it.

"I'm glad," I murmured.

Then he read aloud my story about the typist. To me, it sounded like a fairy tale from a distant land.

. . .

"Does it tire you out to be doing something you're not used to?" asked the old man as he arranged the teapot and cups on the table. He was wearing the sweater I had given him over a thick shirt, with wool slippers on his feet.

"No, everyone is very nice to me," I told him, "and I'm enjoying the work."

We were meeting for tea on the boat for the first time in a while. What's more, we were having pancakes. I had found eggs and honey, both great rarities, and we cooked together. We divided the batter in thirds and made three cakes, one of which I'd wrapped in a napkin to take to R.

Don, who had been dozing under the sofa, must have smelled the pancakes, since he appeared suddenly and began to nudge the tablecloth with his muzzle.

"Typing is hard, but I enjoy practicing. As soon as your fingers start to move, a sentence appears almost effortlessly—it's like magic." The old man poured the honey over the pancakes, careful not to waste a single drop.

"And the business seems to be going well. Herbs grow in the least bit of soil, and you can harvest them even with all this snow. Food is so hard to get that people are selling half-rotten meat and vegetables, and everyone wants something fragrant to kill the smell—so my coworkers are expecting big bonuses."

"That's good," said the old man as he lifted the lid on the pot to see whether the tea had finished steeping.

We chatted about this and that as we sipped our tea, laughed at Don's antics, and slowly ate the pancakes. Cutting just one bite at a time, we let it dissolve on our tongues in order to appreciate every bit of the sweetness, and as the remaining pieces of pancake grew smaller, so did the size of the bites we cut.

We each gave a bite to Don, who inhaled them with no thought for their sweet flavor and then stood looking at us expectantly, as though unwilling to believe that there was nothing more.

Light poured in through the windows, bright enough to make you think spring might be just around the corner. The sea was calm, and the boat, which was usually creaking as it rocked on the waves, was quiet. The great pile of snow melting on the dock shone in the sunlight.

When we'd finished eating, the old man went to find the music box hidden in the bathroom. He set it on the table and we listened together. As always, it faithfully repeated its tune, over and over. We stopped chatting, sat up straight, and closed our eyes. I had no idea where or how one was supposed to listen to a music box, but I had decided arbitrarily that closing my eyes would enhance the effect R had hoped it would induce in us.

The melody that flowed from the box was simple but pure and sweet. That much I could feel. But I had no confidence that it would be able to check the exhaustion that was overtaking my soul. Because once it had been sucked beneath the surface of that bottomless swamp, it left no trace at all, no ripple, no fleck of foam.

Don, too, eyed the music box with some interest. Each time we would rewind the mechanism and the music would start again, his ears would twitch and he would back away, belly pressed to the floor. It seemed as though he was barely able to contain his curiosity, but when I picked it up and held it in front of his nose, he ran for cover between the old man's legs.

"How has your . . . novel been going?" he asked, after finally closing the lid of the music box. Even pronouncing the word had apparently become difficult for him.

"I'm trying," I told him, "but it's not going very well."

"It's difficult when something has disappeared. To tell the truth, I feel a kind of emptiness every time I wind the spring on this box. I try to tell myself that this time I might discover something new, but I'm always disappointed. Still, it's a precious present so I force myself to wind it up again."

"I know. I put a fresh sheet of paper on my desk, but no matter how long I stare at it nothing comes to me. I don't know where I am or where I want to go ... as though I'm lost in a thick fog. Then I tell myself I'll find a way around it and I turn to my machine and just start typing. I have a typewriter I borrowed from work on my desk. They are beautiful things, when you look at them. Complex yet delicate, quite lovely. Just like a musical instrument. Which is why I listen for the sound the levers make as they move the keys, hoping for something that will connect to my novel ... but nothing seems to help."

"Those terrible flames would paralyze anyone—it seemed like the whole island was burning ..."

"I thought I could hear the sound of my memory burning that night."

Don gave a little yawn. We hadn't realized it, but he had been moving a bit at a time to keep himself in the warm rays of the sun.

We could hear the voices of children in the distance; no doubt they were delighted by the first nice day in a long time. Some men in work clothes were playing catch in front of the warehouse on the dock.

"Still . . . ," I continued, "why do you suppose I thought of writing a story about a typist? I'd barely ever used a typewriter or had any friends who were typists. It's strange."

"Is it possible to write about something in a novel even if you've never experienced it?" The old man looked a bit skeptical.

"I suppose it is. Even if you haven't seen or heard about something, it seems you can just imagine it and then write it down. It doesn't have to be exactly like the real thing; it's apparently all right to make things up or even lie. At least that's what R says."

"Even lie?"

The old man man's eyebrows twitched, as though he was growing more and more confused.

"That's right. Apparently no one blames you for lying in a novel. You can make up the story out of nothing, starting from zero. You write about something you can't see as though you can see it. You make up something that doesn't exist just by using words. That's why R says we shouldn't give up, even if our memories disappear."

I tapped my fork on my empty plate. Don seemed to be dozing, his head resting on his front paws. Their break over, the men who had been playing catch walked back toward the warehouse, their gloves dangling in their hands.

"I'm not sure whether I should be asking this," the old man said after staring at the sea for a moment. "But you're in love with him, aren't you?"

Unsure how to answer, I reached down and put my arms around Don's neck. The dog's eyes opened with annoyance, and he let out a sound, half cough and half burp. Then he slipped out of my embrace, ran once around the cabin, and came back to the same sunny spot.

"I suppose," I said, my tone intentionally ambiguous. "But do you think he'll ever be able to come out of hiding? Do you think he'll be able to see his wife and child again? I doubt it. I think he'll be able to live only in the hidden room. His soul is too dense. If he comes out, he'll dissolve into pieces, like a deep-sea fish pulled to the surface too quickly. I suppose my job is to go on holding him here at the bottom of the sea."

"I understand," the old man said, nodding, his eyes staring at his hands.

Don, apparently hoping to nap a bit more, rubbed his paws on his jaw and then stretched out with a satisfied air.

Just then, a terrible noise rumbled through the heavens. We hopped up instinctively and braced our hands on the table. Don jumped to his feet.

The boat began to rock violently. The dresser, the dish cabinet, the radio, the lamp, the pendulum clock—everything in the cabin crashed down around us.

"Earthquake!" the old man cried.

When the shaking stopped and I opened my eyes again, the first thing I saw amid the debris was Don, hiding under the couch, trembling with fear.

"It's all right," I told him. "Come here."

I pushed aside the drawers that had fallen from the dresser and the toppled lamp and pulled him to me through the narrow space.

"Are you all right?" I called to the old man. The room was so completely ruined that it was impossible to tell where he had been sitting just a moment before. Don began barking, as though he, too, were calling the old man.

"Yes, I'm here," I heard him say, after what seemed a long time. His voice was weak.

He was trapped under the dish cabinet and covered with shards from the shattered plates. His face was bloody.

"Are you all right?" I asked again. I tried lifting the cabinet, but it wouldn't budge, and I was afraid I might hurt him.

"Don't worry about me. Get away as fast as you can." His voice was barely audible under the rubble.

"Don't be silly. I can't leave you here."

"But you have to. The tsunami will come."

"Tsunami? . . . What do you mean?"

"A huge wave that comes from beyond the horizon. They come after an earthquake. If you stay, you'll be caught up in it."

"I don't understand, but I'm not leaving without you."

He waved the fingers of his one visible hand, as if to urge me on my way. I tried again to lift the cabinet, but I couldn't move it more than a few inches. Don watched us with a worried look.

"It may hurt, but you have to try to crawl out as soon as I move the cabinet." I said this as much to reassure myself as to explain my plan. A piece of glass had torn my stocking and cut my knee. There was blood everywhere, but I felt no pain. "I'll tell you when, and then you move. I'm sure we can get you out of here."

"Please, you have to leave me . . ."

"Don't say that! I'm not leaving without you," I yelled, almost angry with him for giving up so easily. I saw the pole and hook that had once been used to pull open the skylight in the cabin and it occurred to me to force it under the cabinet and use it as a lever.

"One, two, *three!*" I called. The cabinet moved a bit more this time. I heard a creaking sound—from the trembling earth or the cabinet . . . or perhaps from my back?—but I paid no attention and continued to push on the pole with all my might. "All right, one more time. One, two, *three!*"

The old man's left shoulder and ear came into view. And just then the boat began to roll again. Not as violently as before, but I lost my balance and gripped the pole to avoid falling.

"Is that the . . . *tsunami?*"

"No, a tsunami is much worse than that."

"We'd better hurry," I said.

No doubt wanting to help, Don bit the sleeve of the old man's sweater and began to tug at it.

My palms were red, my temples and teeth were throbbing, and my shoulders felt as though they were being pulled from their sockets, but still the cabinet did not move as much as I'd hoped. But as I continued to push, the old man's body gradually came into view.

I tried to keep the tsunami out of my mind, but somehow the word was stuck in my head. What was it? If the old man was frightened, it must be a terrible thing. A monster that lives at the bottom of the sea? Or some sort of force that was impossible to oppose, like the disappearances? I pushed even harder on the pole, hoping the physical effort would keep this fear at bay.

As the old man's right leg came into view, I fell over backward in relief. He immediately struggled to his feet.

"All right, young lady," he called. "We have to go!" I gathered Don in my arms and followed him.

.   .   .

I don't recall how we managed to escape the shattered boat or which way we went after we left the dock, but when we finally stopped to catch our breath, we found ourselves among the ruins of the library, halfway up the hill, surrounded by others who had also taken refuge from the earthquake. The weather, which had been magnificent, had turned gray and gloomy, and the sky threatened snow.

"Are you injured?" asked the old man, turning to look at me.

"No, I'm fine. But how are you? You're all bloody." I took a handkerchief from my pocket and began wiping his face.

"Nothing to worry about," he said. "Just scratches."

"No, there's blood coming out of your ear." A thick, dark ooze trickled from his earlobe to his chin.

"It's nothing," he insisted. "Just a cut."

"But what if it's inside your ear . . . or your brain. It could be serious."

"No, no, it's nothing. No need for you to worry."

He put his hand up to hide his ear, and just then we heard a rumbling in the distance and saw a white wall of water rushing toward the coast.

"What is that?" I gasped, dropping the handkerchief.

"The tsunami," he said, his hand still clasped to his ear. The scene in front of us was transformed in an instant. It seemed as though the sea were being simultaneously drawn up into the sky and sucked down into a hole in the earth. The floodwaters mounted higher and higher, threatening to wash over the entire island, and the people around us began to wail and moan.

The sea swallowed up the boat, washed over the seawall, and smashed the houses along the coastline. All this must have happened in a moment, but I had the impression that I was able to observe individual scenes, one at a time—the deck chair where the old man took his naps being carried away; a baseball abandoned on the docks being tossed on the waves; a red roof being folded like origami and sucked under the surging waters.

When the wave at last subsided, Don was the first one to open his mouth. He leapt up on a stump, faced the sea, and howled long and low. Then, as if this were a signal, everyone began to move again, though slowly at first. Some headed back downhill. Others went in search of a phone or water. Some simply sat and cried.

"Is it over?" I asked, gathering up my handkerchief.

"Probably, yes," said the old man. "But we should stay here a while yet, just to be sure."

We turned to look at each other . . . and found we were both in an awful state. The old man's sweater was hanging in tatters, his hair was covered with dust, and he had lost both shoes. In his hands he held just one thing: the music box—totally unharmed despite all we had been through. For my part, the hook on my skirt had come loose, my stockings were in shreds, and the heel had come off one of my shoes.

"Why did you bring the music box?" I asked him.

"I don't know. It was under me when I was pinned by the cabinet, but I have no idea how I managed to get it here. Clutched in my hand, I suppose, or shoved in a pocket . . ."

"I'm glad you were able to save something. The only thing I brought with me was Don."

"But Don is most important of all. An old man like me doesn't need much. I don't mind that everything was washed away. And besides, the ferry itself had disappeared a long time ago."

He gazed out at the sea. The shoreline was buried in splintered wood and debris. Cars floated here and there. Farther out, the boat was knifing into the waves, sinking, bow down.

"And I'm afraid we've lost R's pancake," I said.

"I suppose so," he answered, nodding.

. . .

Some neighborhoods in the town were damaged as well. Walls had caved in and cracks had opened in the streets. Fires were burning. Emergency vehicles and the trucks of the Memory Police raced around us. And now, to make matters worse, it had started to snow.

From the outside, my house seemed to have escaped with only minor damage; a few roof tiles had fallen and Don's doghouse had toppled over. But things inside were far worse. Everything had been tossed from its place and lay strewn about at random—the pots and dishes, the telephone, the television, vases, newspapers, boxes of tissue . . .

As soon as we'd tied Don in the yard, we hurried through

the mess to the hidden room. Our greatest concern was to see how this little space, suspended between floors, had fared in the earthquake. I turned up the rug and tried to raise the trapdoor, but it wouldn't budge.

"Hello! Can you hear us?" the old man called. After a moment, we heard a knock coming from the other side. And then R's voice.

"Yes, I'm here."

"Are you all right?" I got down on the floor and called through the gap. "Are you hurt?"

"No, I'm fine. But how are you? I've been worried about both of you, but I can't tell what's going on out there. I'd just started to wonder what would happen to me if no one came back."

"We were on the boat when it struck. We were able to get away, but I'm afraid the boat sank."

"I'm glad you're safe. I tried opening the door to get some idea of what happened, but it wouldn't move."

"I'm going to try pulling on it again," said the old man, coming over to examine the door. "Could you push from your side?" But the results were the same.

"The earthquake must have warped the floor." Though we were separated from R by no more than the thickness of a single board, his voice sounded distant and weak.

"I'm sure that's it. The door is jammed into the floorboards." The old man put his hand to his chin to ponder the problem.

"What if we can't get it open? He'll starve to death, or suffocate." The words came rushing out.

"Is the ventilation fan working?" asked the old man.

"No, I think the electricity has been cut off." Since it was midday, I hadn't noticed until now, but the power was, indeed, off.

"Then it's pitch-black in there?" the old man called down to R.

"Yes." R's voice seemed to be slowly retreating from us.

"We have to hurry," I said, getting up from the floor. "We'll get it open—I'll go find a chisel or a saw."

. . .

The old man worked quietly and precisely, as he always did, and in no time at all the trapdoor had been opened. I stood by, feeling useless, my one contribution being that I'd gone to the neighbors across the street to borrow the tools. There were chisels among the sculpting tools in the basement studio, but it would have been impossible to find them with everything in such a mess, and the old man's tools had been washed away with the boat, so there was no other choice but to ask. The ex-hatmaker agreed readily, but he insisted that he should come along to help.

"How terrible! Are you all right? Do you need anything?"

"Thank you, but I'm fine. I can manage."

"A young woman, all by herself?"

"No, the old man is there as well."

"You can never have too many hands in an emergency," he said. Smiling, I wracked my brain for an excuse that would avoid hurting his feelings but also keep from arousing suspicion.

"To tell the truth, the old man's face is broken out in a rash— eczema of some sort. He looks terrible and says he doesn't want anyone to see him. He must feel embarrassed, even at his age, and he can be quite stubborn at times."

So it was that I managed to put off the hatmaker.

The trapdoor gave way in a shower of splinters, accompanied by cries of joy from all three of us. The old man and I immediately got down on our bellies and peered into the opening. R, crouching at the bottom of the ladder, was looking up at us with an expression of exhaustion and relief. His hair was flecked with chips of wood from the shattered door.

We made our way down the ladder, uttering meaningless grunts in greeting as we patted and embraced one another. Though it was difficult to see in the dim light, it was clear that the hidden room had been battered by the earthquake. The slightest movement meant treading on the scattered contents of R's shelves. But we did not need to move, content to hold hands and stare at one another for a long time. There seemed to be no other way to reassure ourselves that we had all come safely through the ordeal.

The town never did completely recover. People made attempts to repair their homes, but the cold and shortages of materials slowed the work. Mud, sand, and the ruins of collapsed houses remained piled along the streets, and dirty snow covered all, making for a pitiful sight.

Debris that had been floating near the shore was gradually washed out to sea and carried away on the current. The only thing left visible was the stern of the boat, still protruding above the waves. Its appearance, like an animal that had suffocated by plunging its head into the ground, bore no resemblance to the ship that had once been the old man's home.

On the afternoon of the third day after the quake, I was out walking near my office along the street where the tramway ran when I spotted the Inuis. Or, to be more precise, I saw only a pair of gloves, but I was sure—though I wished I hadn't been—that they belonged to the Inui family.

My boss had sent me to run errands, and I was about to enter the stationery store when one of the dark green covered trucks passed me. The back seemed to be tightly packed with people, and the vehicle rolled from side to side as it lumbered along. Nearby cars and pedestrians moved away and waited for it to pass.

I stood with my hand on the doorknob at the stationer's, trying not to stare at the truck. Still, I caught sight of the gloves, peeking out from the one corner of the canvas cover that had been turned up. Startled, I stared at those gloves—the small sky-blue hand-knit pair with a strand of chain stitching to hold them together.

They belonged to the Inuis' boy. I remembered that I had cut his fingernails for him in my basement. The soft, transparent clippings had fluttered to the floor, and I recalled again the softness of his hands and the gloves that had lain nearby.

The cover over the back of the truck made it impossible to see bodies or faces, but the gloves seemed terribly sad, barely protruding into the outside world. I wanted to follow them, but I knew that it was pointless. A moment later, the truck was gone.

I'd heard rumors that people who had been in hiding were forced to wander the streets when their homes were destroyed by the earthquake or the fires that followed it. And that the Memory Police had been rounding them up and taking them into custody one after the other. But I had no way to know whether the Inui family had actually been in that truck or not. All I could do was pray that someone had continued to cut the little boy's fingernails and that the blue gloves were still protecting him.

. . .

The old man came to live in my house. I'd already decided this would be best and had begun preparations for the move, so it was no trouble for me. But he had seemed strangely subdued since the earthquake and I'd begun to worry about him. Of course, it was natural for him to be in shock—he had lost his home and all his possessions with no warning. Furthermore, though he had spent time at my house and knew it well, that was different from actually living here. He just needed time to get used to things—or so I tried to convince myself.

And, in fact, when it came to the project of putting my house back in order after the earthquake, he seemed to revive and pitch in with great energy. We were fortunate that there was no real damage to the structure, but inside was in such a terrible state that it was difficult to know where to begin. Still, the old man set to work, and in no time at all he had put everything back in its place.

First, he righted all the toppled furniture and fixed the pieces that were broken. If something was beyond repair, he chopped it up and burned it in the garden. Then he sorted everything that had been strewn around the house and put it back where it belonged. He even waxed the floors. Finally, he fixed the frame on the trapdoor to the hidden room and all the other doors and windows that had been damaged, so they worked as well as they ever had.

"The wound on your face doesn't seem to be healing very quickly. You should take it easy," I told him.

"No, no, no time for that. It's easier just to get this kind of thing done all at once. By the way, I ran into the man who lives across the street and he asked me about my eczema, said he could still see traces of it on my face, and told me to take care of myself." He laughed as he went off, tapping here and there with his hammer.

.   .   .

While the old man and I were cleaning up the basement we found some mysterious objects.

The basement had always held random stacks of old things, but the disorder after the earthquake was extreme, and there was barely anyplace to walk when we made our way down the stairs. I had decided I would use this as an opportunity to get rid of things

I no longer needed, but everything I touched—sketchbooks, chisels, everything—reminded me of my mother, and in the end I was unable to make any progress at all.

"Young lady, could you come over here for a moment?" said the old man. He was squatting next to a cupboard.

"What is it?" I asked, my gaze following his pointing finger. Inside the cupboard were my mother's sculptures, the ones the Inuis had left with me for safekeeping, fallen now from the shelves where they had been stored. The tapir she had given them as a wedding present, the doll she'd made when their daughter was born, and three more abstract objects she'd sent them before she was taken away.

"Look here," the old man said, still pointing. While the tapir and doll seemed to be intact, the other three were cracked or broken in places. But I quickly realized that he had not called me over to inspect the damage, but rather because there appeared to be things hidden inside that were now visible through the cracks.

"I wonder what those are," I said, carefully gathering up the three objects in my hands and setting them on the table. We sat down for a few moments and just looked in silence at the objects peeking out from the broken statues.

"Shall I take them out?" I said.

"I suppose so. We can't tell much just staring at them like this. But please be careful. They might be dangerous."

"I doubt it. Not inside my mother's sculptures."

I pinched them between my thumb and index finger and pulled them out one by one.

One was a rectangular piece of paper, folded over a number of times. It had yellowed and was ripping at the creases. There were letters and numbers barely visible on it.

The second was a metallic square about the size of a chocolate bar. Tiny holes covered one side of it.

210

And finally, there was a plastic bag that contained several white tablets that looked like medicine.

"My mother hid these inside the statues," I said, as soon as they were lined up on the table.

"That certainly seems to be the case," said the old man, moving around the table to examine the objects from every angle. I soon realized that these were all things that had been kept in the secret drawers in my mother's chest. I gathered up the broken pieces of the statues and set them at one end of the table. A careful search for more hidden treasures turned up nothing more. The scrap of paper, metal bar, and white lozenges seemingly had nothing in common, but they all shared a certain gentle modesty.

"I wonder if the Inuis knew about this."

"If they had, I would think they'd have told you about it when they left the statues with you."

"I suppose so. Then that means these things have been hidden for fifteen years without anyone knowing about them."

We sat again at the table, resting our chins in our hands, and studied the mysterious objects. The heater in the basement was working no better today than it ever had, and though it had been running a long time, the room was still cold. Snow beat against the transom window, but the sky was invisible. The ice floes on the river outside made creaking noises from time to time.

"What should we do with them?" I asked.

"I wonder . . ." The old man reached out to pick up the metal bar, but his hand was trembling and closed on nothing but the empty air. The more he tried to reach for the objects, the more his hands seemed to move off in unexpected directions.

"What's the matter?" I asked him, and he quickly used his left hand to pull back his right arm and place it on his knees.

"Nothing, nothing at all. I'm just a little nervous seeing all these unusual things."

"Something's wrong with your arm. Show me."

"No, no. It's nothing, really." He turned, trying to shield his right arm.

"You must be tired. Let's just leave all this and get some rest." He nodded silently. "But we should take these up to R's room. I'm sure they're the kinds of things that can exist only there."

. . .

"Did your mother make other sculptures between the time she got the summons and the day they took her away?" R asked.

"I'm not sure," I said, clutching the quilt as I spoke. "But if she did, I think the three the Inuis left are the only ones here in the house." The three objects were lined up now on R's bed. "The other sculptures she left my father and me were made long before they ordered her to report to the ministry."

"And she didn't store her work anywhere else?"

"The only place I can think of is the cabin we have up near the source of the river, but I haven't been there in years. It must be a ruin."

"Still, I bet that's where they are. She must have hidden her sculptures there, or rather, hidden things that had disappeared inside the sculptures—to protect them from the Memory Police." He pushed his hands down into the bed and recrossed his legs. The springs groaned.

"That's why the things in the secret drawers disappeared at some point?" I looked up at him.

"That's right."

He picked up the piece of paper first. It seemed extremely fragile, so he set it in the palm of his hand and gently unfolded it.

"Do you remember this?" he asked.

"No," I sighed.

"It's a ticket for the ferry." His tone was gentle.

"A ferry . . . ticket . . . ?"

"That's right. Look. It's badly faded, but the destination and the fare are printed here. This ticket would have taken you far to the north, to a very big island. Everyone bought a ticket and boarded the ferry. The same ferry the old man worked on."

I held my breath and stared at the soiled scrap of paper with unblinking eyes. In the center was a picture of a boat sailing over the sea. I wondered what the name of the boat had been. The letters painted on the hull of the old man's ship had long ago faded in the salt spray—just as the print on the ticket was faded and illegible.

"I seem to remember something, but it's very vague." My eyes hurt and l wanted more than anything to close them, but I forced myself to keep looking, afraid that if I didn't the slight stirring in my memory would fall still. "It's nothing specific about this piece of paper, nothing as distinct as that, not like your memories."

"It's not a contest. We just want to gather up every memory you have. Go ahead, try to recall something, anything at all." R set his hands on my knees, and our shoulders touched.

"I remember only one thing. I remember how it looked when I saw it with my mother in the basement. It was folded just as it is now, sitting quietly there in the drawer. When I pulled the handle, the paper seemed to tremble, as if I'd startled it. And I recall my mother, as she unfolded it as gently as you just did. It was always night when I went to the basement, with the moon shining through the high window. The room was strewn with splinters of wood and pieces of stone and plaster. The river whispered outside. My mother's warm, strong hands were dirty, crusted with modeling clay and cuts from her chisels. I think I touched the ticket, too. I took it from her as carefully as I could, looking back and forth between her and the ticket. I felt my heart beating hard, though not from pleasure or excitement exactly. It was more that I was afraid that the ticket would slip through my fingers and be lost. But my mother gave me an encouraging smile. The ticket was nothing more than a worn scrap of paper that might have been rescued from a trash can, and I had no idea why she had guarded it with such care. Still, not wanting to disappoint her, I treated it as carefully as she had."

Having said all this almost in a single breath, I placed my hands on my chest and bent forward. I had concentrated so completely on this memory that I was having trouble breathing. A pain ran through my chest, deep under my ribs.

"Don't overdo it. You should rest a bit." He put the ticket down on the bed and brought me a cup of tea. Supplies of tea were so low now that it was little more than colored water, but it was comforting nonetheless.

"It's always like this. I can never remember anything that can satisfy you."

"It's not about satisfying me, it's about waking up your sleeping soul."

"My sleeping soul. I wish it were just sleeping, instead of completely gone."

"But it's not. Didn't you just remember something about the ferry ticket? The handle on the drawer, the palm of your mother's hand, the sound of the river?"

He stood up to turn down the lamp and then sat on the bed again. The hidden room had been almost completely restored after the earthquake, and the mirror, razor, and bottles of pills were back in their places. The only visible difference was the trapdoor, which had been repaired with new boards.

I realized that the two of us always talked on this simple, sturdy bed that the old man had made in a great hurry. This bed draped in a fluffy quilt I made sure to air out every few days. We had no place to be, other than this small rectangular space. It was here we talked, and ate, and gazed at each other, here where our bodies came together. It was the one space that had been granted to the two of us. It seemed impossibly cramped and vulnerable.

"When the surface of your soul begins to stir, I imagine you want to capture the sensation in writing. Because that's how you've written all your novels," he said. Then he picked up the object that looked like a bar of chocolate wrapped in silver foil and brought it to his mouth. As I was wondering whether it was really something to eat, he began to breathe in and out, his eyes smiling, and as he did, sounds began to emerge from the bar.

"Oh!" I cried out, but R didn't answer, since his mouth was filled with the bar. Still, the noises continued.

The sound was different from the music box. Fuller somehow, and strong enough to fill every corner of the hidden room, and yet, from time to time, it wavered forlornly. Unlike the music box, the bar did not repeat the same melody over and over. Each sound seemed to have its own distinct characteristics.

He gripped either end in his hands, pressed his lips against it, and then began moving it back and forth. The farther he went to the right, the higher the pitch, to left, the lower. The bar had completely vanished into his folded hands, so that it almost seemed the sound was coming from his lips themselves.

"It's a *harmonica*," R said, when he was finished.

"Har-mo-ni-ka," I repeated, as though drinking each syllable from his mouth. "It's a romantic name, don't you think? The kind you'd give to a fluffy, snow-white kitten."

"It's a musical instrument," he said, handing it to me. Once it was in my hand, I could feel just how small it was. The metal was tarnished in places, but it glinted silver in the lamplight. In the middle were letters that must have been the name of the company that had made it. On the side where R's mouth had been were two even rows of holes like a honeycomb.

"You try," he said.

"Me? I can't play it."

"Why not? I'm sure you must have played it when you were young. Why else would your mother have bothered to keep it safe? Go ahead, give it a try. It's simple, just like breathing."

I hesitated a moment but then put the harmonica to my lips. I could feel a bit of warmth lingering from his mouth. A light puff of air produced a louder sound than I'd imagined, and I pulled it away in surprise.

"You see how easy it is?" He smiled. "This is 'do.' Next is 're.' Then 'mi.' If you just keep blowing in and out, you'll be able to play a scale."

Then he played several tunes, some I knew and some I didn't, but they seemed to calm me either way. It had been a long time since I'd held a musical instrument or heard one played, a long time since I'd forgotten their very existence. But now I remembered that I'd taken organ lessons when I was a girl. My teacher had been a fat woman with something of a temper, and when she tested me on scales—always my weakness—I had cowered down behind the keyboard cover. I had no ear for music and could never tell the difference between do, mi, so and re, fa, la. When I had to play with a group, I would just move my fingers without actually pressing the keys, to avoid ruining the performance. I carried my sheet music in a bag my mother had made, with an appliqué of a bear cub with an apple perched on its head.

I wondered where the organ and that bag had gone. I remembered that the organ had been expensive and my mother had grumbled when I'd quit my lessons after less than a year. For a time, she had draped a sheet over it and had used it as a stand

for one of her sculptures, but at some point it vanished. I suppose, over time, that happened to lots of things, even without the
disappearances . . .

He continued to play, his left shoulder drooping slightly,
his eyes shaded. His hair hung down over his brow. He played
extremely well, without ever making a mistake, and he seemed
to know any number of tunes, from bright and fast to slow and
gloomy.

From time to time he handed me the harmonica and asked
me to play again. I hesitated, embarrassed at my lack of skill, but
he told me he wanted to take a break, to be the audience for a
while. So I sounded out the children's songs my nurse had taught
me or the tune we had used to count for tiddlywinks. It was painfully slow, and I had no idea where to find fa or ti or how to judge
the intervals, and since I wasn't used to the breathing, I produced
sounds that were too loud or that were so soft and tremulous that
they threatened to fade away. Still, when I had finished playing a
song, R would applaud my effort.

The room was ideally suited to playing the harmonica. There
were no noises from outside to disturb us, no telephone ringing,
no one to come calling, and the sound spread to every corner.
We could shut ourselves in for as long as we liked—the old man
was sleeping downstairs in the tatami-mat room. Closed off as it
was, the hidden room could become stuffy, and it was sometimes
difficult to breathe by the end of a long tune, but then we would
stand together near the ventilator fan and take deep breaths.

When we had played every song we knew, we set the harmonica back on the bed and turned to the last of the objects that
had been hidden in the statues. R opened the plastic bag and
emptied the white pills into his hands. The bag was yellowed and
had turned brittle with age, but the contents seemed unharmed.

"Is it medicine?" I asked.

"No, it's called *ramune*. I'm impressed that your mother tried to preserve something as ordinary as this." The tablets were round and dusted with white powder, with a slight depression in the middle. He picked up one of them with great tenderness and slipped it suddenly between my lips. Startled, I covered my mouth with my hands, as R grinned.

It was so sweet it burned, but as soon as I moved my tongue to try to taste it, it dissolved instantly.

"Did you like it?" he asked. The flavor had been so sudden and powerful that I merely nodded, unwilling to open my mouth and risk losing the lingering sweetness. "It's a lemon-flavored candy. When we were children, all the stores sold them and there were countless *ramune* on the island, but now there are only these few left here."

R popped one of the remaining tablets in his mouth. No doubt it dissolved as quickly as mine had, but he continued to sit quietly and stare at the few left in his hand. I'm not sure how long we sat there in silence.

"Let's share the rest with the old man," he said at last, returning the remaining pills to the plastic bag.

.   .   .

That evening R told me the stories associated with each of the three objects. The ferry ticket, the harmonica, and the *ramune* were lined up neatly over the bed. When we lay down, I had the feeling that the bed was even narrower than it had been when we were sitting on it. It seemed to gather up around us without leaving any extra space.

It must have been getting very late, but I had no way of knowing since the clock on the shelf was hidden by R's shoulder. The old man had replaced the latch on the trapdoor, and it glittered in the lamplight. The ventilator fan continued to turn.

"There was a pasture on the northern island," he began. "A place at the base of the mountains where they raised cows and horses and sheep. For a fee, you could take a ride on a pony. One of the young women who worked on the farm would hold the bridle and lead you once around the pasture—but it was all over in a few minutes. I would call out to the girl to slow down and make the ride last, and just once she actually took me for a second lap. There was a cheese factory in the middle of the pasture. I used to feel sick whenever I went near the place. As soon as I saw all that cheese churning in that huge tank, I'd started imagining what it would be like if I fell in. Still, the pasture was a wonderful place and I would play there all day long, breaking off only to get back to the dock by five o'clock. The ferry made just four round-trips a day, but the dock on the northern island was as lively as a market. They sold ice cream, popcorn, baked apples, candy . . . and *ramune*. Anything a kid could want. The sea would glow in the evening just as we were sailing back from the north, and as the sun dipped toward the horizon, it would seem so close you could reach out and grab it in your hand. Compared to the northern island, ours always seemed a little quiet and lonely, with the mountain shrouded in haze. I kept my ferry ticket in the back pocket of my pants, carefully folded to make sure I didn't lose it, but it always ended up crumpled and crushed from the pony ride."

R talked on without a pause. It was wonderful to hear him, as though he were reading me a thrilling fairy tale or playing delightful music. From time to time I would raise my head to glance over at the three objects lined up on the bookshelf, but they seemed to be dozing—so very peacefully that it was almost

impossible to believe that they were the source of all these stories. I rested my cheek once more on R's chest.

He told me he had once played the harmonica at a school
concert when the conductor's baton snapped in two and everyone burst out laughing, interrupting the performance. How his
grandmother used to produce *ramune* from the pocket of her
apron and feed them to him one after the other, until one day
they made him sick. How his mother scolded her. How his grandmother had died from a disease that wastes away the muscles of
the heart.

Listening to stories about things that had disappeared usually tended to overexcite my nerves. But there was nothing dis-
agreeable about these stories. And though I wouldn't have been
able to recount much of what R told me, it didn't bother me in
the least. Much as I had done as a girl during those secret times
with my mother in the basement studio, I was content now to
simply listen innocently to everything he said—like a child with
the hem of her skirt spread, waiting to receive God's chocolate
from heaven.

The next Sunday, I decided to visit my mother's cabin with the old man, since R had said she might have left more sculptures there that concealed secrets.

I called the place a cabin, but it was really nothing more than a rough hut that she had used in the summer as a place to sculpt. No one had set foot there since her death, and I suspected it would be in ruins after the earthquake.

The old man and I filled our backpacks with canteens of water and our lunch and left the house early in the morning. We took the train to the base of the mountain and then walked an hour along the road by the river, reaching the cabin just before noon.

"This is terrible," said the old man, resting his backpack on the snow and wiping his face with a towel he had tucked in his belt.

"Worse than I'd imagined," I added, sitting down on a rock by the river and taking a sip from my canteen.

The cabin was barely recognizable as a building. It was difficult to tell where the door had been, and it looked as though the whole thing would come crashing down at the slightest touch. The roof was caved in from the weight of the snow, the chimney had broken off, and brightly colored mushrooms were growing from the moss that covered the walls.

We decided to eat our lunch and rest for a while before setting to work. But not for too long. We didn't want to get home late, since the Memory Police tended to take note of anyone lingering outdoors after dark.

We pulled away the boards of what must have been the entrance and made our way inside. The floor was littered with nails and knives and chisels and carving tools and all kinds of sharp objects, and since our path was blocked by a fallen beam, we made our way cautiously, shining a flashlight as we went.

"What's that?" I called, my voice rising nearly to a shriek. I had spotted a small lump under the worktable—something that seemed different from the rest of the rubble around us, soft and damp, almost slimy, but with spiky bits sticking out here and there, a shape that was melting in on itself . . . and giving off a terrible stench. The old man directed the flashlight toward it.

"I'm afraid something has died," he said, his tone neutral.

"But what?"

"A cat, if I had to guess. It probably made its way in here to die."

On closer inspection we could see that the flesh on the head and body had almost completely dissolved, leaving just the bones. But the paws and ears were clearly those of a cat. We said a silent prayer for an animal we'd never met in life and set to work, trying to avoid looking at it.

The sculptures were scattered about the room, but it was actually fairly easy to tell those that had been designed to conceal something inside. They were more abstract, having been fashioned from scraps of wood and stone arranged in such a way that it would be easy to extract what lay within. A number of them were already broken and their contents spilling out.

We filled our backpacks with sculptures, and when they were full we used the suitcase we had brought along to carry more. There was no time to break open each piece to see what was inside, but we could tell the moment we took one in our hands that it contained something that had disappeared.

We were finished in two hours. Two backpacks and a suitcase completely full. It occurred to us that we should bury the cat, but in the end we left it where it was, knowing that it would soon be interred under the snow and the crumbling cabin. When we reached the riverbank, I stopped, set down the suitcase, and turned to look back at a place I knew I would never visit again.

"Can I carry your bag?" asked the old man.

"No, I'm fine," I told him, and we set off down the valley for the station.

Since the express train was about to arrive, the waiting room was overflowing with travelers and their luggage—families returning from a day in the country, farmers bringing vegetables to the market in town—everyone seemed ill at ease, as though the station itself were filled with anxiety.

"The train must be late," I said, shifting the suitcase from one hand to the other.

"No," said the old man. "They're checking the bags."

.   .   .

The Memory Police had just closed the ticket gate and were ordering the passengers to form two lines. Their green trucks were parked around the circular drive in front of the building. They had the station attendants remove the benches from the waiting room. The train had already pulled up to the platform, but there was no sign it was about to leave.

I looked at the old man, my eyes asking him what we should do.

"We have to stay calm," he murmured under his breath, "and get to the back of the line."

Surrendering ourselves to the wave of people around us, we

gradually retreated through the ranks, arriving at last about ten places from the end. Just in front of us was a farmer shouldering a bamboo basket stuffed with vegetables, canned goods, dried meat, cheese—a mouthwatering supply of food. Behind us were a prosperous-looking mother and daughter carrying suitcases.

The line advanced bit by bit. The Memory Police, guns drawn, kept a careful eye on us as they patrolled the waiting room. It was difficult to see over the crowd, but it seemed that two of the officers were checking luggage and identification papers at the ticket gate.

"They've been doing this a lot lately."

"But they can't be finding much way out here in the country."

"I don't know about that. I've heard rumors that people are leaving hiding places in town because they think it will be safer up here in the mountains. So the police are beginning to shift their activities as well. They apparently found a man in a cave the other day."

"But we're the ones kept waiting. I wish they would hurry up."

The whispered conversations stopped, and the travelers fell silent whenever the Memory Police passed by.

"They're not interested in the luggage, just our papers," murmured the old man as he bent over and pretended to adjust his belt. "Ours are in order, so there's nothing to worry about."

And indeed, they seemed to be taking their time examining each person's identification. They turned over the documents, held them up to the light, repeatedly compared photograph to person, and otherwise checked for fakes, while at the same time matching the identification numbers against their black list. By comparison, the luggage searches took only a moment and were limited to a quick glance inside the opened bags.

Still, the contents of our backpacks and suitcase were not

the usual assortment of underwear and sweaters, cookies and makeup, but a collection of objects that concealed things that had long ago vanished from memory, for which even we did not know the names, much less the functions. I tightened the shoulder straps on my pack and gripped the handle of the suitcase. After sitting for so long in the ruined cabin, the objects we had taken must have been shocked when we pulled them out into the world. I could almost sense their fear, coming through the bags.

"Just leave this to me," said the old man. "You don't have to say a word."

I wondered how he was planning to explain three bags filled with odd sculptures. We had, of course, been careful to put the cracked ones deeper in the bags, but if one of the officers were to reach in to search or empty the contents completely, that would be the end of us. There was nowhere to run. My mouth was dry as dust, my tongue glued to the roof.

Our turn drew steadily nearer. The whistle on the train sounded, and those remaining in the line grew even more impatient. The scheduled departure time had long since passed, and dusk was deepening around us. The would-be passengers were annoyed to have their plans interrupted way out here in the middle of nowhere, but I found myself envying them. No matter how important the appointments they might be missing, it was certain that their lives didn't depend on the outcome of the inspection that was now facing the old man and me.

"Next." The Memory Police said no more than was absolutely necessary, their faces expressionless. Once the inspection was finished, the passengers buckled their bags and pushed through the ticket gate onto the platform. Just three more people ahead of us. Just two. The old man and I huddled close together.

"How much longer is this going to take? We're already an hour late."

The man ahead of us with the overflowing basket of food had
spoken up when his turn came, and suddenly the line came to an
abrupt halt. The rest of us held our breath, wondering whether he
was insane to be addressing the Memory Police that way.

"Do you know who I am?" he continued. "I'm the guy who
supplies your dining hall. I have orders to make my delivery to
the Memory Police headquarters every Sunday by five o'clock.
Here, take a look: my pass, issued by the police. So let's get this
train moving! Right about now, your colleagues back at headquarters will be starting to complain that there's nothing for dinner. And I'm the one they're going to blame."

He had said all this while holding the pass under the nose of
one of the officers. Then, just as he finished, the young woman
behind us pressed her handkerchief to her mouth, staggered a
step, and collapsed.

"Oh dear!" cried her mother. "She's anemic, and her heart is
weak. Someone help me, please!"

The old man immediately passed his bag to me and gathered the girl in his arms. As he did, the people waiting behind us
surged forward, curious to know what had happened, and the
line turned into a crowd, while the farmer in the front continued
his speech.

"All right. The rest of you come forward slowly, but make
sure we can see your papers as you pass. When we've cleared you,
hurry up and get on the train." With a wave of his hand, the officer
who seemed to be in charge dismissed the farmer and ordered us
through the checkpoint. My arms were aching from the weight of
the three bags, but I fumbled in the pocket of my coat and pulled
out my identification as quickly as I could. The old man asked
the girl's mother to retrieve his from his pants pocket. And so it
was that the remaining passengers passed through the ticket gate
in a single mass—with only a cursory glance at our papers and

no luggage inspection at all. Once through, we ran toward the platform, because we'd been ordered to, but also because we were anxious to get away before the Memory Police officers changed their minds. The girl apologized to the old man again and again as he carried her onto the train, and as soon as we had collapsed into seats, the wheels began to turn.

.   .   .

It was after ten o'clock when we finally sat down to dinner that evening. We had parted with the mother and daughter when we changed trains to catch the express into Central Station. From there, we took the bus home, saying barely a word the whole way. The trains and buses were crowded and hardly seemed like the right place for a talk, and we were elated but exhausted from our good fortune at the checkpoint. Even the old man, who was always a tower of strength in a tight situation, seemed almost too tired to sit up.

After we reached the house, we sat, dazed, on the living room sofa for a time, our bags left where we dropped them. We lacked the energy to open them and investigate the contents.

Dinner was little more than a plate of crackers, pickles, and a few slices of an apple that we'd received as thanks from the mother and daughter on the train.

"I'm sorry there's nothing warm to eat," I said.

"No, this is perfect," the old man answered, reaching toward the pickles with his fork. I washed down a dry cracker with a glass of water and stared at the plate without really seeing it. The old man tried several times to skewer a pickle without success, his fork stabbing at the empty air, and just when I thought he had one, he'd miss and hit the plate or the tablecloth instead. Then he tried adjusting his grip on the fork, but that was no better. Finally, he cocked his head and stared at his target with a worried frown, as if trying to swat a nasty insect.

"What's the matter?" I asked, but he didn't seem to hear me. "What's wrong?" I asked again, but he just continued his futile efforts. I could see that his mouth had gone slack and his lips were turning blue. "That's enough," I told him. "I'll get one for you." I took the fork from his hand, stuck it into a pickle, and lifted it to his mouth.

"Ah, ah, thank you . . . ," he murmured, as though regaining consciousness.

"Are you feeling ill? Are you dizzy? Numb anywhere?"

I moved closer and rubbed his shoulder, just as he had always done to comfort me.

"No, not at all. I'm just a little tired," he said, munching on his pickle.

Two weeks had passed and the old man had finally recovered from the exhaustion of the trip to the cabin and the fright we'd had at the checkpoint. He was his energetic self once again, finishing all the housework while I was away at the office and even going out to help the neighbors shovel snow. His strength and appetite and spirits had all returned to normal.

We decided that we would not tell R what had happened at the station. It would have upset him terribly, and there was nothing he could have done about it, even if he had known. No matter what disappeared next, no matter how close the Memory Police came to finding us, he could do nothing but remain in the secret room.

But he was very anxious to see what was inside the statues we had brought back from the cabin. He urged us to hurry, as though he were waiting to meet old friends he had not heard from in decades. For the old man and me, however, the job of breaking open the statues and revealing their contents was far less exciting—not to mention the fact that we were not sure how best to go about it. We knew beforehand that no matter how precious the discoveries we were making, our hearts would remain frozen in the face of them, and it was terribly sad to see R's futile attempts to thaw us, to move us with these objects. For us, the more pressing concerns were whether we would be able to find something for the three of us to have for dinner or when the Memory Police would make their next visit.

Still, since we could not leave the backpacks and suitcase sitting out forever, we decided to set to work on the statues on the following Sunday. First, we carried them to the basement, lined them up on the worktable, and tapped each one with a hammer. The trick was knowing how hard to hit them. For some, a light tap was enough to break the statue neatly in two, but for most of them it was not nearly so simple. We were afraid that striking too hard would destroy the contents along with the statue, and we also worried about making too much noise. Not many people took the path that ran between the house and the river, but there was nothing to prevent the Memory Police from passing through on patrol and hearing suspicious noises.

We took turns with the hammer, one of us trying various angles and degrees of force, while the other kept watch out the door that led to the laundry platform. If anyone passed by, a quick signal halted the work for a moment.

In the end, we found that each statue concealed a single object, different from the others. One was so tiny we almost failed to notice it, another was wrapped in oiled paper, a third had a complicated shape. There was a black one, a sharp one, a fuzzy one, a thin one, a sparkly one, a soft one . . .

The old man and I were completely disoriented. If we held them too tightly, would they break? Should we pick them up with tweezers or some other tool? Would we leave fingerprints? We had no idea. We could do nothing more than stare at each object in silence.

"It's hard to believe they've been hidden away for fifteen years. They seem so new and untouched," said the old man.

"You're right," I agreed.

There were more objects than could have been held in the drawers of the chest under the stairs. My mother must have had other secret hiding places. As I continued to study them, I began

to be able to distinguish the objects I'd seen long ago in the basement and dimly recall some of the stories my mother had told
me. But that was the extent of it. The swamp of my memory was
shallow and still.

. . .

When we brought the objects up to R arrayed on a tray, he
greeted us from the bottom of the ladder, a grin on his face.

"We were worried they'd break if we put them in a bag, so we
brought them like this," I told him.

"You didn't need to be that careful," he said, running his eyes
over the assortment.

The hidden room was too small to set out everything in one
place, so we put some on the shelves and others down on the
floor. Being careful not to tread on them, the three of us made
our way to the bed and sat down.

"I feel as though I'm dreaming," R said. "I never thought there
would be so many of them . . . Oh! This brings back memories! I
had one just like it, but when the disappearance came my father
burned it. And this! It's worth a fortune. We should take good
care of it—though I suppose we're not likely to find any buyers
even if we did want to sell . . . But look, just touch this one. Don't
be afraid. It feels wonderful."

All this came out in a rush, and then he continued more slowly.
"Your mother hid everything away with such care! We should be
grateful to her." He picked up one object after another and told us
what it was used for, or the memories he associated with it. The
old man and I could only listen, barely able to get a word in.

"I'm glad they please you so much," I said when at last he had
finished his explanations and paused to take a deep breath.

"But that's hardly the point," he responded. "I'm not the one who needs these things—you two are." The old man let out a low sigh, as though lost in thought. "I truly believe they have the power to change you, to alter your hearts and minds. The slightest sensation can have an effect, can help you remember. These things will restore your memories."

The old man and I glanced at each other and then looked down. We had known that R would tell us something like this, but now that we were confronted with his actual words, no appropriate response came to mind.

"If we do remember something," said the old man, struggling to find words, "what do we do then?"

"Nothing in particular. We're all free to do as we choose with our own memories," R said.

"I suppose memories live here and there in the body," the old man said, moving his hand from his chest to the top of his head. "But they're invisible, aren't they? And no matter how wonderful the memory, it vanishes if you leave it alone, if no one pays attention to it. They leave no trace, no evidence that they ever existed. But I suppose you're right when you say we should do everything we can to bring back memories of the things that have disappeared."

"You should," said R, after a moment's pause. "Our memories have been battered by the disappearances, and even now when it's almost too late, we still don't realize the importance of the things that have been lost. Here, look at this," he said, picking up the manuscript pages that had been sitting on the desk. "These exist here and now, no doubt about it. As do the characters written on them. A mind that we cannot see has created a story that we can. They may have burned the novels, but your heart did not disappear. We know, because you're sitting here next to me right now. The two of you have rescued me, so I must do everything I can to return the favor."

I looked at the sheets of paper R had clutched in his hand. The old man held his fingers to his temples, as though trying to follow the train of the conversation.

"But what if everything on the island disappears?" I murmured. The two of them were silent for a moment. I realized I had said something that should not be said, and they seemed stunned to silence by the fear that once these words had been said aloud, it might actually come to pass.

"Even if the whole island disappears, this room will still be here," R said. His tone was even and calm, filled with love, as though he were reading an inscription engraved on a stone monument. "Don't we have all the memories preserved here in this room? The emerald, the map, the photograph, the harmonica, the novel—everything. This is the very bottom of the mind's swamp, the place where memories come to rest."

. . .

Several weeks passed largely without incident. My typing skills improved considerably, and I was given a number of projects at the office. Spices continued to sell well, and with our market expanding to include jams and jellies and frozen foods, we were quite busy. Some days I worked overtime and got home late, but thanks to the old man there was no need to worry about the house. He took care of everything, from shopping and cooking to cleaning and looking after R.

One day, the drain got clogged and we were unable to run the water. Under normal circumstances we would simply have called a plumber, but for us even a clogged pipe could have been fatal. So, instead, the old man spent a day and a half covered in mud and snow before we could use the plumbing again.

There was also a day when Don fell ill. I'd wondered why he was rubbing his head against the wall of his doghouse, and then I noticed a sticky yellow liquid coming from one of his ears. When I wiped it with a cotton ball, he squinted his eyes and looked up at me as if to say he was sorry to be causing so much trouble. But a half hour later his ear was running again.

I thought for a moment, unsure whether I should take him to the veterinarian. He was no ordinary dog, in the sense that his former owners had been taken away by the Memory Police. And I knew they kept a close watch on the doctors and hospitals, hoping to trap people who were forced out of hiding to seek medical care. So if someone realized that Don had been overlooked in a search by the Memory Police, it could mean a great deal of trouble for us. And even if I said that I'd simply adopted him when he'd been abandoned, there was nothing to prevent them from taking me in for questioning anyway.

On the other hand, had they been interested in Don, they could have taken him away with them during the raid, or when they'd come back to search the house. But they had ignored him. So there was nothing to be worried about, I concluded, deciding to take him to the neighborhood veterinarian.

The vet was an old man with white hair and a kindly, almost priestlike manner. He cleaned Don's ear, treated it with an ointment, and prescribed some pills for me to give him for a week.

"Just a minor infection," he said, scratching Don's throat. "Nothing to worry about." Don wriggled with pleasure on the examination table, looking up at the doctor as if to say he didn't want the visit to end. I was relieved to realize that all my worry had been unnecessary.

One other small event was the haircut the old man gave R. Obviously, he had not been to the barber since he'd come to live in the hidden room, and his hair was getting unsightly, but it proved to be something of an ordeal to manage a haircut in the narrow room that was now overflowing with disappeared objects.

First, the old man spread newspapers on the tiny space remaining on the floor. Once R was seated there, he wrapped a towel and a plastic sheet around his neck and fastened them with clothespins. Then he began cutting R's hair, moving nimbly around in the confined space to find just the right angles. I watched from the bed.

"I didn't know you were a barber, too," I said.

"I'm not, really. I just cut here and there, almost at random." As he talked, the scissors moved continuously over R's head. From time to time R would roll his eyes up, attempting to see what was happening to him, but the old man would grip his head. "Hold still please," he told him.

The finished product proved to be quite passable. While it was clear that the old man was not a professional, R seemed satisfied, and the slightly uneven patches had the effect of making him look younger.

Cleaning up afterward was another ordeal. Despite having taken precautions with the newspaper, hair seemed to have made its way into every corner of the room, and we spent a long time sweeping it out from under all the objects.

. . .

After this period of relative calm, I was walking Don one Saturday evening when I happened to meet the old man on the hill, not far from the ruins of the library.

"Ah!" I called. "Done with the shopping already? Did you get anything good?" He was sitting on a pile of charred bricks and raised his hand to wave when he noticed me.

"No, just the usual. A shriveled cabbage, three carrots, some corn, yogurt that's two days beyond its sell-by date, and a little bit of pork."

I tied Don to a tree nearby and sat down next to the old man.

"Well, we can manage with that. At least for the week. But you spend more and more energy just to get enough for us to live on. I suppose it's even worse for someone living alone. How could anyone work and still find time to hunt through the shops and markets for hours a day?"

"It would be impossible. It's awful when food is so difficult to find." He poked at the bricks with the toe of his shoe. Pieces fell from the pile, scattering in the snow.

The library had been reduced to a mound of blackened rubble, and it seemed as though the smoke might start rising again from between the bricks at any moment. The lawn in front of the entrance, which had been so carefully tended, was now hidden under the snow. Far below, the sea spread out to the horizon.

"What are you doing, sitting out here in the cold?" I asked him.

"Looking at the boat," he said. "It's been just the same since the day of the earthquake—half sunk out there, catching the waves as they race to shore. But the part protruding above the water seems smaller today, as though it's being pulled under, though it may just be my imagination."

"Would you like to go back to your old life?" I asked him, knowing that the question was pointless, that the boat would never come back. And I knew how he would answer.

"No, not at all," he said, shaking his head vigorously. "I couldn't be happier living with you. If it wasn't for your kindness, I would be wandering the streets. Why would I ever want to go back to the way it was before? Besides, the boat was worn out. Even without the earthquake, it would have sunk sooner or later. That's the way with the things that have disappeared."

"I know, but I worry that the earthquake changed everything too suddenly, that it was too shocking."

"No, the truth is that I was dying under that rubble and you saved me. There was nothing to be shocked about. I can't tell you how grateful I am for what you've done, and I'm not watching the boat out of nostalgia, but to remind myself how lucky I am."

We stopped talking then and looked out at the sea. The color of the sky began to change slowly at the horizon, and the boat was swallowed up by the dusk. The beach and the docks were deserted, and the only signs of life were the cars running along the coastal road. Don was restless and looking for attention, wagging his tail and staring over at us, licking his chain, scratching at the tree trunk. His ear, which had begun to heal, must have been itchy, and it twitched from time to time.

I turned and looked up the hill at the observatory, half buried under a heavy blanket of snow. It had been unnecessary for the Memory Police to bulldoze it, since it was already in ruins. The sign for the arboretum along the promenade was still standing, but the arrow pointed in the direction of a void. Nothing remained on the hillside except things that were quietly awaiting their ruin.

Since the old man had lost all his clothing in the tsunami, he was wearing things that had belonged to my father that I had kept carefully stored away—corduroy pants, a wool sweater, and an overcoat with a collar of artificial fur. The pants were faded and the fur was a bit worn, but everything fit perfectly and seemed made for him. As I started to talk, he leaned slightly toward me, as if unwilling to miss a word, and placed his large, strong workman's hands on his knees.

I have always loved his hands, from the time I was a little girl. They could make almost anything: a toy box, a plastic model, a cage for a rhinoceros beetle, a beanbag, a desk lamp, a bicycle seat cover, smoked fish, an apple cake. The knuckles were large and knobby, but his palms were pleasantly soft. One touch of these hands was enough to reassure me that no one was going to hurt me or leave me all alone.

"Do you think we'll have trouble keeping the things we got from the sculptures, just as it was impossible to keep the boat?"

"I don't know . . . ," he said, sitting slightly back on the pile.

"R seems to think he can keep anything in the hidden room."

"Yes, he believes in the power of the hiding place we've made. But I have my doubts. Of course, I wouldn't think of telling him about them, and what good would it do if I did?"

"You're right, none at all. But he's the only one on the island who truly understands the disappearances. You and I don't even understand the things from the statues . . ."

"So even if we resist the Memory Police, we can't resist the fate that separates us from R," he said.

"Sometimes I find myself wishing that the next thing to disappear would be the Memory Police themselves. Then no one would need to hide ever again."

"That would be wonderful. But what if the hidden room disappears before that happens?" he said, rubbing his hands together in front of his chest. Perhaps he was trying to warm them—or perhaps he was praying. I was at a loss at these words, never having imagined what it would mean if the hidden room disappeared, if a time came when I no longer knew what was there, under the rug. How to raise the trapdoor. Why R was there beneath our feet.

Don began barking insistently, no doubt upset that I had taken him for a walk only to tie him up under a tree for so long.

"I'm sure you don't have to worry about that," I said as cheerfully as I could, trying to cover my confusion. "We've managed to cope with all kinds of disappearances in the past, but no one has suffered terribly, no one even seems to mind much. I'm sure we'll be able to cope with whatever comes next."

The old man rested his hands on his knees once more and smiled at me.

"I'm sure you're right," he said, his smile seeming to dissolve into the evening shadows.

I rose from the pile of bricks I'd been sitting on and wrapped my scarf tightly around my neck. Then I went to get Don.

"The sun will be setting soon. Let's head home. We don't want to catch cold," I said. Elated to be free, Don took off running and rubbed his nose against the old man's feet.

"You go on ahead," he said. "I'm going to rest here awhile and then stop in at another butcher shop on my way home. I found a place on the other side of the hill that's well stocked. I'm going to buy a nice ham."

"But haven't you done enough for one day? You shouldn't overdo it."

"No, I'm fine. It's just a little detour."

Suddenly remembering the *ramune*, I retrieved the plastic bag from the pocket of my skirt. "Here's something to give you a little lift," I said.

"What's this?" he asked, tilting his head and blinking.

"It's called *ramune*. It was in one of the sculptures the Inuis left with me." I emptied the contents of the bag into my hand. R and I had each eaten two, so there were three left.

"It's dangerous walking around with something like this. What if you came to another checkpoint? . . ." As he spoke, his eyes were fixed on the tablets.

"Don't worry, when you put them in your mouth, they dissolve almost instantly. Here, try one."

He gingerly picked up one of the pills and brought it to his

mouth. Held between his thick fingers, it looked still smaller than
it had before. His lips curled and his eyes blinked even harder.

"It's very sweet," he said, rubbing his chest as if to reassure
himself of the fact.

"But delicious, don't you think? Here, you have the rest."

"Really? Something so precious? You're too kind! Far too
kind!" With each succeeding *ramune,* he pursed his lips and
rubbed his chest. When they were gone, he joined his hands
together and bowed. "Thank you."

"I'll go on ahead, then," I told him, "and see you at home." I
waved. Don gave two short barks and pulled me away down the
hill.

"Until later, then . . ." The old man smiled at me, still seated
on the bricks.

That was the last I saw him alive.

Around seven thirty that evening, a call came from the hospital saying that the old man had collapsed in front of the butcher shop. Worried that he was late, no matter how far out of his way he might have gone, I had just been going out to look for him when the phone rang. The woman—a nurse or a secretary—spoke quickly and the connection was poor, so I didn't understand everything she said. Still, I knew I had to get to the hospital right away.

After telling R the news through the funnel speaker, I ran out of the house with nothing but my wallet. I thought I'd be able to find a taxi at some point, but not a single one appeared and I ended up running all the way to the hospital.

The old man was not in a bed but rather had been laid out on a plain metal table with wheels that resembled a kitchen cart. The room was tiled and very cold. His body was draped with a cloth, a frayed, faded blanket that looked rough to the touch.

"He apparently collapsed on the sidewalk and was brought here by ambulance, but he had already lost consciousness by the time he arrived and his heart stopped; we did everything in our power to revive him, but he passed away at seven fifty-two p.m. . . . As for the cause of death, we found an intracranial hemorrhage, but we'd need to do additional tests to discover why it occurred."

The doctor stood next to me and talked, but I understood

almost nothing of what he said. The flat voice of this unknown man droned in my ears.

"Had he recently received any sort of trauma? A sharp blow to the head?"

I looked up at the doctor and tried to answer, but the pain in my chest kept the words from coming out.

"The hemorrhage was not deep in the brain but close to the surface, just under the skull. In those cases, the cause usually turns out to be head trauma. But it's also possible that he had a heart attack and hit his head as he fell, in which case . . ." He continued in the same monotone.

I lifted the corner of the blanket. The first thing I saw were the old man's hands folded on his chest. Hands that would never make anything again. I remembered the dark blood that had come from his ear when he'd been pinned under the dish cupboard after the earthquake. I remembered how much trouble he'd had skewering a pickle or feeling the objects inside the statues. Had the bleeding started slowly back then?

"But he fixed the drainpipe. And what about R's haircut? He did that so beautifully," I murmured. But my words were absorbed by the tiles on the walls and did not seem to reach the doctor's ears.

The old man's shopping basket had been left next to the cart, carrot greens and a package wrapped in butcher's paper peeking out from the top.

. . .

The funeral was modest. Those in attendance included a few distant relatives—the grandson of a cousin, a niece and her husband—some old friends from work, and a few neighbors. R, of course, could offer only his prayers from the hidden room.

I found it terribly difficult to come to terms with the old man's death. I had lost many people who were important to me in the past, but somehow my parting with them had been different from what I experienced now. I had of course been terribly sad when my mother and father and my nurse had died. I missed them, and wished I could see them again, and I regretted the times I'd been selfish or cruel when they were alive. But that pain had lessened with the passage of time. Their deaths grew distant with the years, leaving behind only the most precious memories I associated with them. But the laws of the island are not softened by death. Memories do not change the law. No matter how precious the person I may be losing, the disappearances that surround me will remain unchanged.

But this time I had the impression that something was different. In addition to the sadness, I was overcome by a mysterious and menacing anxiety, as though the old man's death had suddenly transformed the very ground under my feet into a soft, unreliable mass.

I had been left alone, with no one to comfort me, no one to reach out and take my hand, no one to share the terrible void in my heart. Of course R would sympathize with me, would console me, but he was locked away forever in that tiny space, and I found it difficult to descend from my unstable, unbalanced state into the hidden room. Likewise, once I was with him I found myself unable to stay for long. It always proved necessary to return to where I'd come from. And always alone.

The materials of the world that surrounded R and me were simply too different—as though I were trying to glue a pebble I'd found in the garden to an origami figure. And the old man, who always reassured me at such moments, who promised we could find a different type of glue, was no longer here.

In order to boost my courage, I threw myself into the activities of daily life. I rose early in the morning and prepared the most elaborate meals possible for R. At the office, my head was full of schemes to get my work done as efficiently and accurately as possible. At the markets, I persevered, no matter how long the lines, navigating my way through the crowds and somehow managing to fill my shopping basket. I carefully ironed the laundry, recycled old blouses as pillow covers, unraveled a frayed sweater and reknit it into a vest. I scrubbed the kitchen and bathroom until they sparkled, took Don for his daily walk, cleared snow from the roof.

Yet when I crawled in bed at night, what came was not sleep but deep exhaustion and anxiety. Closing my eyes, I would feel a kind of panic, and tears would begin to flow. Certain I would never get to sleep, I would go to the desk and take out my manuscript. I could think of no other way to pass the night.

I would take some of the objects from the statues that I'd hidden next to the funnel speaker and arrange them on the manuscript pages. Often, when I was visiting him in his room, R would tell me to take any that interested me and keep them with me. To be honest, nothing was likely to interest my soul in its weakened state, but in order not to disappoint R, I chose one or two that happened to be close at hand.

Now, in the middle of the night, I would stare at them. And when I tired of that, I touched them, smelled them, opened their lids, wound their springs, rolled them about, held them up to the light, blew on them. I had no idea how they were really meant to be used.

From time to time, for just a moment, one of the objects would show me something more. A slight curve in the shape or a depth of color would catch my eye—and I would startle, wondering whether this could be the revelation that R was hoping for. But whatever it was, it never lasted more than a moment. Nor was it within my power to bring it back. Worse still, only a small fraction of the objects ever showed these special traits; the rest were content to remain sitting modestly on the manuscript pages.

Passing my nights this way did not relieve the anxiety I'd felt since the old man's death, but it was better than weeping in my bed. Occasionally, these flashes of recognition were sparked by some object two nights in succession—once it happened three times in one night—but then I might go four nights without encountering even one. I began to wait for these brief moments with increasing impatience, seeing them as luminous signposts that would lead me to R. And I, too, hoped the light would illuminate the cavity in my heart.

One night I made an effort to write some words on the manuscript paper. I wanted to leave a record of what I saw in that dimly illuminated void of my memories. It was the first time I had done such a thing since the novels disappeared. I held the pencil awkwardly, and my characters were either too large to fit within the lines or too small and misshapen. Nor did I have any confidence in the things I wrote—and yet my fingers were moving—however slowly.

I soaked my feet in water.

It had taken me an entire night to write that one line. I tried reading it aloud a number of times, but I had no idea where the words had come from nor any guess as to where they might be leading. When I returned the objects to R the next day, I held out my manuscript along with them. He stared at it a long time, though it was no more than a single line.

"It's just scribbling," I told him. "Not something you need to read. I'm sorry. Just throw it away." He had been quiet so long, I was sure he was disappointed.

"Don't be silly!" he said at last, placing the page carefully on his desk. "It's extraordinary progress! This is the first thing you've written without tearing holes in the paper with your eraser."

"I don't know if you can call it progress. It's more like a whim. And tomorrow, I may be unable to write anything."

"No, don't say that. The stories have begun to stir again."

"I wonder if you're right. I don't expect much, but what do they mean? I have no idea. They make no sense to me."

"The meaning isn't important. What matters is the story hidden deep in the words. You're at the point now where you're trying to extract that story. Your soul is trying to bring back the things it lost in the disappearances."

He went on encouraging me. In all likelihood he was telling me lies, unwilling to hurt me further and deepen the damage done by the old man's death, but I didn't care. If he was willing to be kind to me, the reason didn't matter.

Not a speck of dust floated on the water.

I looked out on the grassy meadow.

When the wind blew, it made patterns in the grass.

Patterns like those in cheese nibbled by mice.

Still without feeling the sense of a story, I continued to put together strings of words, one line each night.

The size and balance of my characters gradually improved, but my hand still shook when it came time to select a word.

"That's wonderful! You're doing fine." R took each piece of paper and added it to the pile.

.   .   .

The first disappearance since the death of the old man. I lay in bed collecting my wits, trying to determine the nature of the thing that no longer existed. It was quiet outside, no sign that the neighbors were stirring. Which might mean that it was something relatively insignificant. I tried to get up, but I felt as though dense air had coiled around my body. Weak sunlight filtered in through the curtains, promising a gray day. Perhaps another heavy snowfall. I should get out of the house early and catch the seven o'clock tram. There were always delays on the day of a disappearance.

I pulled back the quilt and made a bizarre discovery—something was stuck fast to my hip. And no matter how much I pulled or pushed or twisted, it would not come off, just as though it had been welded to me.

"What in the world?" I said, gripping the pillow with frustration. I had the feeling I would fall out of the bed if I didn't hold on to something. At the slightest movement, the thing attached to my hips threw my body off balance.

I held still, my face against the pillow, trying to calm myself. A chilly sensation lingered in my hands from where I'd touched whatever it was that was attached to me a moment earlier. Had I come down with some sort of disease? Perhaps an enormous tumor had developed overnight? How could I get to the hospital with this sort of affliction? I glanced down again at my body, which was still stretched out in the same position on the bed.

Since I couldn't remain where I was indefinitely, I decided to get up and get dressed. First, I put my weight on my right leg and slowly sat up. But as I did, the thing fell with a heavy thud and I was thrown to the floor. I fell against the wastebasket, knocking it over and spilling the contents, but I managed to crawl to the dresser and pull out a sweater and some pants.

The sweater went on easily. The problem was the pants, which seemed to have two openings. Once I'd slid my right leg into one of them, I had no idea what to do with the other. The thing was still there on my hip, as though it were looking at me, waiting for something. I wasn't exactly afraid of it, but it did seem somehow rather ominous. But the more I studied it, the more I realized that it had a shape that would exactly fit the other opening in my pants. The right length, the right thickness, it was perfect. I tried taking it in both hands and putting it into the opening. It was heavy and difficult to work with, but after some time, just as I'd imagined, it slid neatly into the pants. As though someone had measured it in advance.

It was then I finally realized what had disappeared: my left leg.

I had trouble getting down the stairs without falling. Holding on to the railing, I had to drag the thing—my disappeared leg—one step at a time. Outside, the snow piled up on the ground made things even more difficult. Fortunately, however, after hesitating for a moment, I had decided to put a shoe on my left foot as well.

The neighbors were gradually beginning to gather in the street outside. They all seemed to be wondering how to deal with their own bodies, as though fearful that the least motion would cause them pain. Some walked holding on to walls or fences, others moved in family groups, using one another's shoulders for support, and some, like the former hatmaker, were using umbrellas or other objects as crutches.

"How can this be happening?" murmured someone, and there were nods of agreement. It was the first disappearance of this sort, and we were at a loss, unable to imagine what might happen next.

"A lot of unexpected things have disappeared, but never anything as shocking as this," said the woman who lived across the street. "What's going to happen to us?"

"Nothing at all. That's the point. It's just one more cavity that has opened up on the island. How is it any different from the others?" said the old man in the house next to mine who worked at city hall.

"But something isn't right about this. My body feels as though it's gone to pieces and won't go back together again." This time it was the hatmaker, who was digging in the snow with the tip of his umbrella.

"You'll get used to it. It may be a bit tricky at first, but that's been true for other disappearances as well. It takes time to get accustomed, but there's nothing to be afraid of."

"I guess I'm actually lucky," laughed the old woman who lived two houses down the street. "Half the arthritis in my knees is gone!" I could manage no more than a faint smile.

As we talked, from time to time each of us glanced down at our left leg. Would the cold creeping up from the snow bring feeling back to it? Perhaps this was all a mistake . . . Or so the vaguely hopeful expressions on our faces seemed to suggest.

"I wonder," I said, screwing up the courage to ask the question that had been on my mind for some time. "How can we get rid of them?"

The man from the mayor's office let out a low moan, the old woman with knee trouble sniffed, and the woman across the street spun the handle of her umbrella. But no one said anything for a moment. Perhaps they were considering the problem, or perhaps they were simply waiting for someone else to say something.

At that moment we saw three members of the Memory Police come toward us from the other end of the street. We moved closer together on the sidewalk to get out of their way. What would they do if they found us here, still in possession of our legs?

They were out on patrol, dressed in their usual uniforms. The first thing I did was look at their left legs. I could see they were intact, so I felt somewhat relieved. If the Memory Police didn't know how to get rid of their legs, they could hardly blame us for still having ours. But they were walking with their usual even gait, perfectly in balance, as though the disappearance had caused them no difficulty—as though they had been training for just this eventuality.

When they had passed by and we were sure they were out of sight, the hatmaker spoke up.

"I suppose there's no need for us to get rid of our legs, then."

"You're right. No need to get out the saw just yet . . ."

"Burning, burying, washing away, abandoning—I guess for some things, there's just no appropriate way."

"Though I imagine they'll come up with one soon enough."

"Maybe they'll just fall off by themselves, like leaves from a tree."

"I'm sure you're right."

"So there's nothing to worry about."

When we'd all had our say, we made our way home—though we were less sure-footed than the Memory Police. The old woman fell by her gate, and the hatmaker's umbrella got stuck in a snowbank.

Don had come out of his house and was pacing in front of the door, wagging his tail nervously. When he saw me, he came running, kicking up snow and snorting with pleasure, but as he approached I realized that his back left leg had disappeared.

"You too, boy? Don't worry, you'll be all right."

I wrapped my arms around him. His hind leg dangled limply.

.   .   .

That night in bed, R massaged my disappeared leg. He worked at it for a long time, as though he thought his efforts might bring it back.

"When I was a little girl and had a fever, my mother would rub me like this," I murmured.

"You see?" he said. "How can your leg have disappeared when you still have a memory like that?" He smiled and pressed harder with his hand.

"I suppose so," I said, nodding vaguely and looking up at the ceiling.

In fact, the feelings I remembered from my mother's hand and those from R's now were completely different. No warmth, no sensation at all came to my leg from his touch. Just the uncomfortable feeling of one thing grating against another. But I worried that it would hurt him if I told him the truth.

"Look," he said. "Here you have five toenails lined up neat as you please. Smooth and translucent like the skin of a fruit. And here's the heel, and the ankle. All the same as your right leg. And the lovely curve of your knee fits perfectly in the palm of my hand. You can feel the intricate bone structure. Your thigh is amazingly white, your calf is soft and warm. I can feel every part of your leg, each scratch and bruise and bump. How can you say all that has disappeared?"

He knelt at the edge of the bed, his hands continuing to move.

I closed my eyes, more conscious than ever of the new cavity that had opened up in my body. It was filled to the brim with clear water that retained no trace of any memory. R's hand stirred the water, but no more than a few tiny bubbles rose to the surface and popped silently.

"I'm happy you're here," I told him. "Happy to know you'll go on looking after my leg even though it's gone. The other legs on the island must feel sad and abandoned."

"I can't imagine what it must be like in the outside world, with things disappearing one after the other . . ."

"I doubt the changes seem as great to us as they would to

you. We shrug them off with as little fuss as possible and make do with what's left. Just as we always have. Though this time people do seem a bit more concerned. Maybe because we haven't been able to dispose of the thing that's disappeared and have to keep carrying it around with us. Though I'm already getting used to that, thanks to you."

"You go to great lengths to get rid of these things, don't you?"

"I suppose we do. But this time there's nothing to be done. We can't burn them or crush them or throw them in the sea. We just try to avoid them as much as possible. But I'm sure that will pass soon enough. I don't know how, but sooner or later every-thing will fall back into place."

"Fall back into place? What do you mean?"

"Eventually, the hole left by our legs will find a place in our hearts and minds that fits it perfectly, a place to fall into."

"But why would you do that? Why would you want to get rid of these things? I need your leg as much as I need the rest of you . . ." He closed his eyes and sighed. I started to reach out to touch his face but then froze when my leg threatened to slip off of the bed. He took it in his hands and brought it to his mouth, kiss-ing it on the calf. A quiet kiss that was almost like a whisper.

I thought how wonderful it would be had I been able to feel his lips, to sense them on skin and flesh that had not disappeared. But on my left leg there was only a slight pressure, like the weight of a bit of modeling clay.

"Stay a bit longer, like that," I told him. Though the feeling was empty, I wanted to watch him holding on to that void.

"Of course," he said. "As long as you like."

Gradually we became accustomed to living without our legs. Needless to say, things did not go back to the way they had been before, not exactly, but our bodies acquired a new sense of balance, and a new kind of daily rhythm took hold. Eventually we stopped noticing people who were unable to stand without holding on to something, or who were too tense to walk naturally, or who fell at random moments. We learned to control our bodies without too much inconvenience.

Even Don began running around again at full speed. He would jump up on the roof of his house to bask in the sun or leap at the branches of trees in the yard to bring the snow tumbling down. From time to time he proved too successful at this game and would come running to me for help after an enormous lump of snow had fallen on his head. But once I had wiped his face and rubbed his chin, he went right back to the tree, aiming this time for even heavier branches.

No matter how much time went by, there was no sign that our left legs were going to rot and drop off. They remained firmly in place, fixed to our hips. But no one seemed to care.

The number of people who were taken away by the Memory Police suddenly increased. Those who had used all sorts of tricks in the past to blend in could no longer fool the police after the disappearance of their left legs. It was surprising to see how many people had managed to hide in plain sight without being captured or resorting to safe houses, but now they found it impossible to imitate our new sense of balance. No matter how much they tried, something was slightly different about the distribution of the weight or the alignment of the muscles or the movement of the joints. And the Memory Police could spot it immediately.

This crackdown, and the loss of the old man, meant that our communication with R's wife had now been suspended for some time. There was always the fear that the phones were tapped, and sending me for a face-to-face meeting seemed still riskier. Letters and packages from his wife were R's only ties to his former life, but receiving them was dangerous, and the best way to keep him safe was to keep him completely isolated. Still, at some point we decided we could use the telephone to communicate if we managed to settle on a code. We decided that we would let the phone ring three times at a predetermined hour before hanging up—the signal that R was healthy and doing well. Three rings from the other end meant the message had been received and understood.

But in order to set up this system, I needed to go back to the elementary school for the first time in a long while. When I did, I discovered that the meteorological box was no longer mounted on its post. I found it in pieces on the ground, perhaps destroyed in the earthquake or crushed under the weight of the snow. I could see the thermometer, shattered and half covered by a pile of boards. I hesitated, wondering what to do, but in the end I decided to push the letter in among the remains of the box. This tiny meteorological station had long ago been forgotten, and now that it was in ruins, it was even less likely to attract attention—making it all the more ideal for our purposes. My one concern was whether R's wife was still coming to look for letters here.

Still, at the appointed hour, I dialed the number and let it ring three times before hanging up. Then I waited in front of the phone. After a moment, it began to ring. Three rings that seemed to dissolve into the shadows and then silence. I had the feeling that the receiver had been trembling.

. . .

I continued with the task of writing strings of words that made almost no sense. The feeling of purpose I'd had during my time as a novelist was gone, but compared to the emptiness I'd felt after the burning of the library, things were going more smoothly. At any rate, I'd gotten to the point where the shapes of certain words seemed to be returning. I could vaguely recall the fingers of the typist locked away in the clock tower, the pattern of the parquet floor, the mountain of typewriters, the sound of footsteps coming up the stairs.

Still, it was extremely difficult to fill the boxes on the blank manuscript paper with characters, and the number of words I produced for an entire night's effort was painfully small. At times I grew so weary and frustrated that I wanted to throw the stack of paper out the window, but then I would choose one of the objects I had borrowed from the hidden room, set it on my open palms, and breathe deeply to calm myself.

Little by little, the boat slipped lower. When I took Don out for a walk, I stopped at the ruins of the library to sit and gaze out at the sea. It was lonely but peaceful there, with the sound of cars on the coastal road barely audible in the distance. The rumor had continued to spread that they were planning to build a headquarters for the Memory Police on the site, but the piles of burned bricks had not been removed and there was no sign that construction would be starting anytime soon.

"Do you remember how the old man looked sitting right here?" I asked Don. "I never imagined that would be the last time I'd see him." Don galloped about, clearly unconcerned with what I was telling him. "I should have noticed something was wrong that day. But he looked fine, his usual self. Though I suppose he did seem a bit sad, and he was never willing to ask for help. I wish I could put my arms around him and tell him there's nothing to fear, that everything will be all right—the way he always did for me. But he's gone, Don."

I took a cracker from my pocket, broke it in pieces, and tossed them to Don. He jumped and twisted, deftly catching them in midair, and as I clapped my approval he raised his nose and capered about, begging for more.

"If I'd realized sooner what was happening, we might have saved him."

I tried to put into words the regret that lingered in my head, though I knew that saying this aloud might only make things worse. Don noisily chewed his cracker.

Now, when the waves were high, they hid the last bit of the boat still visible. And it seemed clear that it would soon vanish entirely beneath the surface. My heart ached when I thought about that day. Would I remember how we had eaten cake in the wheelhouse? Or made our plans to build the hidden room? Or stood on deck, leaning against the rail, watching the sunset? It was more than my empty heart could stand.

.　.　.

By the time their right arms disappeared, people were less troubled than they had been with the disappearance of their left legs. They didn't linger in bed, wondering what had happened, or spend long hours trying to figure out how to get dressed, or worry about how to dispose of the disappeared item. To be honest, we had been certain something like this would happen sooner or later.

The disappearances of body parts were, in fact, easier and more peaceful than earlier ones, as no one had to gather in the square to burn the objects or send them floating down the river. There was no uproar, no confusion. We merely went about our usual morning routines, accepting that a new cavity had opened in our lives.

Of course, this disappearance brought subtle changes to my daily routine. I could no longer apply polish to my nails. I had to come up with a new way to type using only my left hand. It took inordinate amounts of time to peel vegetables. I had to move the rings I had worn on my right hand to my left . . . But none of this posed any real problem. I had only to surrender to each new disappearance to find myself carried along quite naturally to the place I needed to be.

I was no longer able to carry a tray of food and climb down the ladder to the hidden room. I would hand the tray carefully down to R and then descend the rungs, one by one, leaning on him for support. Nor was climbing back up any easier, as I struggled with the ladder and the trapdoor before pulling myself through the narrow entrance. As I did, R would watch me from below with a worried look.

"The time will come when I won't be able to get in and out of this room," I told him.

"Don't be silly. I'll just pick you up and carry you, like a princess," he said, holding out his arms toward me. They still seemed surprisingly strong, though they'd had no more taxing exercise than organizing receipts, shelling peas, or polishing silver. They were supple and alive, unlike my right arm, which seemed to have hardened like plaster.

"That would be wonderful," I said. "But how can you hold something that has disappeared?"

His hands dropped to his knees and he looked up at me and blinked as though he hadn't grasped the meaning of my question.

"I can hold you, I can touch any part of you I want."

"You can touch me, but what does it mean if I don't feel anything?"

"What do you mean? Look, what about here? And here? . . ." As he spoke, he took hold of the limp rods that hung from my shoulder and hip. The hem of my skirt swayed. My hair fell across my face.

"Yes, I know you take good care of my body. And I know you can summon up memories of the music box and the ferry ticket, the harmonica or the *ramune*. But that doesn't mean the things themselves come back. It's no more than a momentary flash, like the tip of a sparkler when you light it in the dark. When the light's gone, it's instantly forgotten, and you can scarcely believe what you saw just a moment ago. They're all illusions—my leg and arm and all the rest of the things lined up on the shelves."

I looked around at the objects in the room and then tucked my hair behind my ears. R let go of my arm and leg, and I scuffed my foot in and out of my slipper. The traces of his fingers on my ankle and calf vanished almost immediately as they reverted to their plaster state.

"My body will go on disappearing bit by bit," I said, shifting my gaze from my toes to my knees, from my hips to my chest.

"No, you mustn't say that."

"It doesn't matter what I say, the disappearances will continue. There's no escape. I wonder what will be next. Ears? Throat? Eyebrows? My other arm or leg? Or maybe my spine? And then what will be left? Or will nothing be left at all? I suppose that's it, every last bit of me will disappear."

"No, that's impossible. Aren't we here together, right now, in spite of everything?" He put his hand on my shoulder and drew me to him.

"But the arm and leg you see aren't really mine. No matter how much you care for them, they're just shells, empty skin. The real me is disappearing as we speak. Slowly but surely being sucked into thin air."

"But I won't let you go."

"And I don't want to go. I want to stay with you, but that won't be possible. Your heart and mine are being pulled apart to such different, distant places. Yours is overflowing with warmth and life and sounds and smells, but mine is growing cold and hard at a terrifying pace. At some point it will break into a thousand pieces, shards of ice that will dissolve."

"But you don't have to go," he said. "You just have to stay here. You'll be safe here, where all the lost memories are preserved, hidden along with the emerald and the perfume, the photographs and the calendars . . ."

"Me? . . . Here?"

"Why not?" he said.

"Because it's impossible," I said, shaking my head in confusion at this unexpected idea. My arm slipped from the bed and struck his knee.

"But it isn't. We're protected here—you, me, all the things that were hidden in the sculptures. Even the Memory Police haven't been able to find us."

"But I know the end is coming. The disappearances used to happen suddenly, without warning, but I had premonitions before my leg and arm disappeared. I could feel my skin stiffening and growing numb. So I can tell something is going to disappear. It may be a few days from now or a few weeks, but it will come. And I'm frightened. Not because I'll disappear and cease to exist, but because I'll have to leave you. The thought terrifies me."

"You mustn't be afraid," he said, laying me down on the bed. "I'll keep you safe, here in my secret room."

Sometimes it strikes me as strange that I don't hate him more. I should curse him and beat him, find any way I can to do him harm, though I know it would do no good. After all, he deceived me, stole my voice, and shut me up in this place.

But for all that, I don't really hate him. In fact, when he shows me the occasional kindness, I even feel a certain affection for him: when he turns the handle of my spoon to make it easier to pick up, or wipes away soap bubbles that threaten to get into my eyes, or untangles my hair from a zipper as I'm changing my clothes. Compared to the truly horrible things he has done, these are trifles barely worth mentioning. And yet, when I see his fingers working just for my benefit, I can't help feeling a kind of gratitude. I know it's foolish, but that's my honest reaction and there's nothing I can do about it.

Perhaps these feelings are proof that I'm becoming more and more attached to this room. Things I felt in the outside world have faded away here, transformed into emotions more suited to this place.

I find, too, that my eyesight has recently started to fail. The mountain of typewriters, the bed, the bell, the various items in the drawer of the desk—all of it appears only dimly, as though shrouded in a dark veil. As does the outside world, glimpsed through the crack by the clock. Even on a bright and sunny afternoon, the grass in the church garden seems gray and hazy, the people gathered there indistinguishable from the shadows.

As a result, I'm forced to move with added care no matter what I'm doing—even things as simple as washing my face or changing my clothes. I find I'm constantly tripping over the tools used to care for the clock or bumping into the chair. I'm particularly tense when he's here. Not that he gets angry when I show my clumsiness. But by the same token he never helps me, content always to watch in silence with that peculiar smile on his face. A cold smile, like the stroke of an icy brush down my side.

Though my eyes get progressively weaker, for some reason I can always see him with great clarity. I can see every movement his fingers make, while everything else is dim and vague.

One day, something unusual happened. Not long after he had gone down to teach a class of beginners, I heard the sound of footsteps coming up the tower stairs. They were slower and more deliberate than his, and they seemed to stop on one of the landings below, as if hesitating, before starting up again.

I wonder who this could be. Do they intend to come all the way up here?

I had no idea what to do. Was this person a friend or an enemy? What sort of relationship did she—for the sound of the footsteps made me certain it was a woman—have to my captor? Did she know about me? In just a few seconds, these questions ran through my head, throwing me into a state of confusion. I realized that in all this time no one but he had entered this room. Nor had it ever once occurred to me, while I was a student, that I might want to ascend to the top of the tower.

From the sound of the footsteps I was sure not only that the person approaching was a woman but that she was young. The tapping on the wooden stairs, like the pecking of a bird's beak, suggested that she was wearing high heels.

Her footsteps seemed to convey her hesitation, as though she was fearful of what she might find at the top of this endless staircase. As she approached the clock room, the interval between each step lengthened. Perhaps she was weary, rather than confused or afraid, since the stairway to the clock tower was narrow and steep and terribly long. In any case, she had at last reached the door.

She knocked three times. I was sitting on the floor, my arms wrapped around my knees. I had never noticed the clear, dry sound of the old wooden door, since he never knocked but made his appearance after a great rattling of the keys on his ring.

I realized this might be my best chance to escape. A student in the typing class had come all the way up here, perhaps having heard suspicious noises or perhaps out of simple curiosity. Even though I couldn't call out, I could run to the door and knock on it to let her know of my existence. Then, surely, she would go and find help in the church or call the police. She would force the lock or take some other action to rescue me. And I would rejoin the outside world.

But I remained crouched on the floor, unable to move a muscle. My heart was pounding, my lips trembling. Sweat beaded on my forehead.

Hurry now! If you aren't quick she'll go away!

In my head I screamed these words to myself. But something held me back.

No! Keep still! How can you explain this to her? Would she believe you? And how would you even tell her? It's not just words you lack. Your eyes and ears, every part of your body has been deformed to fit this room—that is, to fit his purposes. And even if she did help you, do you really believe you'd get back all the things you've lost?

Covering my ears with both hands, I hid my face in my lap, held my breath, and prayed the girl would give up and go back down the stairs. I knew now that I lacked the courage to rejoin the outside world.

I'm not sure how long I stayed that way. She jiggled the lock and turned the handle, and then, with a sigh, she moved away from the door. The echoes of her footsteps receded, spiraling down the staircase. I was still unable to move, even after they had long since vanished altogether, frozen by the fear that the slightest noise would bring her running back up the stairs.

It was not until evening that I found myself wanting to peek out from behind the clock and look down on the churchyard. Needless to say I was unable to pick out the woman who had knocked on my door. In the garden below, the students leaving the afternoon classes mingled with those arriving for the evening. But they were no more than shadowy masses, my weakened eyes unable to distinguish their features or clothing or shoes. The only thing that was clearly visible—indeed painfully etched on my retinas—was his form as he sat on a bench, chatting pleasantly with his students.

That night, he appeared, bringing with him more strange articles of clothing, though these were not as elaborate or refined as the earlier ones had been. Like the other garments, these were not the kind of things being worn in the outside world, but the fabrics were more ordinary than usual, there were no decorations of any kind, and the stitching was crude. I found myself feeling disappointed.

"Did someone pay you a visit today?" he asked abruptly. Startled, I dropped the clothes he had just handed to me. How did he know about the woman who had come to the door? If he did know, why hadn't he stopped her? Why risk revealing such an important secret? . . . Confused, I looked down at the floor.

"Did someone knock at the door?" he asked. I gave a slight nod. "Then why didn't you ask her for help?" he added as he began gathering up the clothes I had dropped. "You might have found lots of ways to alert her that you're here. You could have knocked back, or dragged a chair across the floor, thrown a typewriter against the wall."

I stood still, unsure how to reply.

"Why didn't you run away? She could have helped you get out of here, and you would have been free by now." He reached up to touch my cheek before continuing. "But you did nothing. You stayed here. Why?"

He continued pressing me for a reason, though he knew that I was incapable of providing one. So what was he really seeking? I stood frozen to the spot.

"She's a new student at the beginner level," he said, the stream of questions finally coming to an end. "She hasn't much technique yet, and I don't even have her typing complete sentences. She just taps out single words, and even then she makes mistakes. But she came to me out of the blue today and asked about the top of the tower. She said that when she was a child she used to be friendly with the old man who tended the clock and she wanted to climb up here again, for old time's sake, as she put it. I told her I had no objections. That the old man was no longer there and that the room was used for storage, but she was more than welcome to go up and see."

Why didn't you stop her? What would you have done if she'd found me?

I stared at him.

"You see, I was absolutely sure. I knew that you were no longer capable of going back out into the world. It would make no difference if someone came knocking at your door. You've already been absorbed into this room."

The word "absorbed" hung for a long while in the air between us. Then I took the clothes from him and changed into them. The fact that these garments were simpler than the others made

changing simple, too. I had only to bend over slightly and the
material coiled around me as if of its own volition.

"Did she call out from the other side of the door?" he asked. I
shook my head. "That's too bad. I would have liked to have you hear
her voice. It's quite charming. Not beautiful in any classical sense.
More unusual and impressive. Like nothing I've ever heard—deep
resonance in the nasal cavity combined with moisture from the
tongue and a wavering tremolo on the lips—sweet enough to melt
the eardrums."

He turned to look at the mountain of typewriters. The lamp that
hung from the ceiling was set swaying by a gust of air from the gap
around the clock.

"Her progress with her typing lessons is only average.
Perhaps not even that. She hunches her back, and she's constantly
mixing up letters. Her fingers are short and stubby, like a child's,
and she hasn't learned to change the ink ribbon yet. But the instant
she opens her mouth, everything around her seems to glow, as if
lit from within. As if her voice were some wonderful living
thing."

When he had finished with this speech, he picked me up and
carried me to the bed.

*What do you plan to do with her? And why are you telling me all
this?*

I tried to struggle out of his embrace, but the strange clothing
made it impossible. He pinned both my ankles with one hand and
held me down.

"She needs a great deal more practice with her typing. She
needs to develop speed and accuracy. So I can capture her voice.
Until it's completely absorbed and the keys no longer move."

. . .

After that, his visits became much less frequent, and I spent long periods of time alone. The gifts of strange clothing ceased, and the food he prepared was inadequate. Once a day, or even less often, he would leave a plate of cold boiled vegetables and a slice of bread just inside the door and go away again. Without so much as a glance in my direction, without opening the door any more than was necessary to slip in the dish, he left behind no more than the clatter of porcelain.

My eyes and ears became weaker and weaker. My body, cut away from my soul, lay prone on the floor in the shadows of the clock room. When he had cared for me, my body had retained a plump freshness, a certain grace, but now it was just a lump of clay. Were those really my hands? My feet? My breasts? Even I wasn't certain. If he wouldn't touch them, they would never come back to life.

He is the only one who comes to see me, here in this room that has absorbed me. But what would I do if he turned his back on me? I trembled just to think about it.

One night I filled the sink with water to soak my legs—in order to be sure they still existed. The water was pure and clear, and it looked extremely cold. I slowly slipped my feet into it, toes first.

But I felt nothing. Just a slight cramping somewhere in my calves. My legs seemed to be floating in air, and I was no longer able to recall how it had felt when they had been real.

Still seated on the edge of the sink, I looked out the little bathroom window. There was a full moon, but its pale glow was of little use to my weak eyes. The city looked like a vast meadow of blurred lights stretching out to the horizon. I tried soaking my hands and face and chest in the water, but the result was the same. My very existence was quickly being sucked away to some remote and inaccessible place.

How long has it been now since he's visited me? And how long since I've eaten anything except the stale bread and jam he brought days ago? It's too hard now anyway for someone as weak as I am. But my weakness is not because he doesn't feed me; it's because I'm being absorbed deeper and deeper into the room. I give up on the bread—which has begun to mold in any case—and merely lick the jam on the spoon from time to time.

I lie in bed and listen, waiting to hear his footsteps climbing the stairs. The slightest creak gives me a start.

He's coming!

But I'm always disappointed. Deceived by the moaning of the wind or mice scuttling across the floor.

Why doesn't he come to see me? Why doesn't he realize that my voice, my body, my sensations, my emotions—everything exists only for him.

Is he giving that other girl a typing lesson at this very moment? He might be touching her fingers, patiently, gently in order to speed the process of capturing her voice.

I close my eyes, realizing that the end is coming soon. Just as I did when I lost my voice, I pray it will come without pain or sadness. But I suppose there's no need to worry. It must feel much like a typewriter key falling back into place after rising for a moment to strike the page.

. . .

I hear the sound of footsteps. He's coming. And behind him, someone else, someone wearing high heels. The two sets of footsteps overlap with each other, blend together as they approach the door. She must be carrying a typewriter. One with keys that no longer move.

I am absorbed silently into the room, leaving no trace. Perhaps I'll find my voice again, lost so long ago. The footsteps stop. He turns the key.

The final moment has arrived.

I put down my pencil and rested my head on the desk, utterly exhausted. In addition to the difficulties I'd had finding the words and putting them together, I had struggled to write them down with so few parts of my body remaining to me.

The characters were awkward, written with my left hand, the lines growing weak and shaky and in places vanishing alto- gether, as though the words themselves were weeping. I gathered up the sheets of paper and fastened them with a clip. I had no real confidence that this was the story R wanted, but at least I had reached the end of the chain of words. I had completed the one thing I would be able to leave to him.

Though it was not so long ago that novels had disappeared, I had taken an extraordinarily circuitous route to bring the story to this point. Everyone on the island had a vague premonition about what awaited them at the end, but no one said a word about it. They were not afraid, and they made no attempt to escape their fate. They understood the nature of the disappearances, and they knew the best way to deal with them.

R alone was determined to find every possible means to keep me here, and though I knew all his efforts were useless, I did little to dissuade him. He would rub the various parts of my body that no longer existed and try to call up memories of the objects he kept in the hidden room. One after another, he tossed pebbles into the swamp of my mind, but instead of coming to rest on the bottom, they continued to drift deeper and deeper down without end.

"I know how hard you've had to work," he said, "but I can't tell you how happy I am to be holding this manuscript." He gathered up the pages, running his hand over the stack.

"But it doesn't seem to be enough to stop my soul from winding down. I may have managed to finish the story, but I'm still losing myself." I rested my head on his chest, overcome by a weariness that made it impossible to hold myself upright.

"You should rest, then. Sleep here for as long as you like. You'll feel better soon."

"I wonder whether the story will remain after I disappear."

"Of course it will. Each word you wrote will continue to exist as a memory, here in my heart, which will not disappear. You can be sure of that."

"I'm glad. I'd like to leave behind some trace of my existence on the island."

"You should sleep now."

"I suppose so," I said, closing my eyes. In a moment I was fast asleep.

.   .   .

When our left legs first disappeared, we were thrown off balance and didn't know how to manage. But once our entire bodies were gone, no one seemed particularly upset. They seemed more coherent now that they had fewer parts, and they adapted easily to the atmosphere of the island, which was itself full of holes. They danced lightly in the air like clumps of dried grass blown along by the wind.

Don was no longer able to jump at the tree branches to knock down the snow, but he found new ways to amuse himself with

nothing but the front left leg, jaw, ears, and tail that remained to
him. When it was time for a nap, he would curl up and try to rest
his head on his back paws, as was his habit, only to look puzzled
for a moment when he realized there was nothing there. But he
soon gave up and dragged over his blanket to use as a pillow.

A deep stillness was rapidly spreading over the island. The
gap grew ever larger between the rates at which old things decayed
and disappeared and new ones were created. No one had ever
come to repair the cracks in the streets that had been left by the
earthquake, and the restaurants, movie theaters, and parks in
town were deserted. The number of trains had shrunk, and the
boat at last sank completely beneath the surface of the sea.

Among the new things to be created were small crops of
daikon radishes, Chinese cabbages, and watercress that poked
their way out of the earth, some sweaters and lap robes made
by the ladies who worked at the knitting factory, and a supply of
fuel that came by tanker truck from somewhere. Not much else.
Except the snow that continued to fall without respite. There was
no sign whatsoever that snow would disappear.

It occurred to me suddenly that it was fortunate that the old
man had died before the disappearances of the body had begun.
That meant that I could still recall the feeling of his dear hand in
mine.

He had already lost enough as it was, and rather than live on
with the expectation of more disappearances, it was easier that
he died still in possession of his own body. When I'd seen him
laid out on the cart, his body had been stiff and cold, but his arms
and shoulders, his chest and feet had retained traces of the gentle
strength with which he had protected R and me.

But I suppose the order of the disappearances made no real
difference—if in the end everything disappeared anyway.

The days flowed by monotonously and uneventfully. I went

to work. Typed with my left hand. Took Don for his walk. Prepared simple meals. Aired the sheets on the rare sunny days. And spent my nights with R in the hidden room. I could think of nothing else I needed to do.

It became more and more difficult to climb down the narrow ladder into the room. I cried out as I let myself fall into his waiting arms, and he was always able to catch me with great skill.

But no matter how tightly we held each other on the bed, we could not escape the fact that the distance between us continued to grow. No part of our two bodies—his so perfectly symmetrical, strong, and alive and mine so sickly thin and lifeless—seemed in accord. Yet he never stopped trying to draw me as close to him as possible. It made me terribly sad to see how eagerly he held out his arms and drew them back, and often I found tears coming to my eyes.

"There's nothing to cry about," he would tell me, wiping my cheeks with his palms. At such times I thought how lucky I was to still have cheeks. But in the same moment I grew uneasy wondering where the tears would go when my cheeks disappeared, how his hand could wipe them—and the tears would flow even harder.

.   .   .

The hand that had written the story, my eyes overflowing with tears, the cheeks that had received them—they all disappeared in their turn, and in the end all that was left was a voice. The citizens of the island had lost everything that had a form, and our voices alone drifted aimlessly.

I no longer needed to fall into R's arms to descend to the hidden room. There was no need to lift the heavy trapdoor, since I was now able to slip through the narrow crack around it. In that sense, the complete disappearance of my body was actually a form of liberation. Still, if I was not careful, my unreliable and invisible voice might be swept away with the wind.

"It's peaceful with just a voice," I said. "With just a voice, I think I'll be able to accept my final moment calmly and quietly, without suffering or sadness."

"You mustn't think like that," R said. I could tell that he wanted to reach his arms toward me, but he remained still. With nowhere to go, his hands seemed to float before him.

"You'll finally be able to leave here," I told him. "You'll be free to return to the outside world. The Memory Police have given up their hunt. Of course, how could they go on hunting people who are no more than voices?" I wanted to smile but then I realized that it would be useless. "The outside world is in ruins, crushed under the weight of the snow, but you'll manage. I know you'll be able to melt the frozen world bit by bit, and I'm sure others who have been in hiding will come out to join you."

"But none of it will mean anything if you're not here with me." He seemed to be trying to caress my voice.

"I'm afraid I won't be able to be with you."

"Why do you say that?"

He reached out and grabbed at the air where he imagined my voice to be, but he missed the mark. Still, I could feel the warmth of his body.

The air current in the room changed directions, and, as though at that signal, my voice began slowly to disappear.

"Even when I'm gone, you must take care of this room. I hope my memory will live on forever here, through you."

It was becoming more difficult to breathe. I looked around. My body was now included among the objects arranged on the floor. I lay there between the music box and the harmonica, my two legs protruding at odd angles, my hands crossed on my chest, my eyes lowered. In the same way he had wound the spring on the music box or blown into the harmonica, I imagined R would now caress my body in order to call forth memories.

"Do you really have to go?" he asked, gathering to his chest the air he held in his hands.

"Good-bye . . ." The last traces of my voice were frail and hoarse. "Good-bye."

For a very long time, he sat staring at the void in his palms. When at last he had convinced himself that there was nothing left, he let his arms drop wearily. Then he climbed the ladder one rung at a time, lifted the trapdoor, and went out into the world. Sunlight came streaming in for one moment but vanished again as the door creaked shut. The faint sound of the rug being rolled out on the floor came to me from above.

Closed in the hidden room, I continued to disappear.